THE DRAGON'S LULLABY

Bret James Stewart

Table of Contents

Dedication

This novel has been many years in the making. When my sons were young, and I was working on this manuscript in the evenings, they asked me to dedicate my first published book to them. Promise kept. I lovingly dedicate this, my first full-length work, to my sons, Alexander James Stewart and Barron Christopher Stewart, both of whom love fantasy nearly as much as I do.

Druidwood

The Unknown Lands

Vale of the Wyrm

The Broken Lands

Wildwood
(Unruled)

Feywood

Barony of
Crystalmere

Elven Kingdoms

Perilous Mtns.

Realm of the Lich King

Rockham

Hrothanheim

The Northern Realm

Rockstead

The Forgotten Lands

The Borderlands

Shadowbender's
Tower

The Emerald Moors

Barony of Trevor

Fields of Blood

The Sundered Mtns.

Th Barren Lands

Duran

Dwarven Kingdoms
Stone Hold

Granite Hills

The Desolate
Lands

Seahall

The Dragon's Lullaby

Canticle of the Wyrm

I have lived for centuries;

More time than you

Can comprehend--

Through the time of the elves,

Through the dawn of men,

When our only enemies

Were ourselves.

Now I sleep

Nestled deep

Within the earth

Coiled 'round the coins

Older even than my birth.

But, one day, the earth will shake

And, then, shall I awake.

So let the sages scheme,

The bards sing,

The witches scream,

The poets dream,

And the elves flee,

To no avail—

I still shall be their destiny.

Prologue

Splintering wood and shattering glass wrenched Cwylln ap Dyrn away from his pleasant dream. He blinked quickly, trying to banish the sleep-induced numbness in his eyes, attempting to see in the inky darkness of the chamber. Had the noise been a part of the dream? He wasn't sure as the dream had already flitted away from waking conscious as nocturnal reveries often do so that, within seconds, he could not quite remember what the dream had been about. The sound had seemed to be outside the dream. His senses were tingling, and the last wisps of slumber were melted away as adrenaline coursed through his system, making him feel warm, awake, and scared. From a distant part of the house, the study, he surmised; the sound of glass breaking occurred again, softer and shorter than the first crash, and Cwyllyn knew he had not been dreaming the sound.

Two muffled thumps followed, and the man sat up, reaching for the nightgown hanging neatly on its hook beside the bed within easy reach, simultaneously turning and placing his feet on the small rug upon which his slippers rested. He donned the shoes by feel, stood up, and slipped on the nightgown. Several winters before, a tree, the victim of an ice storm, had fallen into the study. That had certainly been startling, not to mention messy and somewhat destructive. The tree, however, had manifested its presence in one loud crash rather than two or three individual sounds. Another thump drifted through the darkness, and he realized something alive had violated the sanctity of his study.

The man was not as affected as other elderly men awakened from a sound sleep in the middle of the night might have been, and he quickly reigned in his emotion and began thinking, for Cwyllyn ap Dyryn was a wizard and wizards, trained in an art thriving on mystery, recovered from surprise and fear at an astounding rate. He reached for the candlestick holder on the night stand beside the bed, then thought better of it. Light might provide him with a sense of propriety, creating a false sense of safety within the radius of its golden glow, but that would be a false comfort. Any light would serve as an unmistakable warning the wizard was awake as well as pinpointing his position. Fortunately, Cwyllyn had resided in the house for more years than he cared to remember, and he knew the location of every piece of furniture, every door, and every creaking floorboard. The darkness would provide greater safety than the light source to him and would also serve as a foil to an intruder. He moved quietly towards the chamber door.

As he crept along, the mage took mental stock of the spells he currently had memorized. Ensconced in the apparent safety of his own home, he had devoted the majority of his spell complement to day-to-day spells focused on research. His "home repertoire," he called it: spells that repaired or cleaned dusty and damaged tomes, divination spells, spells allowing one to translate unknown tongues—none of these were much use to a mage raided at night by unknown adversaries. Cwyllyn had lived a long time, and old mages rarely

5

attained such status if they were careless. Thus, even at home, Cwyllyn kept several combat-oriented spells on hand. One was a spell protecting a person from magical effects. He cast it on himself before opening the door.

Before him, though he could not see it, was a small landing bare except for a standing clock, an oddity crafted in the Barony of Trevor and presented by a grateful student to his master a quarter century ago and, on the opposite side, an ornately carved oak door leading to the study. The ticking of the clock seemed jarring as the old man moved slowly across the spartan chamber toward the study door. Cwyllyn had a fleeting hope the shuffling within was that of an animal of some sort but discarded the notion with a wry smile. Animals didn't break through windows into people's houses. Whatever was rustling around in there was sentient and potentially deadly.

He wished he had a weapon of some sort, but both his staff and the brace of daggers he always carried with him when he went out-of-doors were in the study. He was old, and his strength was not what it had been several lustra before. He would have to rely on magic and wit for protection. As he moved toward the door, the mantle of clouds that had drifted across the moon moved away, allowing a faint but clear light to spill through the windows, creating two rectangles of light on the floor and permitting Cwyllyn to see. He was not sure if the light was a boon or not, but he knew the study, featuring large windows on the two outside walls, would be illumined as well. He lifted the latch and allowed the door to creak open of its own volition, frowning at the noise that announced his presence.

The study was weakly illuminated, making everything look grey. A faint breeze stirred and the curtains framing a broken window and its shattered frame flapped eerily in the night air. The breeze bore the smell of freshly-cut grass and, beneath it, the almost imperceptible aroma of the wild flowers Cwyllyn himself had so carefully planted in beds beneath the window casements. The silhouette of a hooded and cloaked figure stood on the opposite side of the room, its cloak stirring faintly in mimicry of the curtains.

"Who are you?" Cwyllyn barked, "Who dares violate the sanctity of my home?"

The figure did not reply, and Cwyllyn took a cautious step forward, intending to scan the rest of the room, much of which was lost in shadow. From the darkness of one of the opposite corners, he heard the unmistakable twang of a bowstring, and he jumped to the side in a desperate attempt to avoid the missile.

He smacked squarely into the door jamb, but the resulting pain in his shoulder was overwhelmed as the arrow he could not see embedded itself in his stomach. The impact doubled him over, and he gasped as the shaft sank deep into his vitals. Two more cloaked figures leapt from the darkness, moonlight flickering on their sword blades.

To the surprise of himself and his attackers, Cwyllyn was still in the fight. Seeing only two shapes hurtling toward him from the encompassing darkness, Cwyllyn, augmented with fear and desperation, unleashed a spell on instinct. He felt the heat of the raw energy coalesce momentarily in the palm of his hand before it flowed through his fingertips and leapt from his outstretched fingers to snap across the darkness and disappear within the layers of one of the assailants' billowing cloak. The man screamed, the impact knocking him backward against the large desk that was the centrepiece of the room before he fell writhing to the floor.

Cwyllyn's elation was short-lived. The other man's sword bit deep into the old man's chest, and the blade of a third attacker who had been hiding along the wall behind the door flickered in the moonlight as it neatly and efficiently decapitated the mage. The room was filled with the smell of blood and burnt clothing and flesh.

"Find it!" the man beside the window hissed.

"What about the bodies of my master and our brother?" queried the bowman as he emerged from the shadows.

"Find it!" repeated the other.

Four figures spread out across the room and began rustling through the mages' books and papers. A cloud bank, driven mercilessly across the stormy sky, engulfed the moon and the chamber was again cloaked in darkness.

Chapter 1

Quint Longbow stopped, taking advantage of the opportunity to catch his breath. His body relaxed, and he tilted his head back as he took in deep draughts of air. He smelled the surrounding forest, the musty smell of decaying humus, the sharp tang of pine, and, from somewhere, the clean freshness of water the ranger identified as much by instinct as actual smell. A refreshing breeze ruffled his clothes, and he felt cool where perspiration had formed. The man lifted his hat, ran his fingers through his damp hair, then replaced the hat. He smiled in exhilaration and turned to survey the view.

He and his companion had worked hard to get here. They were now quite high up, and the ranger knew such a view would be a shame to miss. He stood solidly, legs apart, with his left hand on the pommel of his sword. He was in the habit of resting his hand thus and the leather wrapping of the pommel had been worn smooth and was darker than the rest of the handle from frequent contact with the oils and sweat from the man's skin. The feel of the trusty weapon was reassuring.

He smiled. He had spent years in the wilderness, and he had seen few scenes more beautiful than the one now before him. Looking out at the last (and much lower) mountain range they'd crossed, Quint could see the mountain ranges, row after row fading into the distance in various shades of green and blue like a painter's pastel palette. The light greens of deciduous trees mixed with the darker greens of pines and, occasionally, the grey promontory of a rock face forced its way through the vegetation. The sun shone yellow before him yet faded to an orange tinge on the farthest peaks. Running through the nearest valley, a shimmering silver cord of a waterway gleamed like a mirror, forcibly reminding him of a similar sight he had witnessed once while traversing the Emerald Moors far to the south west: a line of distant knights wearing mail that had also been shining in the sun. The memory was still clear though it had occurred some years ago. An eagle cried in the distance, its tone fierce and proud, and the ranger smiled, envisioning the noble bird gliding the gentle thermals, crying out in indomitable freedom and the sheer joy of existence.

Quint jealously shook his head; the eagle was accustomed to the altitude. The air was thinner in the mountains and even the experienced ranger was adversely affected. Rest breaks were longer and more frequent. Quint took it all in stride; after all, being a hero wasn't supposed to be easy.

Quint and his companion had travelled many long miles, he had forgotten exactly how many, through wilderness, along little used cart paths, along a clean river brimming with tasty speckled trout (so far, that had been his favourite part of the trip), and, finally, along the tortuous route through the mountains. Largely unsettled, the mountains were difficult to traverse as the lack of suitable paths, propensity for thick undergrowth, and simple geography, combined to make such travel tedious at best and only those devoted to the task would be likely to make it. Certainly, no one out travelling for pleasure would have made it as far as they had.

Several times, they had been forced to backtrack in order to wind around some impenetrable obstacle. At each delay, his companion grew increasingly vocal in his opposition to continuing their journey and, at the fourth (or, was it the fifth?) obstacle, a narrow gorge cleaving their selected path like some ancient giant's massive sword-cut, his companion had threatened to throw the man in and save them both the misery of mountain travel and return home where, he emphatically maintained, people knew better than to scramble around on a bunch of hellish mountains even the gods had forsaken.

Quint, himself, was rather daunted by the effort required to get here, but he maintained enough hope to bolster both of them up in the face of adversity. Quint's hopes had risen with the altitude and, now, despite being bone-wearily tired, the ranger was elated they had climbed so high. He liked measurable goals, and the view before him was a handy (and beautiful) gauge of their accomplishment. By the gods, he felt like a *man*, having (nearly) completed the virtually heroic task of scaling the mountains!

Below him, he heard his companion long before he saw him. Loud gulping sounds accompanied by frequent stumbling gave the impression his companion was a lame bull fighting its way up the mountainside rather than the armoured dwarf he was. The two of them had travelled many hundreds of miles together, and the ranger had grown accustomed to the other's racket. Soon, the dwarf came into view.

Roland Bloodaxe was moving slowly. Below his helm, reddish hair blew softly in the breeze and his long beard, worn braided in traditional dwarven style, swung back and forth in time to the dwarf's movements. Roland was hunched over, eyes cast upon the ground, and was using his axe handle-side down, like a staff, as he half-walked, half-pulled himself along. Quint was struck by the image: Roland was some tottering old grandfather humping and wheezing along, and the ranger tipped his head forward in order to hide his laughter behind his hat. Roland was irritated enough as it was; he'd complain all night if he knew Quint was laughing at him. Finally, the dwarf reached the ranger who had, by then, composed himself.

Roland Bloodaxe plopped down on a large stone, panting. At this rate, we'll suffocate before we get there," he complained, "I don't know about you, but I didn't come all the way up here to suffocate. Why did you stop, anyway?" he wheezed, "getting a little old for such physical exertion—huh!"

"Hardly," the ranger laughed.

"What are you now," the dwarf queried, tilting his head so that his eyes were shaded by his helm, "about forty?"

"About thirty," Quint scoffed.

Roland made no reply, but spat on the ground between his feet, then ground his foot over the spot. "How old are *you*?" Quint asked. He considered the topic had been broached by the dwarf and was, therefore, fair game; "you huff and puff like someone's grandfather," he added in afterthought. He was mildly curious as to

12

the dwarf's age. The two of them had been on a number of adventures over the past few years, but Quint had never considered how old the dwarf might be. Dwarves, in the rare instance their normal lifespan wasn't cut short by violence or accident, lived several hundred years, or so the ranger understood.

"Old enough to whip *your* tail," Roland replied.

"Oh, come on, Roland," Quint laughed, "you know you'd never catch me."

"Whatever," Roland answered, "but I notice I had to stop here in order to allow you to catch your breath, youngster!"

"Oh, right!" Quint said incredulously. He had stopped a full five minutes before Roland had reached his present position, "I actually stopped to show you something."

"What?" the dwarf demanded.

Quint pointed. Several yards ahead stood a sign upon a wooden pole stuck into the ground and further supported by a pile of rocks set around its base. Written upon a piece of wood in the trade language used by most literate beings in order to communicate across racial boundaries, it read: "No trespassing by decree of the lord of the mountain. You have been warned."

"Well," asked Roland, "what does the sign say?"

The ranger looked thoughtfully at the sign for a moment then turned back towards his dwarven companion.

"It says," the ranger replied, "Shadowbender's Tower ahead." The human ranger bowed to the sign, "We must not keep the learned sage waiting. Come on, Roland!"

With that, the pair continued their arduous climb.

"What's wrong?" Oceana asked. The elf maid paused from her writing and looked at the solemn elf sitting at a small table in the centre of the large study. Sunlight poured through several skylights, creating three large rectangles of sunlight upon the semi-reflective surface of the polished wood floors. The rectangles moved with the position of the sun, and she had learned to tell the time by their location. According to the rectangles, it was mid-afternoon, almost tea time. She was sitting within one of the rectangles enjoying its warmth and light, two things of which the maiden thought one couldn't get enough. *And* books, for a third, she noted with a glance at the shelves flanking the room. They were filled to overflowing with folios, librams, scrolls, maps, and tomes; not surprising, considering both elves were wizards and wizards have a hard time functioning without books. Of the pair, her brother was the more scholarly, though Oceana enjoyed books in her own right.

Their Tower housed the largest library south of the Elven Kingdoms, but Oceana wasn't concerned with books at the moment; the other elf had not responded. He ignored her question and continued to peer into the crystal ball that was the sole occupant of the scrying table. From where she sat, Oceana could detect movement within the globe, but could not make out anything specific. She gently set her quill down beside the scroll she had been transcribing for the past four hours and walked, stretching broadly, toward the scrying table.

At her approach, the other elf muttered under his breath, and the crystal ball winked out, now an ordinary glass ball to all appearances. Oceana was used to such foibles and smiled inwardly at her brother's habitual guarding of knowledge. She knew from past experience that he would share information if he deemed it important to do so. He turned in his chair to face the approaching woman, a puzzled look on his features.

"Two travellers. A man, apparently a woodsman by the attire, and a *dwarf*!"

"A dwarf!" Oceana laughed, "They must have a task of great importance if a dwarf has crossed the Sundered Mountains because of it. I wonder what they want."

"So do I," said the other. The elf got up and walked toward the stairway that would lead him, ultimately, to the tower entrance. He disliked visitors as they always interfered with study. Antisocial to the extreme, the elf magically scried on the path to the Tower at least once per day to make sure his privacy was secure.

Finding a pair of travellers irritated him. He was a cautious elf, and he wanted to be prepared when the strangers arrived. Making sure his spell components were in order and loosening his dagger in its sheath, he walked out the study door and down the stairs.

"Homey, isn't it?" the dwarf said sarcastically as he peered at the tall, slender tower, neck craned to take in its full height. The edifice stood in the middle of a small clearing, the red glow of the sunset shining on the white marble making the structure appear pink

15

like the tile floor he had seen once that some fat human merchant had paid to have made out of rose quartz in order to keep his fat, nagging wife happy.

"Quiet," the other said, "I wonder how they got all that marble way up here?"

"Not by any normal means, I can assure you," answered the dwarf. He glanced uneasily at the lengthening shadows. He thought again about the merchant. The man was oily and fawning as his type was prone to being, but much safer than mages. Merchants generally didn't kill you or turn you into a frog or steal sleeping babies out of their cradles. Of course, the dwarf thought, they do occasionally hire someone to kill you like the one in Duran whose daughter Quint had taken a few liberties with. Dangerous business, that. *And* this, he reminded himself. He never thought it safe to come here in the first place, and now it was getting dark. They would soon be in the dark in a strange forest on some isolated mountain no respectable dwarf had ever set foot on and, to top it all off, there was this odd tower with some dainty-footed spell-spitting elf skulking around in it, to boot! "There's probably no one here, anyway," Roland said, "perhaps we should just head on back!" Roland turned, fallaciously hoping the ranger would have a change of heart and follow him off the mountain. He stopped short, drawing his axe.

"Quint!" he hissed, "company!"

At the dwarf's words, the ranger spun around and drew his sword in one fluid motion. Behind them stood a human, an old man in homespun, leaning on a hoe. Quint lowered his weapon but did not sheath it. Roland, always suspicious and not caring who knew it, never even lowered his axe.

"Who are you?" Quint asked.

The old man shifted a little, glaring at the pair. From somewhere in the forest, a squirrel chattered loudly.

"I think it is I who should ask you that question," the old man replied, "but I am Carrick the grounds keeper."

Quint looked around. The Tower sat within a small clearing virtually covered in knee high grass and brambles. A narrow, white-gravelled path appeared to be the only unnatural feature about the clearing; if there were any grounds here to keep up, they were few and far between. The old man gazed at them in silence. Roland, likewise, glared wordlessly at the old man. Quint shook his head. Between Roland and the old man, he could take a nap and not miss anything.

"Um," said Quint, "is there one Shadowbender, a learned scholar and sage by reputation, here at the moment?"

"Who seeks him?" the old man queried.

"Quint Longbow and," he laid his hand on the dwarf's shoulder, "Roland of clan Bloodaxe. Perhaps you've heard of us?" The ranger straightened to full height, took a deep breath, and continued, "I am also known as Quint the Fearless, Quint the Troll-Slayer, Quint the…"

"Never heard of you," the old man stated.

"Ah. Well, yes," said the crestfallen ranger, "anyway, we do need to see him. We have an… item of considerable interest to him, I understand. We were sent by one Cwyllyn ap Dyryn, who, I believe, is known to the illustrious Shadowbender."

"You may enter," said the old man simply.

"Do you think, maybe, you should check first, or something?" asked Quint.

"No."

"All right," Quint was surprised at the directness of the man. He had feared he would have to tell the old man everything before being allowed inside. The old man had really asked nothing. Quint certainly didn't mind talking about his exploits, but now didn't seem to be the appropriate time, standing, as they were, on the doorstep of a powerful wizard within an unknown wilderness. Besides, what did some old codger know about heroics, anyhow? Hearing a sound behind him, Quint turned to see the only door to the tower swing open on its own accord. Roland groaned. Quint turned to thank the groundsman and gasped in surprise. Carrick had vanished.

"I am not going in!" Roland said flatly. Quint could wheedle all night if he wanted to, but Roland wasn't going to set foot in the weird tower. First, there is a disappearing old coot floating around some place and, secondly, there was an elven wizard sneaking around waiting to ensorcell them both, no doubt. Nope, let the ranger whine all night if he cared to. Roland was *not* setting foot in the tower.

Twenty minutes later, Roland paced the floor in what was evidently a parlour. *Curse that ranger,* he thought. *Why is it he can talk me into anything?* Quint had talked him into entering Feywood, too, and that was what had started this whole thing. Roland threw up

18

his hands in a silent display of resignation. He may have entered the Tower, but he would be prepared should the lord of the tower pull any elven tricks.

Quint pointedly ignored the sulking dwarf. They had to enter the Tower and talk to the wizard; Cwyllyn had stressed that, due to the discovery of the ancient scroll. Quint stood in front of the large mirror opposite the door. The room was filled with comfortable yet functional furniture, and the ranger noted the faintly pleasant odour of oiled leather. Beautiful things had to be properly cared for in order to maintain their beauty and functionality. Quint went to the mirror to spruce himself up a bit. After all, you only have one chance to make a first impression.

Oceana stood on the other side of the mirror, amused despite her curiosity. She laughed out loud as the human smiled and winked at himself in the mirror (not realizing, of course, anyone could see him from the opposite side). The enchanted mirror allowed the inhabitants of the Tower to spy on any infrequent visitors; it was one of Oceana's favourite devices. At her laugh, the male elf approached. He was solemn-faced as always, but Oceana could detect a twinkle in his grey eyes.

"Mr. Vain looks comfortable enough though the dwarf is upset enough for both of them," she said.

"They match the descriptions sent by Cwyllyn ap Dyryn, at any rate. I detect no magical dweomer indicating they are anything beyond what they seem," said the other.

"What are you waiting for, then? Go and greet our guests!" said Oceana. "I'll be watching from here, of course," she added in afterthought. A little moral support wouldn't hurt. Her brother might be a powerful mage, but he was as antisocial as a hermit and welcomed guests to the tower with as much enthusiasm as he welcomed the onslaught of a toothache. She knew he would have had her run the visitors off if it weren't for the message from Cwyllyn.

She had received the message earlier in the week. Cwyllyn ap Dyryn always sent tidings via a huge hawk, his familiar she supposed. She had been on the roof that morning practising weather-altering incantations. She had just begun a new one that, when correctly performed, bestowed upon one the ability to summon rain, when the hawk came screeching from the sky. She had untied the message from the hawk's talon and had considered opening it herself (they received news so rarely), thought better of it (due largely to the unfortunate fact Shadowbender's name was on the outside in Cwyllyn ap Dyryn's cramped scrawl), and had taken it (alas—unopened) to her brother. He had seemed upset, but, then, he was always nervous. The message had said two travellers, a human and a dwarf, were en route to the Tower bearing information they would find interesting. There followed a description of the travellers. Cwyllyn would have elaborated, the note said, except the information was much too secret to risk being lost should the hawk fail to arrive. Personally, she was curious.

"Well, I suppose I had better find out what is going on," her brother said at last. With that, he walked from the room, heading for the waiting room, as they termed the parlour. She turned to face the mirror, not wanting to miss anything.

"Well, it's obvious no one is coming," the dwarf was saying, "I say it's time to go." The dwarf walked toward the door. Before he could lift the latch, however, the door to the interior opened. With a sigh, Roland turned to see who or what had arrived to greet them.

Chapter 2

An elf stood in the doorway between the entry room and the interior of the Tower. Lithe and willowy, common enough traits among elven kind, the elf seemed taller than his five and one-half feet. Quint thought someone as strong as himself could lift the elf with one hand. His blonde hair, worn in customary elven style—tied in the back with long sweeping bangs, was offset by the soft, dark grey robes that billowed to the elf's feet where the toe of a supple boot peeked from beneath the hem. Quint noticed how pale the elf's supple fingers (resting conveniently near the pommel of an unadorned dagger) looked against the dark robes. The elf was much fairer than the darker wild elves Quint had encountered during his travels. The faint smell of cinnamon emanated from somewhere within the robes, but it was the elf's eyes that caught the ranger's attention. They were stern grey, and Quint barely withheld a chuckle as he pondered which was colder: the elf's eyes or the stones forming the archway the elf stood within.

"I am Shadowbender. Welcome to my Tower," the elf said in a quiet voice, looking back and forth between the man and dwarf. "Might I inquire as to your names and business?"

"I am Quint Longbow," the ranger said hurriedly. He had seen Roland open his mouth, and he wanted to prevent what was sure to be a caustic reply from the dwarf. "This," he nodded at the dwarf, "is none other than Roland Bloodaxe. We were sent…"

"I am aware who sent you and why," the elf interrupted, "if you will please follow me, I am sure you need refreshment after your long journey." Without another word, Shadowbender turned and walked further into the Tower's interior, glancing oddly at the mirror as he turned.

Well, the mage wasn't overly friendly though the ranger acknowledged he might not be very friendly himself should two strangers show up unannounced in *his* parlour. On second thought, they weren't "unannounced" as Shadowbender had indicated an awareness of their purpose (having found out from Cwyllyn, no doubt). The elf's standoffishness, then, must have a different source. Considering their seemingly unwilling host was an elf *and* a mage, there were multiple possible sources as both the race and the profession were prone to aloofness.

To all appearances, Shadowbender was a northern elf, sometimes called "Fey" elves by others and "Pure" or "True" elves by themselves. As a rule, the northern elves, virtually all of whom lived in the Elven Kingdoms, avoided association with other races. Quint didn't know why this was, though the habit was generally interpreted as self-perceived superiority by non-elves. The dwarves, possessing a relatively strong disdain for elves (Quint didn't know exactly why), had a proverb to the effect it is easier to melt stone than to pry an elf away from his own reflection. As a dwarven maxim, Quint assumed this to be an exaggeration, though elven aloofness, at least among the northern elves, was legendary.

Northern elves rarely left their own country and, when they did, usually kept apart from other races. Unlike the wood elves of the south, who freely associated with other peoples and occasionally even married humans, the northern elves almost never married outside their own communities, much less outside their race. According to rumour, elves of mixed heritage, in the rare instances they did occur, were exiled from the Elven Kingdoms. Perhaps Shadowbender was one of these; that would explain why he lived outside the borders of his homeland. However, Quint had seen a few half-elves (the other parent being human) and Shadowbender displayed none of the features common to the half-breeds. Perhaps he was of mixed heritage in that both parents were elves, but of two different branches. Well, whatever the elf's' heritage, it didn't really matter as the important element of Shadowbender's terse welcome wasn't his theoretical background, but his factual offer of refreshments.

An old campaigner, Quint had developed the habit of securing food and shelter on a daily basis before considering life's more esoteric concerns. Quint had been eating trail rations and drinking water for over a week, and his mouth watered at the thought of something a little more palatable. A mug of cold ale accompanied by cooked meats and fresh vegetables served by an attractive barmaid is what he really wanted, though he had no illusions about getting it here. First, Shadowbender's Tower wasn't a tavern, so barmaids weren't likely to enter the equation. Also, although not strict vegetarians (as far as he knew), elves had little propensity toward meat and even the wood elves, whose taste for meat was considered greater than that of other elves, generally subsisted on bread and vegetables. The good thing about elven preferences, as far as Quint was immediately concerned, was their appreciation of wine.

The wood elves were fond of fruit wines made with orchard fruits such as apples and pears or wild fruits such as blackberries. If the northern elves carried their appreciation for the finer things of life into wine appreciation, they would most likely have finely cultivated wine made from grapes. Roland categorically despised wine as "fit only for infants" and teased Quint for drinking it; but the ranger, though he appreciated malt beverages, enjoyed wine as it appealed to his sense of refinement and extravagance. Based on Shadowbender's choice of delicate white marble to construct his home, Quint felt refinement was one of the elf's primary traits. Yes, wine was definitely in his future.

"What kind of twisted parents name their kid 'Shadowbender', anyway?" Roland muttered to no one in particular after the mage had stepped through the doorway and out of sight. Roland was brave but wasn't foolish; mages might be freaks of nature, but they were dangerous freaks of nature and it wouldn't do to rile one up unnecessarily. Thus, the barb *after* Shadowbender had left the room.

Quint ignored Roland's barb but not the elf's strange glance at the mirror. He turned to face the looking-glass. Nothing amiss there; maybe the elf was surprised by his image, as pale as it must have been. Perhaps Roland's proverb about elves being in love with their own reflections had some merit, though narcissism wasn't necessarily a bad thing. Looking at his reflection, Quint squared his shoulders and turned so he could inspect his profile. Fit and trim, the ranger sported a stubbly beard of two day's growth which made him look rugged and adventurous. He might be 'about thirty' as he had told Roland, but he looked "about twenty", if he did say so himself. What a shame there are no women here, he thought. Sighing, he turned and, with Roland tripping along reluctantly at his side, followed Shadowbender into the interior of the Tower.

Quint was excited. The ranger had been all over the world, the less civilized portions, anyway, and had seen a great many things, some of them rare and mysterious. Quint had seen the exterior of a wizard's tower, once, in the Barony of Crystalmere, but the interior of a wizard's tower was something he had never experienced, and the ranger looked forward to adding such an experience to his repertoire of "camp-fire tales," as he labelled his observations that made an interesting story. Quint could make almost any tale interesting, but the mysterious nature of wizardry lent itself to a particularly good yarn, or so he thought.

Quint wasn't sure what to expect. Wizards were not, and for good reason, a very open bunch, and everything they did (he was a little hazy about exactly what they did) seemed cloaked in secrecy. Mage-craft was sometimes reviled and usually feared. Mages were few, Quint had met only two as far as he knew, and their rarity merely added to their mystique.

According to peasant superstition, in which Quint was steeped, wizards were a combination of madman and sage living in remote places such as caves unfit for normal habitation. Exactly how they functioned was unclear but, if the tales were believed, it involved lots of candles, mysterious powders, and bizarre equipment which were used to summon demons, storms, and pestilence. Using unsavoury components such as bat-wings, blood, and skulls (there were always skulls in the tales, it seemed), wizards ironed out pacts with fell entities to prolong their lives, pry into the secret affairs of men, and steal young virgins (he remembered the part about virgins quite distinctly). Few saw the inside of a wizards' hovel and returned unscathed, if they returned at all. Nearly every village had tales of a wizard who lived "away in the wood" and, through arcane rituals, curdled milk, deformed children, and generally caused mischief. Thus, Quint knew tales involving a wizards' residence would be eagerly received, though Shadowbender's Tower was a far cry from a hovel.

Of course, Quint was astute enough to understand rumour was an unreliable measurement of truth. First of all, if there were as many wizards skulking around in the woods as the tales claimed, certainly he would have encountered some, somewhere. He had met two and neither seemed to fit the description assigned to them by folklore.

The first of these was an elderly man he had met in the Emerald Moors. This man's hair had stuck out wildly in all directions, but that had been the only odd thing about him as far as Quint could tell. The man gathered roots to brew ointments and potions and seemed more like a cleric than a mage. He had talked with the man briefly and had left with the impression the man was like any villager (except for the hair).

The second mage Quint had met was Cwyllyn ap Dyryn, who seemed fairly ordinary. The man played a dulcimer he always carried, and Quint would've assumed the man to be a bard had reputation not held him a wizard. He had not seen the homes of either of these men. Shadowbender's Tower, then, was a first for him. He hoped to see something nefarious (though not particularly dangerous—Quint wanted no part of being magicked into a toad or anything else bad) so as to have a good story. Maybe he could convince the elf to turn *Roland* into a toad (temporarily), which would be incredibly funny as well as making an interesting tale.

The elf led them through what appeared to be an informal dining room and then up a spiral staircase. The Tower itself was surprising. First of all, it seemed larger on the inside than the outside dimensions would indicate. Clearly, there was some sort of powerful magic responsible for this anomaly. The presence of magic, while not inherently a bad thing, did tend to make one a bit uneasy.

Secondly, to be so isolated, every conceivable luxury seemed to be present. Elegant pottery, glassware, and even what appeared to be crystal candelabra were all to be seen among other furnishings of elegant taste. The furniture in the first room had been comfortably functional, but the dining room displayed beautiful maple furniture decorated with realistic carvings of natural things: leaves, trees, animals, and Quint could even see the playful faces of faeries grinning from the intricately wrought mantle. Fabric covered cushions were in the seats of the chairs and several bouquets of fresh wild flowers graced the room with their scent as well as supplying a splash of colour. Overall, the room was light, bright, and happy. It seemed out of character for the gloomily clad mage; perhaps he was married, and his wife was responsible for the 'hominess'. Quint also wondered how the mage had acquired all these fine things, as isolated as he was.

Thirdly, the entire interior seemed filled with light despite the lack of windows and artificial light. From the outside, the tower seemed to be solid marble, beautiful, but certainly opaque (and 'dainty,' as Roland had disparagingly remarked). From the inside, however, the walls appeared almost translucent and glowed warmly with soft light. Quint was awed.

"Come on, Quint!" Roland whispered, bringing the ranger back to his senses, and the ranger hurried to catch up as the elf led them up the spiral staircase.

On the second level was a landing. The stairs continued upwards, soaring toward the sky, or so it appeared as the light grew brighter the higher one progressed. Perhaps the Tower was open to the sky or, at least, featured a skylight somewhere above them. Quint suspected the latter as there were no signs of weathering to indicate the elements (except light) had access to the Tower's interior.

Shadowbender stepped onto the landing, walked to a closed oaken door and turned to the pair, "This is the music room, a bit informal, perhaps, but one of the more comfortable rooms in the Tower," Shadowbender opened the door. The sound of a skilfully played dulcimer spilled onto the landing. Quint wondered if Cwyllyn ap Dyryn was here, though he had no idea how the man could have arrived before he and Roland. Taken aback, the pair entered the room cautiously.

Quint found the room was designed with comfort in mind. Soft, comfortable chairs and sofas were strategically placed throughout the room. Large pillows were also lying about should one prefer them to the furniture. Thick rugs covered the floor and colourful tapestries portraying bards, minstrels, dancing satyrs, and other festive characters covered the walls. Several candles in silver holders were lit in various locations, their light augmenting the natural glow of the chamber. Various instruments lay scattered around the room: flutes, lyres, drums, bagpipes, and several others. A small marble-topped table stood in a corner, covered with wine bottles, jugs, and assorted breads and cheeses. Sitting on a velvet cushion in the middle of the floor was the source of the beautiful music.

It wasn't Cwyllyn, but a man in a simple cloth tunic and brown trousers sitting cross-legged strumming a beautifully carven dulcimer. A few loose sheets of parchment, a bottle of ink, and a quill lay on the floor beside him. He had apparently been composing a song as the uppermost parchment displayed the odd shaped designs of musical notes scattered across it, some of which were crossed out and rewritten in a slightly different order. The man stopped playing the moment he noticed them enter the room. He had shoulder-length brown hair worn untied, brown eyes, and was of average height. He smiled broadly as he bowed, "The illustrious Quint Longbow and Roland Bloodaxe, I presume. Well met! Your exploits have preceded you. I am honoured. Drake of Allendale, at your service."

The dwarf nodded curtly, but Quint was pleased with the man's politeness. A polite demeanour indicated a cultivated mind.

"So, you've heard of us? And you are a bard?"

"Of course," Drake answered with a smile.

"Ah!" Quint said enthusiastically, "then perhaps I should detail some of our finer adventures, so you can compose a little something about it in fine epic tradition!"

"Perhaps you should detail your present adventure as it pertains to your visit here," Shadowbender interrupted before the bard could reply.

"Quite so!" Quint replied nonplussed.

After a few general pleasantries (between the ranger and the bard; Roland and Shadowbender were silent), Shadowbender poured them all drinks. They all sat down comfortably, even Roland who was in somewhat better spirits after learning Shadowbender kept a fine brew of dwarven ale on hand (for Drake), a large mug of which the dwarf had already consumed in the short interval. Roland could (and had, on many occasions) consume as much ale as several men. Usually, this resulted in trouble as Roland grew cantankerous when drinking, but, as drinking kept the dwarf occupied and happy, at least in the short run, Quint felt the drinks might serve a useful purpose in negating Roland's acerbic tongue as the dwarf would be unlikely to lash out at a host who was supplying him with ale, at least until he got drunk. Quint, for his part, gratefully accepted a glass of wine.

"Drake here," Shadowbender said, "is a bard and scholar. He is a friend of mine and an occasional adventuring partner. Anything

31

you can tell me can be said in his presence." Shadowbender settled comfortably in one of the chairs, a goblet of light elven wine in one hand and a generous slice of cheese in the other. "Please tell us your story."

"It's a long tale," said Quint, "it will take most of the night to tell it."

"Wait!" chirped a voice behind them, "don't start without me!"

Quint spun around. Roland drew his axe in surprise, nearly (but not quite) spilling his ale. Before them stood a female elf dressed entirely in blue. Her blonde hair was fastened into an elven ponytail (both sexes wore it in the same fashion—a trait Roland found contemptible) with a sapphire-studded clip gleaming in the translucence. Quint knew he looked upon the perpetrator of the Tower's décor. The woman promptly plopped into a large armchair, "Go on, then!" she giggled, her blue eyes sparkling.

"My sister, Oceana, is not as polite as some would wish," Shadowbender began.

"But polite enough!" she laughed. She stood up and bowed, "I am pleased to meet both of you."

Quint bowed in return, "It is certainly a pleasure to meet such a beautiful maiden," he said flashing a bright smile. In contrast to her brother, the maiden displayed none of the stereotypical elven aloofness, and he was delighted the beautiful woman was the mages' sister, not his wife—which would have been most unfortunate. He heard the dwarf snort behind him in response to his compliment.

32

Roland always found Quint's romantic overtures funny, which didn't matter to Quint, who operated on the theory that associating with non-romantic men only enhanced his own chances with the ladies. Ignoring the dwarf, Quint sat back down, a hint of regality etched upon his features.

"Cwyllyn ap Dyryn sent word you have something I should see," said the practical Shadowbender. The elf was a successful mage. He owned this success to motivation, practicality, and a rigorous programme of study. Measuring his life by accomplishment, Shadowbender was irritated by any waste of time and, as far as he was concerned, the meaningless pleasantries between people who had no meaning or bearing on one's life or career, was a tremendous waste of time. If not for Cwyllyn's strange missive, Shadowbender would have sent the ranger and his uncouth companion packing without a second thought. As if inviting the pair into his Tower was not bad enough, the ranger appeared content to flirt all night and moon like a human girl. If he did not prompt something out of the ranger soon (the tight-lipped dwarf was probably intractable) they would be here all night. He was mildly annoyed with the ranger's response to Oceana, not that it was an uncommon response among men first meeting her. Humans found elves hauntingly beautiful and exotic, and Oceana was considered beautiful even among elves.

Quint turned to face Shadowbender. "We have discovered an ancient scroll of some sort in our adventures. We took it to Cwyllyn, whom we have dealt with in the past. He kept it overnight. When we returned the next day, Cwyllyn insisted we bring it to you, giving us directions to your tower. Roland didn't want to come and, to be honest, I didn't, either. But Cwyllyn said it would be worth our time, so here we are." Quint reached into a pocket and withdrew a scroll case and handed it to Shadowbender.

The scroll tube was of the common sort constructed of bone (or, perhaps, ivory) and yellowed with age. The mage unscrewed the cap at its base and withdrew a yellowed scroll. It was obviously old; it was brittle, and the writing had faded so as to be almost unreadable. The elf walked over to one of the scattered candles that lit the room and peered at the scroll for a full ten minutes.

While the mage was so engaged, Quint appraised the elf maid. He had known a number of attractive women, but the elf possessed an unearthly beauty beyond any a mortal woman might possess. Her hair was slightly darker than Shadowbender's, a cascade of warm summer honey spilling down her shoulders. Her eyes, too, were noteworthy. They were faintly luminescent and were easily the brightest blue he'd ever seen. They were an odd (ah! —make that *unique*) hue: the brilliant blue of a spring sky after a cleansing rain shower when the whole world seems fresh and sparkling. Intently watching Shadowbender, she caressed one of a pair of dangling earrings featuring small sapphires that merrily reflected the soft candlelight. Quint was suddenly aware Drake, too, was closely watching the elf maiden, and the ranger was surprised to feel a twinge of—what? Jealousy? Certainly, it was too soon for that.

"It seems strange," Quint said demurely, "that such a radiant maiden should be so blue." He laughed softly, pleased with himself for being so coy.

"I like blue," Oceana laughed.

"Why?" Quint asked; long ago, the ranger had learned the way to learn about women is to ask open-ended questions and pay attention to the responses.

"Blue reminds me of the sky and freedom and tempestuousness and the ocean," the woman replied, "have you ever been to the ocean, Quint?"

"Oh…yes," answered Quint, who had been trying to work out the word 'tempestuousness' in his head, "I have seen the ocean on several occasions. It is beautiful, though not as beautiful as some things I've seen." Quint waited to see if Oceana would take the bait. Unfortunately, she didn't, and Quint missed an opportunity to make an extremely romantic statement.

"The ocean is wild," said Oceana gaily, "but, when I see it, it makes me want to sit and think about, well…a lot of things."

"The ocean makes everyone a philosopher," said Drake, a faraway look in his eye.

"Ah, yes," said Quint, slightly irritated the bard would horn in on his carefully orchestrated seduction; he was going to follow up with something fitting, but couldn't think of anything, which further irritated him.

Shadowbender returned to his seat, casting a pall over the others. "I must study this thoroughly," the mage said, "I shall relieve you of your obligation to tell your story tonight. I know you are weary and guest quarters have been prepared for you."

Both adventurers seemed somewhat unhappy to be dismissed without an explanation, and the dwarf seemed ready to argue. Hurriedly, Oceana stood up, offering to lead Quint and Roland to their guest chamber, a pleasant room with two large beds. "I shall call you in the morning," promised the elf maiden, "and I'll bring a cask of ale to your chamber." Reluctantly, Roland and Quint followed the elf maiden from the room after bidding the mage and bard good-night.

Meanwhile, in the music room, Drake turned toward Shadowbender.

"What is it my friend?" he asked. He knew Shadowbender and the elf's reaction was cause for concern.

Shadowbender ignored the question. Instead, he walked toward the staircase, "Come with me to the study, Drake. I shall be wanting your help, I think. We shall be wanting all the help we can get." With a frown, Shadowbender walked from the room, the bard following.

Chapter 3

Shadowbender didn't so much as show his face the next day. Or the day after that. One of the mage's guests was not comforted by his absence. Quint, though satisfied with Shadowbender's hospitality, was bored just sitting around as he, unlike Roland, had no desire to drink himself into a stupor.

Quint walked over to the small, narrow window of the chamber and gazed out. The room featured a pair of wooden beds, a night stand, a wardrobe, and the window. Angled, the window allowed one to look out but did not allow someone at ground level to see in. In fact, Quint had deduced the window itself, as cunningly constructed as it was, could only be seen from the outside from an angle; someone looking from directly in front of it would miss it entirely, believing he looked at a solid marble wall. Like the rest of the tower, the room he and Roland had been given was lighter than it should have been. Quint had already devoted thought to this conundrum since he first noticed it but was no closer to a solution (other than magic) than he had been when they first arrived. The Tower appeared translucent from the inside though not nearly enough to allow one to see through the walls; rather, it was translucent enough to let in light yet opaque enough to block vision. If nothing stranger was to be seen during his tenure here, the translucence should make a pretty decent tale.

Outside the Tower, the ranger could see a large copse of laurel, many of the bushes in bloom. He knew each individual bush bloomed only every other year. Bees swarmed around the blooms, dipping into the individual flowers systematically. Nature was such a work of art in its combination of stark efficiency and sheer beauty. He could smell the flowers and surrounding forest. When the wind was right, he could smell water, probably the mountain freshet he could only just hear beneath the distant droning of the bees. Each individual drone knew its place in the hierarchy of the hive; each had a purpose and, in serving its purpose, contributed to the well-being of the entire hive and, indeed, considering the role the bees inadvertently filled in cross pollinating the flowers they visited, the entire ecosystem. Each drone contributed to the entire world and didn't even know it.

Quint wondered about his own purpose. What was he contributing to the world at large? Perhaps he, like the drones, unknowingly set in motion events that benefited the entire world. Perhaps not. His position was much less ordered than the drones, harder to label with any finality. There were two types of rangers in the world: rangers by profession and rangers by happenstance, and he was one of the latter.

Rangers by profession were men who made a traditional living from the forest. Some worked for a lord tending the forested areas for their liege. These generally fulfilled secondary roles such as acting as game wardens protecting the lord's game from poachers or hunters supplying meat to the lords table. Sometimes called Foresters, these men spent a good deal of their time in the woods but had a regular home and were bound to the area the lord controlled (or a portion of it if the area was sufficiently large). Quint had once considered this career but baulked at being confined within a certain boundary and the accompanying charge of acting as a sheriff policing a lord's resources. Mostly, this lifestyle didn't appeal to him because he belonged to the second classification of rangers: rangers by happenstance.

Rangers by happenstance made their living within the forest. Such men happened to live in a forest and were rangers by default. Serving no lord (at least in regard to their careers), these men were hunters or trappers who made their livelihood from the forest's bounty but were not officially charged with overseeing an area. Some lived within established domains, but most lived beyond them in the so-called uncivilized areas of the world. Some were forced into this lifestyle, fleeing the law or evicted from their previous homes. Some chose to live away from the civilized areas for various reasons. Many, basically living as free-homesteaders, "claimed" an area as their own and protected and oversaw this area much as a commissioned forester would only there was no official sanction to do so. Others, such as himself, roved at will.

Some who roved had a purpose, and those whose purpose was protecting the woodland from encroaching civilization, often violently, were the most talked-about but, in Quint's experience, the least common. Most roving rangers were men such as himself, chasing their own dreams and freedom and, more or less, just happened to do so in the wilderness as wilderness, unclaimed by any established authority, was a conducive setting for this particular endeavour. Quint had no particular area he considered his own, and he wasn't opposed to civilization as were some of his more embittered contemporaries. Like many rovers, Quint was driven by curiosity and a sense of freedom. Perhaps, one day, he would find what he was looking for and, like Shadowbender and Oceana, settle down to "do his thing"—whatever it might be. Taking a deep breath of the fragrant air, Quint turned from the window and stepped back into the room.

"I don't even know why we're here, I didn't want to come in the first place," Roland said when Quint turned, "but, as long as the ale holds out, I guess it don't matter no way!" The dwarf laughed loudly at his jest. Roland had not been idle during the absence of their elusive host. It was only early morning of their third day and the dwarf had already emptied a full barrel of Shadowbender's dwarven ale. He didn't know why the elf would have dwarven ale in the first place, but who cared? 'Where there's ale, there's friendship' was a popular dwarven maxim. Roland was feeling downright hospitable. Quint just hoped the ale would hold up, otherwise the dwarf would become tired of waiting around and demand they leave.

Quint didn't want to leave. The ranger was curious as to the scroll they had discovered in Feywood. He knew the scroll was a rarity and of some interest, but was it really a magic scroll? Quint didn't know for sure, but he was anxious to find out. The fact that the elven mage had spent two entire days examining it in his study (so Drake had said during the latest of his infrequent visits) merely added to the ranger's curiosity. Quint had no idea what, if anything, he could do with such an item, though the discovery of a magical scroll would provide a nice boost to his reputation and give him yet another story of derring-do to share around the camp fire. A knock at the door interrupted the man's pleasant thoughts.

"What's that?" Roland demanded. The dwarf rose to his feet after three tries, and stood on wobbly legs, his axe in hand. He peered at the door, a look of surprise on his face. "Why is the door moving?" Roland had seen a lot of strange things during his adventuring career and anything that even hinted of magic worried him.

Quint tried unsuccessfully to cover a smile. "Too much ale is the most likely answer, my friend." The ranger walked to the door and opened it cautiously, stepping to the side as he did so. Old habits die hard. No danger stood across the threshold on this occasion, however.

Oceana, clad in a pale green tunic and soft leather knee-boots, smiled and entered the room like the appearance of a woodland dawn. Her beauty was greater than Quint could comprehend, despite the fact he knew she was there, she seemed like a dream. She bowed slightly, "I'm sorry to intrude, but I thought you might be bored cooped up in here. I thought I might offer you a tour or something."

The dwarf shrugged and plopped back into his chair. Quint hadn't heard a better offer since, well, ever. The dwarf, Quint knew, didn't care about such things. In this case, Quint was glad for the dwarf's indifference as the rangers' heart leapt at the thought of being able to be alone with Oceana. He only hoped she had not invited Drake.

"A charming idea," Quint said, "It is rather tedious, the waiting, I mean."

"My brother is a great elf but attending to a guest's comfort is not one of his better qualities. How about a walk around the Tower?"

"What do you say, Roland? Up for a tour?" Quint asked the dwarf. He wasn't surprised when Roland waved his hand dismissively. Quint turned to the elf, "I guess it's just the two of us," he smiled, "though I'd rather see the grounds if you don't mind. I've been inside for over two days now, and a taste of fresh air would be most refreshing."

Quint and Oceana strolled around the exterior of the Tower. Quint gazed at the sparkling marble as it reflected the late morning sun. 'Dainty' Roland had called it. The dwarf had remarked how he and ten of his clansmen could topple the entire structure in an hour's time.

"Your home is beautiful," is what he said to Oceana.

"Yes," she replied, "Shadowbender had it erected in his youth, not long after he acquired the robes of mage hood. The rare marble came far from the south, along the coast of Duran."

"I've been to Duran." Quint replied. "It's a nice place. Not many forests left, though. Civilization has spread almost to the border of the Sundered Mountains."

"You prefer the forests, then?" Oceana glanced curiously at the ranger. Most humans disliked the wilderness, seeing it only as a place of danger or a resource to be plundered. She knew not all humans were that way anymore than all elves were gentle and good or all dwarves were alcoholic war-mongers. Well, she thought as an image of Roland popped into her mind, maybe there was some truth to the dwarven stereotype.

"Of course. I am a ranger, after all. The forest is our home, such as we have," he added. Puzzlement crossed the man's features, "You said Shadowbender erected this Tower in his youth, but he appears young now. I know elves are longer lived than humans, but Shadowbender certainly couldn't be considered old," he queried.

Oceana giggled, "That depends on what you consider 'old'. That varies from race to race, but humans would consider him old, I think. He is a little over four hundred." The elf maiden laughed at the disbelief on the ranger's face.

"Four hundred. But that's older than most of the world's kingdoms!"

"Ah, but you are undoubtedly thinking only of the human kingdoms, which are still in their infancy by elven standards."

Feeling a little foolish, Quint decided to change the subject.

"Where is Carrick the grounds man?" he asked, glancing around, again struck by the absence of cultivated grounds. Except for the path itself, the forest seemed unaltered.

"Who?" Oceana asked.

"Carrick—the man who met us the day of our arrival," Quint said. Oceana smiled strangely, "You've seen him, though you may not have known it. Carrick is rather reclusive, but he is never far away."

"What's that supposed to mean?" Quint asked. The ranger didn't like the sound of Oceana's mysterious reply. Was the old man hiding, spying on him from the forest?

"It means Carrick is my brother."

"What?" Now the ranger was thoroughly confused. "But, Carrick is human. How could he be your brother?"

"Shadowbender is an illusionist. Didn't Cwyllyn tell you?" Oceana shrugged, turning toward a white gravelled path leading into the forest.

"Well, no." Quint followed her down the path, his boots crunching on the glittering stones. "If Shadowbender is an illusionist, how do I know you aren't Shadowbender in disguise?" he asked as the disconcerting thought occurred to him.

Oceana (if that's who it was) stopped and turned to face the ranger, "I guess you don't, do you?" she giggled. Abruptly, she turned, flounced her hair playfully, and strolled down the path. Quint hesitated for a moment, trying to work out things in his head. The possibility of mage-craft at work, especially illusion-based magic, left him questioning his own perception. Was Oceana Oceana or was Oceana Shadowbender or was she someone else entirely? Roland was right, these people were weird. Shaking his head, Quint followed who he hoped was the elf maid down the path.

He soon caught up with her, and they walked together. Oceana's hair was flowing gently in the breeze and smelled faintly of lilacs. Quint wanted to say something witty and desperately romantic, but, frustratingly, couldn't think of anything suitable. Thus, in order to have something to distract him, he began to study his surroundings.

He had never been so high in the mountains before, and the terrain was similar to that found in regions much further north. The forest was largely evergreen. There were a lot of hemlocks, he noted, his favourite tree. Most of the trees were short and gnarled and tended to be thick in diameter due to the constant winds, heavy snowfall, and short growing season. Impassable laurel thickets abounded and, if not for the path, they would have had some difficulty moving around. He noticed many of the larger trees displayed broken limbs. Snow and ice were harsh to hard woods; their rigid limbs simply broke under the weight. Evergreen limbs were limber and tended to shed the accumulated snow when it became too heavy, the supple limbs snapping back into place. The forest was fascinating, the ranger thought. Different, somehow. Wild. Wilder even than the uncivilized woods in the lowlands. This forest seemed more distant; isolated from the rest of the world. *Apart* was the word he was searching for. Lack of suitable farmland on the mountain slopes as well as general inaccessibility kept settlers away. Even explorers were rare; the occasional adventurer merely crossed the mountains to get to the valleys opposite, and they used the passes lower down the mountain range. He recalled the absence of humanoid signs on the way here. Orcs and goblins often inhabited semi-inaccessible regions, using them as bases for their raiding forays into more populated regions. There weren't really any populated areas close enough to raid, though Quint suspected his hosts had as much to do with the absence of raiders as the lack of suitable victims. His train of thought turned toward his strange hosts.

Who were they, anyway? He had met a few elves in his travels, wood elves in the deep southern forests. They were unlike Oceana and her brother. The general features, build, and facial structure were similar, of course, but the similarity ended there. The wood elves he had seen were shorter than the willowy elf maid beside him. Oceana was fair-haired and skinned. Wood elves were darker and almost invariably had brown or black hair. His hosts seemed more civilized, too. The wood elves were more rustic; in fact, wizards were rumoured to be extremely rare among them, although druidic magic was not. Many of the southern druids were wood elves who were renowned for their herb-lore and their aggressive quashing of human encroachment into any lands they considered their own. Fortunately, such areas tended to be deep in the inland forests far from the areas settled by men and violence between the two races was rare, though rumoured to be brutal when it did occur. Most stories, except those of dwarven origin, maintained elves were generally peaceful, living in the twilight between the mortal and the fey— neither yet both. Quint knew there were different races of elves, and he decided Oceana and Shadowbender were a different type. But, he thought, all elves were clannish, not so much as dwarves, to be sure, he thought with amusement of Roland and his genealogical rules about who was at war with whom and with whom one could conduct business. Dwarves were clannish to the extreme, fighting entire wars over suspected slights to some distant, long-dead ancestor. Oceana and Shadowbender, though, presumably lived outside a clan environment unless there were other elves nearby of whom he was unaware.

The ranger had travelled extensively and, consequently, had picked up the odd bit of lore. Elves, by and large, were peace-loving though it was whispered the elves, in the forgotten days of antiquity, suffered a schism of some sort. The majority, wanting to avoid contact with the other races (the exact reasons behind this varied from telling to telling), remained in their hidden civilization in the Elven Kingdoms. The minority wanted to expand and migrated over most of the southern forests. As a result of a semi-nomadic existence, they gradually became less learned and wilder than their brethren. They became known as wild elves or rustic elves and lived much like the frontier human did except for their propensity for druidic magic which was a rarity among humans.

Quint pondered the enigma that was Oceana. Lithe and beautiful, Oceana moved fluidly as if she were actually composed of the element that was her namesake. Oceana was real and women, despite their race, were women. The ranger was relatively certain the elf maid was playing coy, tripping around the forest like a nymph in all the tales. She was obviously attracted to him, a concept he heartily supported, and was playfully stringing him along in that mysterious, light-hearted way women had. The elf maid had done nothing overt to encourage him, he acknowledged to himself, but one needn't be a sage to possess wisdom enough to understand there is more to a woman's style of camouflage than merely colour and shape. Witty, beautiful, and a cultured conversationalist, Oceana seemed more like a talented courtier thriving on flirting and intrigue than someone who lived an almost hermit-like existence in the middle of an uncivilized forest. Her social talents (which he much admired) hinted she had once moved in quite a different circle. It seemed odd for Oceana to live way up here apart from other elves. He opened his mouth to ask Oceana why she did live way up here when the elf maid suddenly stopped, head cocked to one side in concentration, and motioned for Quint to stop. Quint did so, his question momentarily forgotten.

"Enemies!" Oceana screamed. The elf maid jumped from Quint's side, landing behind a young hemlock, and drew a slender wooden stick from her belt. Quint cursed himself for being so lost in thought that he had nearly walked into something hostile without even realizing it. Some ranger and guardian he was! Quint drew his long sword and peered into the surrounding forest.

Quint could see nothing. What was the elf talking about? A bow twanged, followed by several more in rapid succession. "Get down!" Quint yelled to Oceana as he threw himself to the ground, desperately trying to avoid the half-dozen arrows whizzing through the clearing. The arrows suddenly stopped in mid-air as if stuck in some invisible wall. Quint gasped in amazement; he had never seen anything like this before. After a moment, the arrows, freed from whatever force that had held them, dropped to the ground. Quint wondered if Shadowbender was surreptitiously aiding (and, therefore, spying on) them.

A cry sounded from the surrounding forest, and six shapes waded into sight. Quint jumped to his feet, prepared for assault. Oceana also stepped into the clearing, a small vial in her hand. They faced their attackers.

Quint shook his head in dismay. He heard Oceana's surprised gasp. Quint had seen a lot of strange things in his life, even a hydra once, in a swamp in The Broken Lands, but he had seen nothing like the creatures he now faced. They were human sized and looked like humans except each had a glaring reptilian face. Some sort of lizard man, the ranger guessed, but what were swamp-dwelling lizard men doing in the mountains? Each held a long sword and a parrying dagger in gauntleted hands, much higher quality weapons than the club-and-bone wielding barbaric lizard men with which he was familiar. They also moved with the grace of skilled fighters; the few lizard men the ranger had encountered were poor fighters who generally relied on surprise and overwhelming numbers rather than fighting finesse. The lead figure said something in a language Quint had never heard. Screaming wildly, the figures launched their attack.

The assailants split up, three attacking Quint, the other three running for Oceana. Quint wondered desperately how he was going to be able to protect the woman, decided he could not effectively do so as the attackers were too many, and started to tell Oceana to flee. Suddenly, from the corner of his eye, Quint saw Oceana point toward the foremost of her attackers, mumbling something he couldn't understand. The creature was lifted and thrown violently into the trunk of a twisted oak. The creature's screams were cut short as it

49

struck the tree with a horrible bone-shattering crunch. It fell lifeless to the forest floor. His mouth snapped shut. By the gods, Oceana was a mage! Then, battle instinct took over and Quint concentrated on his own battle.

Hoping to even the odds a bit, Quint palmed the dagger hidden in his sleeve and threw it with a quick motion as the lizard men raised their swords to attack. The dagger caught one in the throat. It fell gurgling, blood oozing around the hilt of the dagger. Quint nodded with satisfaction, bolstered with the knowledge these creatures, though mysterious, could be killed like any other. The combat was joined with clanging blades, and Quint focused on the battle before him with the intensity of a seasoned warrior.

The first of the attackers moved before him, deftly parrying Quint's responsive attack. The second moved to flank him. Quint stepped away from the flanking creature, using the one before him as a barrier to the second. As he drew another dagger, Quint again struck out with his long sword and was again parried. The lizard men exchanged positions as the one before him took a step to the right, becoming a flanker, and the other moved forward, taking the place of the former.

Sometimes, Quint enjoyed fighting skilled opponents; such combat kept one sharp and provided an opportunity to learn new tactics and, providing one survived, increased one's skill. Now, however, was not one of these times. One, he was outnumbered. Two, the attackers were just plain weird, and he didn't like fighting unknown assailants. Third, he felt an overwhelming urgency to assist

Oceana (whom he just couldn't envision to be a skilled warrior) and becoming entangled with two skilled adversaries was not conducive to a quick hack-and-slash solution. However, possessing a numerical advantage, the lizard creatures soon had Quint on the defensive.

Whatever else they might be, these creatures were skilled warriors. Quint fought bravely but made no progress. The ranger had been nicked several times, the pain fuelling his blood rage. He hammered at his foes relentlessly, but he knew the odds were against him. The pair worked well together, coordinating their attacks. Quint was forced to fall back, the creatures pushing him off the path and into the forest.

From his new vantage point, he could see Oceana. A second attacker lay motionless on the ground. Oceana was grappling with her final attacker. At least she was alive. His own situation was getting desperate. The undergrowth was entangling his legs, threatening to trip him. An opportunity presented itself and Quint took it. Backing into a limb, the ranger stepped back quickly. The branch recoiled behind him. Blocking a sword thrust, Quint ducked, snapping the branch into the faces of his opponents. One of the creatures was struck in the face and fell backwards, momentarily stunned. The other ducked forward, losing its balance. Quint stabbed, allowing the creatures own momentum to impale itself on Quint's blade. He sprang forward, pressing his advantage. Still stunned from its fall, the last creature was easily dispatched.

Breathing heavily, Quint ran to Oceana. She was still grappling desperately with her assailant. Quint attacked from behind, slashing so as to minimize the danger of injuring the elf. With a scream of rage, the creature whirled on Quint. The blow had been lethal, and the creature knew it; Quint could see it in its eyes. It raised its sword. Suddenly, the creature shuddered, its sword falling from its nerveless hand. The creature crumpled, Oceana's dagger buried in its back. Over the body, their gazes locked. Quint wasn't sure if the look on Oceana's face was shock or sorrow; he decided it was both and cringed inwardly in sympathy for the elf maiden's pain.

Quint leapt forward concerned for the elf maid. Oceana lifted her arms, "Get back to the Tower!" she hissed. She mumbled a word and vanished in a crackling sound reminiscent of static electricity. Quint was alone.

Quint stood in surprise; knowing the elf maid possessed a mysterious power he couldn't hope to understand was both exciting and a little frightening. Shaking his head at this new-found knowledge, Quint inspected the clearing. The creatures were scattered about the clearing like broken dolls; it seemed no more were forthcoming. Quint turned toward the Tower, and then hesitated. What were the creatures? He bent over one of the bodies. Upon closer inspection, the ranger realized they weren't lizard men at all; the reptilian visage was a mask. Carefully, he removed the mask to reveal the tattooed face of a fearsome and very dead human. The tattoos were in the stylized pattern of scales.

Chapter 4

Quint ran back to the Tower; for all his speed, his thoughts raced faster. The men in the masks were a puzzle and puzzles had to be solved. Unfortunately, he couldn't think of a solution. Mages were strange and dabbled in many things. It was likely they created a few enemies in the course of their work and it was entirely possible the masked men were such.

He reached the Tower door, found it locked, and began beating on it frantically.

"Who's there?" called a gruff voice.

"Roland! It's me—Quint!"

The door opened. Roland peered from the doorway, eyes squinting into the light. Quint pushed past him, and the dwarf quickly closed the door and bolted it.

"I'm glad you made it, Quint," the dwarf shifted uncomfortably. "I'm sorry... I should have been there..." the dwarf began.

Quint laid his hand on the dwarf's shoulder.

"Don't worry, my friend. There was nothing you could have done. Besides," he added squaring his shoulders, "I was never really in danger, anyway."

The dwarf snorted, regaining his normal grim expression.

"I should have known it was you pounding on the door. As if my head weren't pounding enough on its own."

"You've got to go easy on the ale, Roland."

"Tell me about it," the dwarf moaned.

"I take it Oceana arrived?" Quint asked.

"Did she ever! Just appeared—poof!" the dwarf snapped his fingers, "It's unnatural the way these elves do. She's a *mage,* Quint, you hear me? A blinkin' mage!"

"I know." The ranger turned toward the Tower's interior, "Come on, Roland, we've got to talk to Shadowbender and make sure Oceana's all right."

"We need to make sure *we're* all right!" the dwarf replied, "Oceana told me what happened and, if this attack was coincidental, I'm a drunken goblin!"

"Well, you do smell heavily of ale," Quint laughed.

"Very funny." Roland's face hardened, "Quint, this is serious. This attack had something to do with that cursed scroll we found. Now, you take a magic scroll, two crazed wizards (and elves, let's not forget), you add some weird lizard-men, and then throw in a dwarf and an insane ranger and what do you get?"

"We don't know the scroll is magical and we certainly have no proof Oceana is crazy," Quint replied, refusing to take the bait. He knew the dwarf's distaste for magic but didn't inherently share Roland's view. However, he hadn't considered the attack related to the scroll.

"Trouble. That's what you get," Roland continued, "and we need no part of it." Quint continued walking, pointedly ignoring the dwarf. "C'mon, Roland," he called.

Roland hesitated for a moment, in the throes of a silent debate.

"Great!" he waved his arms in disgust, "just great." Shaking his head, the dwarf followed his friend deeper into the Tower, muttering the whole way.

It was an odd and mixed assembly gathered in the music room half an hour later. Shadowbender and Drake sat together on a sofa smoking curiously carved ivory pipes. Comforted in the discovery, Shadowbender had tobacco and delighted in the elf's willingness to share, Roland sat near the mage, smoking a simple clay pipe. Roland's opinion of Shadowbender was much improved, and the dwarf appeared as happy as a dwarf sitting near an elven mage could be. Quint sat on the floor gazing alternately upon Shadowbender and Oceana. He smoked occasionally in social situations but had no particular fondness for tobacco. He had been offered a pipe but declined in favour of a glass of wine. Oceana completed the assembly. Sitting in a chair facing the others, she managed to appear amused and concerned at the same time.

No one spoke for a good while. Oceana, impatient with 'this masculine posturing' as she considered it, finally broke the silence, "Well, I suppose we better get started before too many days have passed," and crossed her arms expectantly.

Shadowbender threw her a cursory glance and set his pipe down. He got up and paced the floor in an agitated manner. Pipe smoke swirled around his robes and about the room, creating a surreal effect. He inspected the two visitors. Their puissance was fairly evident, especially after Oceana's description of the battle with the men in the lizard masks; or, perhaps, it was more accurate to say dragon masks. Intelligence, however, at least in the intellectual sense, did not seem to be a strength for either of them. The possession of a scroll such as the one he had inspected seemed out of character for two adventurers who could not read it.

"It would be helpful," is what Shadowbender said, "if I knew the story behind your discovery of the scroll." It was a thinly veiled question and the elf looked at Quint, of the pair, the most likely to talk.

The human seemed eager to communicate his own exploits and happily launched into the tale: "Roland and I," Quint explained, "had journeyed to Feywood following a rumour of a black unicorn. Unicorns, as you know, are generally white or pearlescent—not black.

"Yes, I am aware," Shadowbender interjected.

"Anyway," Quint didn't miss a beat, "we combed the wood for a couple of weeks, exhausted all our leads, and were pretty well disappointed in not finding the unicorn. Or, I was disappointed; I don't think Roland cared that much one way or the other." Quint smiled, and his face filled with wonder at the idea of glimpsing the legendary beast.

"Fortunately," he continued, "we heard about an old abandoned keep over the course of our inquiry into the unicorn."

"Why was that fortunate?" Shadowbender asked.

"Because," Quint smiled, "it gave us something to do, eh— Roland." Roland didn't respond as he had learned long ago it was better to let Quint run his mouth until satisfied. A speaker would have to be pretty deft to get a word in edge-wise when Quint was talking.

Roland would interrupt the ranger if something important was left out, but generally avoided such conversations. Quint usually embellished quite a bit, particularly if a woman was around, but, as it didn't really matter, Roland let the embellishments go. After all, such colourings often made the dwarf seem more heroic, too. Roland had nowhere near the female attention the young, energetic, handsome (and tall) ranger had, but he still had his pride (which was what Roland, like many a dwarf, inaccurately called his ego). If the occasional lass were star-struck over the dwarf's exploits—well, that was a good thing.

Not expecting a reply from the taciturn dwarf, Quint continued immediately, "Way out in the middle of nowhere, looking like it had been abandoned for a thousand years, was the keep. It was made of stone (though not of particularly skilled workmanship as Roland had pointed out). The entire structure was vine-covered and littered with debris. Part of the building had actually toppled over, and it was rather dangerous scrambling around it.

We had heard about the keep two days earlier from a travelling druid and thought we'd check it out as it wasn't far from where we were at the time. We weren't told about the scroll or any treasure for that matter, but it is interesting to see an old keep being reclaimed by nature—it is sort of mystic. Roland, in any event, was much more interested in the keep than the continued search for the elusive unicorn and, being free men upon the earth, we changed plans in midstream, so to speak. Thus, we found ourselves poking around the ruins of a keep we had not known existed.

I still don't know anything about it other than what we could glean from the building itself. It's strange how something as important as a keep could be forgotten when it was once so real. I wonder if some curious adventurer might one day say the same about this very Tower," Quint gestured at the stones around them.

"That," said Drake, "is a fascinating concept."

"Though unlikely," Shadowbender mildly countered, "after all, elves have long memories."

"As do dwarves!" Roland chimed in.

"Yes," said Drake, "but neither puts much energy into knowing enough about humankind to remember anything about them."

"Too chaotic and short lived," remarked Roland.

"You were exploring the keep?" Oceana prompted.

"Yes. Thank you." Quint took a deep breath and resumed his tale. "Roland and I poked around the outer perimeter. Nothing seemed amiss—meaning a battle or anything. The rocks seemed to have aged and toppled over on their own with roots and vines bearing the primary responsibility. Then, we heard a sound. I felt a little stupid, being so absorbed as to let something surprise us.

Roland drew his axe and sprang to attention. About fifteen feet away, stood a man with his chest and arms visible over the remains of a wall. He was thick, and his arms were knotted with muscles. He had piercing black eyes focused on Roland and black hair tied back and a long, bluish-black beard. Both hands were placed atop the broken stones and his demeanour was boisterous.

"Halloo, little ones!" he bellowed. Then, I noticed what had escaped me at first— he was tall. The wall stood almost five feet tall and his chest was completely visible above the stones. He must have been seven feet tall! Thus, 'little ones' wasn't out of order— especially regarding Roland." The dwarf quickly frowned, and Quint smiled broadly. His face again became serious and the ranger continued— "Roland said nothing, merely stood shifting his axe from hand to hand and looking around warily. I answered saying, 'Greetings.' Then, I waited for a reply. I didn't feel comfortable being accosted by some pseudo-giant in the process of salvaging an abandoned keep. I figured the swarthy stranger had no claim to the property but, then, neither did we. I didn't know if this guy was hoping to cash in on some imagined treasure or was merely inquisitive.

'Who be ye?' he said genially, but his eyebrows bristled at the question.

'We're curious adven—er, travellers—drawn to these odd ruins,' I said. Roland said nothing.

'And why would ruins draw a curious traveller in the first place? Ruins are dangerous places,' he said, 'in more ways than one,' he added in afterthought.

'No particular reason,' I said. I didn't like the way the conversation was turning but wasn't yet hostile. Roland, on the other hand, was openly hostile as is his nature.

'It is important that we know!' he urged.

'We?' I questioned. I listen pretty closely when someone talks and caught the slip.

For an instant, the man appeared to be caught off guard. His eyes betrayed him, flickering with anger at being found out. Resolve replaced uncertainty and he raised his index and middle finger to his mouth and whistled—two short notes followed by one longer one. Obviously, a signal of some sort.

"Obviously!" the dwarf added his rare input to the story. Drake laughed out loud at the joke and clapped the dwarf on the back. Even Shadowbender smiled.

"Anyway," Quint ignored the joke, "almost immediately after the signal, three centaurs trotted into view. I had seen centaurs before, but I am always struck by the intriguing paradoxical effect they have on me. They are graceful, combining the speed and power of a horse with the agility and precision of a man. The combination of the two species is disconcerting, as if the mind can't reconcile the two separate halves into a believable whole." The ranger shook his head, "It's difficult for me to describe exactly what I mean. I often wonder how such hybrids came into existence.

Two of the centaurs were brown—both the horse part and the hair colour of the human portion. The third was somewhat different. He was black on the lower half, but his human half was fair. The brown ones had swords strapped to their backs and the strange one carried a spear. They stopped about sixty feet away and said nothing.

The man we had been speaking with moved to his left where the wall ended. The resulting clicking sound caused the realization that was verified when he came into view—he, too, was a centaur!

'Roland,' I said in dwarven, 'we can ask them about the black unicorn—they'll know where it is.' I don't know why I spoke in dwarven except for a general uneasiness.

'Why would they help us?' Roland responded in dwarven. The centaurs' eyes narrowed as Roland and I spoke, and I assumed they couldn't understand us.

'Because I'm a ranger and because we can offer them that small cask of ale you bought at the inn last week. You know, no one loves alcohol like a centaur. . . except maybe a dwarf'.' I waited for Roland to laugh, but he didn't. "It'll be as easy as baking a pie,' I added. Roland snorted again, but didn't disagree, so I continued in common: 'Gentle woodland-folk, we are seeking the black unicorn...'

'Black unicorn!' the original centaur said. The others looked puzzled.

'Yes,' I replied.

'We know and care nothing about unicorns, black or otherwise.' Before I could respond, he went on, 'What is it you seek here?'

'We seek the unicorn,' I said, which was partially true, in a general sense. The centaurs, unfortunately, did not buy it.

'You expect me to believe a human and a dwarf are looking for a unicorn in a pile of rubble! Only a fool would believe that!'

I was going to respond in a witty manner when, without warning, the first centaur ordered the others to attack.

We weren't caught completely off guard. Roland had his axe in hand and I was uneasy enough to be wary. Thus, we were able to respond when they made their move.

Fighting with centaurs is certainly an experience. You would think it to be similar to combat with a mounted human, but that isn't the case. First of all, the man portion of a centaur is at the front of the creature while a mounted human is pretty much centred on a horse. Thus, weapon range and use are different. Secondly, a centaur, as one being, possesses a speed and agility that even the most talented combination of horse and rider cannot match.

The centaur that had been speaking leapt for Roland. At a full gallop, the others would be engaging us within moments. The first centaur landed in front of Roland and stumbled as the rocks and rubble threw him off balance. Roland took advantage of the incident to take a swing as he moved to a more defensible position near me. His blow caught the centaur across the flank, blooding him, but doing no real damage.

Roland and I stood back to back; we held the low ground, so to speak, as the centaurs enjoyed a height advantage. Roland took on the first centaur and the odd- coloured spear-bearer while I fought the two brown ones. I kept thinking how strange it was going to be to kill centaurs, creatures a ranger is more apt to be allied with than battling against. The centaurs pressed us, and we quickly found ourselves in a bad way. Or, at least, Roland was in pretty bad shape; I was holding my own pretty well."

"Right!" Roland cried.

Quint chuckled, "Anyway, the centaurs had three weapons apiece—two hooves and a human weapon as well. This abundance of weapons combined with their height and strength had me a teeny bit concerned. I took a hit in the shoulder from the fair one's spear and I really became worried.

Suddenly, a loud cracking sound filled the air. I saw the two centaurs I was fighting stumble and then they fell into the ground! Before I realized what was happening, the ground beneath me buckled, I spent a few moments falling with chunks of earth and stone cascading all around me, then I hit something solid. I felt earth and stone fall on top of me, then I blacked out.

I awoke to find Roland splashing me with water from his canteen. He had dirt, rock chips, and pieces of roots all over him and clinging to his beard. I thought it fairly fitting, for a dwarf.

'The centaurs?' I asked, still a bit groggy.

'Dead beneath us,' he answered.

I looked and saw two of the bodies or, rather, parts of their bodies as they were mostly buried. We had been fighting over an underground chamber and the weight had caused the ground to collapse. The centaurs, far heavier than us, had fallen through first. As the ground gave way around Roland and I, the section we were on lost its support and collapsed on top of the centaurs. I guess you could say the chaps killed themselves.

Upon seeing I was okay, Roland busied himself with inspecting the partially exposed bodies of our opponents. I looked around and realized we fallen into some sort of room carved out of stone (and, now, somewhat filled with stone).

'Where are we?' I murmured.

'A chamber of some sort,' Roland answered, 'there's a tunnel leading further into the earth.' He pointed behind me. Turning, I saw a carved passage.

'This must be the lower level of the keep,' I said, 'we have to explore it.'

'We have more important things to consider first,' Roland said. He handed me one of the swords the centaurs had wielded, 'Look at that symbol!' he demanded. At the hilt was a rune formed in sort of a squiggly line with a horizontal bar through the centre.

'What?' I asked.

'The necromancer,' Roland said simply. My blood ran cold. Roland had fought goblins allied with the necromancer and recognized the rune. A shiver ran through me for I had heard about the evil of the necromancer and his allegiance with goblins, orcs, and lawless men.

'Why would centaurs be allied with the necromancer?' I asked.

'Beats me,' Roland said.

'Why would they be after us,' I asked, 'did you do something?'

'Yeah,' answered Roland, 'I declared war on all centaur-kind when you weren't paying attention.'

After thinking about it for a while, Roland suggested we were being paranoid, that the centaurs weren't hunting us to begin with, and the centaurs must be protecting or looking for something at the keep and encountered us only coincidentally.

Well, this train of thought led us to wonder what it was the centaurs were after. Obviously, they hadn't found it yet or they wouldn't have still been around. Anything agents of the necromancer were after would be valuable to find or to prevent the necromancer from finding, so we decided to continue searching the ruins.

The short of it is we found only a handful of books and scrolls in a chamber deep within the bowels of the keep. Suspecting they might be magical, we opted to take them to Cwyllyn."

"How do you know Cwyllyn?" Shadowbender queried.

"He hired us, once, to obtain some rare herbs for some sort of experiment he was conducting, and we began employing him whenever we needed to know something or have an item identified."

"And why did you suspect these books and scrolls were magical?"

"Everything else in the keep had decayed into nothingness, but these books were intact. That, in itself, made me suspect they were magical."

"I see," said the mage, "please go on, then."

"Well," Quint said, "that's pretty much it. Cwyllyn inspected the items we had discovered and bade us bring the scroll to you. By the way, were you able to identify it?"

Shadowbender cleared his throat and began speaking in a soft voice: "A thousand years ago, the world was embroiled in what we now call The Mage War. I am sure everyone here is generally familiar with the history…"

"I am more than generally familiar with The Mage War," Roland interrupted, "all dwarves are. It was during The Mage War that the elves destroyed our homelands and drove us into exile!" Roland gnawed the end of his pipe in agitation.

"Gently, Roland," Quint chided, "I want to hear what our host has to say."

Roland muttered something, but sullenly complied with the ranger's request.

Though clearly irritated by the dwarf's outburst, Shadowbender was not willing to be drawn into an argument.

"Yes," he said to Roland, "it was because of The Mage War the dwarves were driven from their ancestral home," Shadowbender shook his head sadly, "but so were some of the elves," he added. Shadowbender lit his pipe and continued, "Magic, in those days as now, was rare. There were few mages and they were separated geographically and racially. Over many years, mages began to band together in order to enhance their knowledge and for the betterment of arcane lore. They learned from one another and learning was greatly increased. In time, all serious mages were so allied and the organization, due to the crystals embedded in the walls of its council chamber, became known as The Crystal Conclave. The Conclave was rather isolated from the rest of the world. People fear what they do not understand, and the populace mistrusted the magic they did not understand, although The Conclave was never actively opposed. Few people other than mages knew the organization existed and The Conclave preferred it that way as it allowed them to focus entirely on the arcane arts. For many centuries, the members of The Conclave cohabited peacefully with their neighbours and among themselves. Unfortunately for the world and everyone in it, this peace did not last.

Over time, a group of mages led by Keldar the Black tried to persuade The Conclave that mages, due to their knowledge and wisdom, were destined to rule the civilized yet ignorant nations. They claimed civilization would flourish with the guidance of the wise. The Conclave, led by Travon the Wise, disagreed. Travon maintained the world was of no concern to true wizards. Only the magic mattered. He also believed Keldar's desire was rooted not in benevolence, but selfish ambition.

For several years, Keldar and his followers, which represented slightly less than half of The Conclave, tried to convince their fellows to support a magocracy. Travon continued to refuse. The situation gradually became tense and continued to worsen. Eventually, Keldar and his followers withdrew from The Conclave and formed their own group known as The Black Hand. They built a fortress in a remote valley; a valley now known as the Vale of the Wyrm.

Travon the Wise and the remaining members of The Conclave believed this was the end of the matter and, although saddened by the schism created by Keldar's departure, resolved to continue as they always had. Unbeknownst to even the most wise among the Crystal Conclave, destruction was about to befall their order and much of the world, besides.

Scholars now believe Keldar had always planned to betray his order. Be that as it may, what matters is he eventually did. The Black Hand was comprised of many learned and powerful mages. The Black Hand, in their jealousy and thirst for power, resolved to conquer the civilized world. Before this ambition could be realized, they felt it necessary to eliminate their major threat (as they saw it): The Crystal Conclave.

Under the pretence of reuniting with their erstwhile compatriots, The Black Hand proposed a meeting of all leading mages. For some reason lost in the mists of time and conjecture, they chose the site of this assembly to be an abandoned keep near the centre of the Granite Hills, the ancestral home of the dwarves.

The assembly was a ruse. Keldar planned a massive ambush to destroy The Crystal Conclave. Somehow, through negotiation or magical means, Keldar had enlisted the aid of the dragons.

"The Crystal Conclave chose the Granite Hills on purpose!" Roland interrupted, "They knew there would be a battle and deliberately chose the dwarven homeland, knowing it would be destroyed in the conflict!"

"No. They did not know," Shadowbender replied, "If they had known Keldar's true intentions, they would never have gone."

"What about the dragons?" Quint asked, "Didn't the Crystal Conclave know about their existence? Keldar obviously did."

"The Crystal Conclave knew of dragons, of course," Shadowbender answered, "but they knew little about them. Dragons were considered faerie tales by and large and even the Conclave knew little dragon-lore. They certainly never considered the dragons would ally with The Black Hand.

Travon and most of the members of the Crystal Conclave walked unwittingly into a trap. As soon as the Conclave arrived, the assault began. The wings of the dragons darkened the skies as the creatures attacked. The countryside burned with the flames of the dragons. As the surviving members of the Conclave began a counter-attack, The Black Hand turned on their former friends in a vicious magical onslaught. The combat was short-lived, but brutal. Hotly fought magical duels spread over much of the countryside. Magical fluxes and combined spell effects resulted in earthquakes, fire, and other catastrophes. Certain areas of the land were torn apart and, in others, the magicks combined with such fury that the land literally melted. The Mage War had begun.

The Conclave fought desperately, but the result was inevitable. In less than half an hour, the bulk of the Conclave was destroyed. Travon himself died in the initial onslaught. Dying, he unleashed such a burst of fire and lightning that the entire area in a quarter mile radius was consumed, along with many dragons. Keldar and many of The Black Hand also died in the explosion. I have been there. All that remains is a crater.

The pitifully few surviving members of the Crystal Conclave fought a running battle in an attempt to regroup at their home in The Longbow Barony, which was in the area known now as The Barony of Trevor and The Barren Lands. Most did not make it. With the Crystal Conclave all but obliterated, the dragons vented their anger and blood-lust on the surrounding territory. The dwarves fought valiantly but were doomed.

Within a month, two thirds of the dwarven population lay dead. The survivors retreated across the mountain range on their western border. Dubbed the Sundered Mountains by the exiles, they never again returned as a nation. The Granite Hills lay smouldering and desolate and, in time, became known as the Barren Lands.

The dwarves subdued, The Black Hand turned their gaze toward The Longbow Barony and the surviving members of The Crystal Conclave. With The Crystal Conclave destroyed once and for all, theirs would be the only relevant mage-craft in the world. The Army of The Black Hand, as it was now known, having allied with the Hrothan tribes of the south, marched against The Crystal Conclave, burning and destroying as they went.

The Crystal Conclave still existed, but barely so. Most of their number lay dead in the Barren lands. They felt they stood a chance against The Black Hand alone but knew they would never fend off the combined strength of the army of mages and dragons marching against them. They spent many long hours in council, desperately trying to discover a way to fend off annihilation. With the death of Travon, the Wise, leadership of the Conclave fell to an astute and talented mage named Pelyon mac Gwhyr. Long admired for his wisdom, the mage came up with a plan. He had a score of the younger (and, therefore, least powerful) mages collect and copy as many of the Conclaves' tomes as time would allow. These images were to depart with these copies and keep them safe so that the knowledge and ideals of the Conclave might survive should the Conclave be destroyed. He sent other mages as ambassadors to Lord Hawk Longbow of the Longbow Barony to request aid. He formed a special committee to deal with the problem of the dragons. He put the remaining mages to work in formulating a battle plan. Many of the mages viewed the situation as hopeless but complied with his requests.

"By the way," Shadowbender looked to the ranger, "your surname happens to be Longbow. Is this coincidence?"

"Yes," Quint responded, "according to my father, our ancestors lived in the Longbow Barony at one time and took the surname from the area in which they lived as opposed to any relation to the Baron himself, though you never know—the Longbow women are comely, and I can easily believe the Baron might have fancied one of them."

"Yes, well," Shadowbender said weakly, "allow me to continue: Fortunately, Pelyon's plans were realized. A score of the younger mages, those who would be the least effective in combat, departed to various hiding places throughout the world long before The Black Hand arrived.

Lord Longbow, whose troops had already fought several small battles with The Army of The Black Hand (and lost), was aware of the enemy army's approach and willingly agreed to an alliance. Longbow's armies were serving to delay The Black Hand as the army crossed Longbow lands. However, they had no real hope of stopping them and Lord Longbow knew it.

Pelyon mac Gwhyr had accomplished much, but the true hope of victory lay with the mages charged with developing a way to stop the dragons. For two long and anxious months, the committee studied and experimented, hardly stopping to eat or rest. Finally, a plan was conceived.

The mages had inscribed a spell. In theory, this spell, if cast from the proper location, would magically cause all living dragons to return to the place of their birth and enter into an enchanted slumber from which they could not be awakened for at least a thousand years. Two problems remained, however. First, none of the mages were sure of the proper location. Several places were proposed, one of which was a huge cavern complex located in the Vale of the Wyrm. Most felt this was the proper site as it was the location in which The Black Hand was based and that was an important coincidence. Several other possibilities existed, however. The second problem was the lack of suitable mages. The Conclave could not afford to send any of their order with The Black Hand threatening their very doorstep.

Pelyon, Lord Longbow, and several others met to formulate a strategy. The strategy decided upon was markedly unconventional. The Conclave enchanted scrolls in the form of musical notes that would be evoked when the notes were played. In this way, a bard could effectively cast the spell although he possessed not the arcane power. It was a risky proposition at best and there was no way to test the scrolls, but it was the only chance they had.

A hundred bards were summoned by Lord Longbow; about twenty survived to arrive at the summons. They were offered the chance to volunteer for the mission. A dozen agreed to the undertaking. They were taught the spell, deployed in great secrecy, and scattered toward the various proposed sites.

The Conclave, knowing their hope for survival rested solely on this handful of courageous bards, resolved to buy them as much time as possible. In order to keep The Black Hand's focus away from the bards, The Conclave and the Longbow army marched to meet the Army of The Black Hand on the field of battle. In autumn, the two opposing armies met on the Delinian Fields, which were later known as the Fields of Blood.

The Black Hand had recruited many men from the Hrothan tribes, fierce barbarians from the south, and had also an army of mercenaries from sundry lands. To the dismay of the Conclave, the dragons were present, wheeling over The Black Hand like a pack of vultures. There could be no retreat. With the resignation of men about to die, the Longbow army and the Conclave decided to stand their ground in the slim hope of buying the bards more time. The greatest and most brutal battle of the Mage War was joined. Many stories could be told of that battle, but suffice it to say, it was long and bloody, ranging back and forth over the Fields of Blood for several days.

The armies clashed for two days and nights without ceasing. A warrior could walk a mile on the bodies of the slain without setting foot on the ground. It is rumoured the river flowing through the field ran red with blood for days. Many dragons were killed, but too many remained. Lord Longbow lay dead on the field, as did most of the Conclave. With most of their number dead, the Conclave and survivors of the Longbow army had no hope of living through another day. Both armies withdrew from the field of battle to organize and regroup. Combat would resume the next morning.

Pelyon mac Gwhyr still lived. He assembled the survivors for the final battle. The next morning dawned much too soon for the beleaguered survivors. At dawn, outnumbered and weary, they marched to what they were sure would be their last battle.

The Black Hand confidently arrayed its forces. The dragons, their wings blotting out the sun, wheeled over the field, their shrieks reverberating in the still morning air. The wyrms soared high, preparing to dive.

The few survivors of the Conclave prepared their most powerful spells in the hope of withstanding the onslaught. Grim faces watched the sky.

The dragons began their descent. Flames surged from their mouths as they plummeted toward their foe. The crackling of magicks mingled with the screams of the dying as the gap between the combatants narrowed. Suddenly, the nearly-unexpected reprieve came. As a body, the dragons veered, wings skimming the helmets of Lord Longbow's cringing soldiers. Without a sound, the dragons flew toward the east (toward the Vale of the Wyrm as one mage later pointed out) and disappeared over the horizon. For the first time in days, silence reigned as both armies stood dumbfounded. The spell, known later as the Canticle of the Wyrm, had worked.

Despite the absence of the dragons, the battle resumed and many more fell on both sides. But the Army of The Black Hand was demoralized by the loss of the dragons and it was the Conclave that took the victory.

As most of the world's mages were now dead, The Black Hand and the Conclave were both disbanded and were never again instituted. The dwarven kingdom was destroyed as were many other communities. Civil War broke out sporadically and the general unrest lasted nearly a decade. During this time, relations between the elves and dwarves became strained and have yet to recover. Magic retreated into the quiet places Pelyon had wisely prepared and the world tried to forget the Mage War ever happened."

"And that," Shadowbender exclaimed, "is the end of the tale."

"The history lesson was nice and all," Roland remarked sarcastically, "but what does all this have to do with us?"

"Everything," said Shadowbender, "the scroll you found is one of the few surviving copies of the Canticle of the Wyrm, the only one I have ever seen."

"What about the men in the lizard masks?" Quint demanded.

"Dragon masks," Shadowbender corrected. The ranger didn't respond, dark realization slowly spreading across his features. "Allow me to explain," Shadowbender continued, "apparently, a remnant of The Black Hand survived and returned to the Vale of the Wyrm. This group hoped to reawaken the dragons and fulfil their goal of conquest. This group remained intact over the centuries and gradually became the Cult of the Wyrm. I found reference to them in a few older writings, although they apparently do not appear in any of the more modern writings. It is my belief the men in the masks are members of this cult."

"Why?" Quint asked, "Why would they attack us. I see no reason for them to have so much interest in the scroll. Why would they want to know how to put the dragons to sleep?"

"Simply put," Shadowbender answered, "they do not want a copy; they want to prevent others from having one. You see, the Conclave created the Canticle, but the Conclave itself is no more. Only individuals with the scroll who also possess the ability to use the scroll can prevent the realization of the cult's goals."

"Could you say that in Common so those of us who are less enlightened can understand?" Roland asked.

"Of course," Shadowbender replied smugly, "the wyrms are going to awaken."

Everyone stood stunned. Oceana finally broke the silence, "You mean the canticle is wearing off?"

"Exactly," said Shadowbender, "the Conclave could not know the duration. Over centuries of analysis, it was determined the

Canticle would last a thousand years. The time is up. It is largely a matter of conjecture what the result of the reawakening will be. Some believe the dragons will continue the conflict, once again plunging the world into chaos. Others believe they will do nothing. The only point on which everyone seems to agree is no one wants to find out, except for the Cult of the Wyrm, that is."

"How come no one knows about this?" Roland demanded.

"Someone does know," Shadowbender snapped, "the mages know. The last time you had a mage over for tea, you could have asked and then you would have known, too!" Shadowbender slapped his forehead in mock surprise, "Oh, that's right! I forgot. No one associates with mages!"

"Let's not forget, brother, some mages would not respond to an offer of tea," Oceana said gently.

"What I want to know is how the Cult knew about the scroll in the first place. After all, it had apparently remained intact all this time. Why try for it now?" Quint wondered aloud.

"That is the question," Shadowbender mumbled. "Unfortunately, I have the answer. Cwyllyn ap Dyryn is dead. He was murdered in his study soon after you left. I sent a message to him asking some questions pertaining to the scroll. One of his students sent a message back telling me about the murder and that one of the other students had disappeared and was suspect of the murder.

Cwyllyn was one of the most learned sages in the world. My guess is a member of the Cult infiltrated Cwyllyn's household knowing the time was nearly here for the reawakening. He learned about the scroll itself as well as its arrival here. He must have killed Cwyllyn in an attempt to keep the knowledge of the scroll secret. Apparently, they did not know much about us, or they would have sent more men to take the scroll."

"Maybe they have," Roland muttered.

Chapter 5

"I fear you may be right," Drake replied to Roland's statement.

"So, what does it all mean?" asked Oceana, looking to Shadowbender.

"I do not know if I can answer that precisely," the illusionist admitted, "the possibilities are virtually endless. There are the historical ramifications, of course, the arcane angle, which should not be overlooked, and there are definitely social as well as ethical considerations."

"Okay," Quint, uninterested in esoteric possibilities, said as he stood, "here's how I see it: First, the dragons, nasty faerie tale beasts that they are, are about to awaken and, maybe, destroy our world. Secondly," he continued, beginning to pace, "we have the means to prevent it. We have been given a tremendous opportunity to prove our mettle and intellect! I think the answer is clear—we save the world and everyone in it by using the scroll!"

"Oh, yeah—good idea, Quint!" Roland snorted. "First, we don't *know* the wyrms will awaken; we *think* they *might* awaken. Secondly, we don't know if we have the means to prevent it," the dwarf glanced at Shadowbender, "seeing how no one here has attempted to use said scroll. Lastly, there is no 'we' involved. You and I," he looked at Quint, "were only supposed to deliver the scroll. I don't remember anything being said about traipsing off into the middle of nowhere to some valley held by a weird wyrm cult *while* being simultaneously hunted by said weird wyrm cult in some hare-brained attempt to use a thousand-year-old scroll no one can read to prevent something we're not even sure will happen." The dwarf plopped his hand against his face, "Maybe I'm asleep and have been having some sort of crazy dream."

"The scroll is usable" Shadowbender said solemnly, "after all, it worked before—it should work now."

"You can use it?" Oceana asked.

"Actually, no. It is transcribed into music; the spell is not detailed—it would take weeks, if not months, to decipher and prepare the music into a traditional magical scroll. Weeks or months, I should like to point out, we do not have. As it stands, only a musician can tap the power of the scroll."

"I can use the scroll," Drake said softly.

"So, I imagine, could you, Oceana," Shadowbender gazed at his sister with penetrating eyes before his features softened and he almost smiled, "You have been trying to teach me to read music. I guess I should have listened!" he shrugged.

"The mages started all this," Roland interjected, "let them figure it out!"

"There are no 'mages' as you say—not as a unified group;" Shadowbender replied, "there is no governing body. Oceana and I are the only people available without months or years of dickering. There is no way to create an association of any sort; if anything is to be done, it will have to be done by an individual or small group."

"We're a small group," Quint offered, "but heroic, I deem," he added hastily.

"We could do it, I'm sure," ventured Oceana.

"I had no intention of you going, Oceana," said Shadowbender, "Drake, as a practising bard, is eminently qualified to use the scroll; I figured on leaving you here where it is safe."

"Yeah. Real safe. Wyrm cultists skulking around everywhere just yearning to kill everyone associated with the scroll—good move, mage!" Roland snapped.

"Hold it!" Drake said loudly before Shadowbender could respond and a full-blown argument ensue, "everyone hold on a minute. First," he went on, looking at each person in turn, "we don't know if *anyone* is going. That will have to be decided. If we go, I think everyone should have his own choice."

"Or *her* own choice," Oceana muttered.

"Secondly," Drake said, ignoring Oceana's comment, "if anyone goes, there are other considerations, namely who should go and who should stay. We all shouldn't go; we're the only people, I presume, who know about this. We don't want to all run off and risk the loss of this knowledge should we all be killed. Someone should stay, if only to warn others." Drake began pacing and rubbed his chin thoughtfully, "I say we send the dwarf to warn his people and leave Oceana here to warn the elves and whatever mages she and Shadowbender are on friendly terms with. Thus, we're warning the world in general, while the remainder actively does something about it."

Roland cleared his throat, "Well, 'the dwarf' has an opinion: I should go to the Vale of the Wyrm. Warning my kin won't do any good. They wouldn't listen. And, should the dragons awaken, they'll know it soon enough, I'll warrant. The only logical choice is for me to accompany the party with the scroll."

"You just said you didn't want go!" Quint said incredulously.

"Well, I changed my mind," the dwarf said stubbornly, "I have a right to do that you know!"

"So do women," interjected Oceana, "although I wouldn't be changing *my* mind, seeing how Drake and my brother have apparently made it up for me—but, I'm going and that's all there is to it," Oceana crossed her arms and pouted. The look in the eyes dared anyone to disagree. No one did.

"First things first," Quint said, "let's figure out who actually wants to go. Once that's settled, we can move on to the secondary issues."

A silence fell across the room as each considered the ranger's words. Several heads began to slowly nod in agreement. Shadowbender faced the group.

"I am going," said the mage, "I am the only one who knows the magic properties of the scroll and the location and history of the vale. I have to go."

"I'm in, too!" said Quint.

Shadowbender looked expectantly at Drake.

"I'm in," said the bard, smiling, "after all, you need a musician."

"Oceana?" Shadowbender said, frowning. Already, he deeply regretted his reckless comment about Oceana being able to use the scroll as it only encouraged the elf maiden to go.

"Count me in!" Oceana laughed.

Everyone looked at Roland. The dwarf picked up his pipe, stuffed it in his mouth, and scowled, "What are you all looking at me for? I'll go. Somebody has to make sure you don't botch everything up."

Looking at the dwarf, Quint smiled.

The next few days were busy ones. Shadowbender prepared magical components and made and sent copies of the scroll to his closest associates in mage-craft. Considering the geographic division and racial and social gulf between the sundry and scattered mages, such a move was virtually useless if it had been attempted in order to procure assistance in their pending journey as there was no hope of any cooperative work occurring in such a short time but, as it was intended as a failsafe to ensure knowledge of the scroll's existence survived should the group fail in their objective, then it was a wise move. Shadowbender was comforted knowing two mages, in particular, Ozmandias of Ebenhill and Nethla'ari of the Ringing Mountains, had been among the few to whom he had sent a copy of the scroll and a brief missive explaining his discovery and intentions. It was too bad about the loss of Cwyllyn ap Dyryn, both as an associate and a friend; Cwyllyn would have been Shadowbender's first choice as a confidant. The others, however, were more than sufficient. Shadowbender felt more secure knowing there was a likely contingency plan should his group fail. Having a sound contingency in effect was one of his trademarks.

Shadowbender and Quint studied every known map in Shadowbender's study to prepare a route to the presumed location of the Vale of the Wyrm. The ranger had a knack for maps as well as for choosing the quickest and safest route to a given destination. They soon selected a route that would offer them speed yet avoided the more travelled paths where they were more likely to be attacked by wandering humanoids or brigands. Brigands were rare in the area due to lack of civilized areas on which to prey, but raiders sometimes used these paths to access the sparsely settled lands of the Barony of Crystalmere. It was also reasonable to assume the Cult of the Wyrm would guard the established paths, but they couldn't guard the entire countryside.

Quint and Drake, when not meeting individually with Shadowbender, prepared the necessary provisions. Drake, as a result of frequent travel, was continually prepared to leave on a lengthy journey upon a moment's notice.

Shadowbender, cautious to the extreme, always kept emergency supplies prepared should he and Oceana need to flee with little time to prepare. Thus, preparing provisions was not a difficult task.

Quint sent, via Oceana's hawk, a summons he dictated to Drake to several of his ranger companions to spread the word about the journey. He also requested whatever help the rangers could send.

A loosely associated brotherhood, he knew the rangers would send little help, if any.

Roland drank gallons of ale.

Drake and Oceana spent hours learning the proper notes of the mystic song that would invoke the scroll's powers. Both Oceana and Drake could read music, and both played a variety of instruments. Drake, in fact, could play, with varying degrees of skill, essentially every instrument known to man and a couple known only to elves. Both wanted to practice the song, so they could flawlessly play it without having to rely on reading the notes. This would enable them to properly cast the spell should they need to do so under stressful circumstances, which both felt was likely to be the case. Obviously, having two members of the group who could play the song was beneficial should one of them be killed or otherwise incapacitated.

"If this is the proper spell," Drake asked Oceana while they were playing on the Tower roof, one morning, "and we're playing it correctly, why won't it work from here?"

"Some spells," answered Oceana flexing her fingers after long practice on Drake's mandolin, "require material components or other factors to work. For example, I can't scry on distant areas without a specially prepared device. In effect, the 'Canticle of the Wyrm' also requires a material component—the birthplace of the dragons. If it is cast elsewhere, such as here, on the Tower's roof, one of the components is missing, thereby preventing the spell from taking effect."

"Why can't you alter the spell, so it will work from anywhere?"

"Well," Oceana laughed, "I could explain that to you (maybe), but it would take a very long time and require you to have a grasp of how magic works. Considering we don't have an extra decade or so for me to teach you, you'll just have to take my word for it that it can't be done that way; if it could," she continued, "Shadowbender certainly would have engineered it that way. The last thing he wants to do is leave the Tower."

"Well, then," said Drake raising a glass in salute, "here's to long journeys and the acquisition of the proper material components."

"And," said Oceana raising her glass, "to the safe return of everyone involved."

On the fourth day, they met in the music room to finalize the preparations. Everyone seemed tense and solemn except Quint who appeared anxious to go and Oceana, who appeared excited.

"Well," said Shadowbender, "I guess we are as ready as we can be. I have sent word to what few mages I respect. Quint has notified the rangers. Our musicians," he said with a flourish indicating Drake and Oceana, "know the proper tune and I *think* we know the location of the Vale. One thing we need to keep in mind is that Drake is the most important member of our group. One bard, working alone, achieved this goal the first time around. The rest of us are here to protect Drake; he is the only one who needs to survive as he could accomplish the goal without us."

"So could I," Oceana quietly chimed in, though Shadowbender ignored her and finished with an appraising look at the small group assembled in the music room, "If ever a party was ready to march off to inevitable destruction, we are." He sat and vigorously puffed his pipe.

"The provisions are ready, and the instruments packed," offered Drake, "is everyone else prepared?"

Everyone more (Quint) or less (Roland) answered affirmatively.

"Just to review," said the dwarf, "we're going to travel to the Vale of the Wyrm, provided we can find it, where one of our musicians, if he survives (Or 'she', Oceana emphatically whispered), will play the proper song in the hope that will prevent the dragons awakening?"

"Right," said Drake.

"It doesn't get any easier!" quipped Quint, "it'll be as easy as baking a pie."

"That's what you said about convincing those centaurs in the abandoned keep in Feywood to lead us to the black unicorn," Roland ventured.

"That wasn't my fault," Quint said hastily, "how should I have known they were buddies with the necromancer? Besides—"

"Okay," Drake interrupted, "we're all ready. Any questions?"

"Who's going to defray our funeral expenses?" asked Roland.

"You should have thought about that before you left," Quint answered.

"When do we leave?" Oceana asked the bard.

"Dawn."

Chapter 6

The next morning dawned clear and bright. The Tower shone in the early morning light. Birdsong poured from the surrounding wood.

"Perfect weather for high adventure," Quint thought happily. Nothing was more invigorating than setting off on an adventure, especially one with potentially world-affecting results. They would all be heroes, for sure! Of course, he was already a hero of renown, but, after this adventure, everyone would know it. That they might accomplish their task, and no one know it had not occurred to the young man. The idea they might fail at their task never would occur to him.

The ranger looked around at the group gathered in the early morning sun. Birds were singing in the wood and the scent of pines filled the air. Quint felt they were inside a song or tale; at least tales, the happy ones, anyway, always started out exactly like this. The bard stood beside Oceana looking thoughtfully at a map Shadowbender had dug up from somewhere. Oceana was certainly pretty enough to be in a tale. She was half-heartedly feigning interest in the map Drake held. Quint noticed how the sun glinted on her blonde hair, gleaming like gold strands. Off to himself, Roland seemed nervous and cast withering looks at the surrounding forest as if he expected the wood to be crawling with cultists. Shadowbender stood near Drake and Oceana fiddling with some sort of spell components or something.

"You got everything, Drake?" the mage queried.

"All ready," the bard rolled up the map and slipped it into his backpack. Beside him, Oceana nodded absently. Shadowbender shot a questioning glance at the ranger.

"Ready," Quint replied, "Roland?" he asked.

The dwarf spat and folded his arms, "As ready as I'll ever be."

"Let's go, then!" said Drake as he began purposefully striding to the northeast.

"By the way," Shadowbender remarked as they left the clearing around the tower and entered the shadow of the wood, "I left a few precautions should any cultists assault the Tower during our absence, I suggest, if anyone should return without me, they not attempt to enter the Tower."

"Great," Roland murmured, "ensorcellment behind us and death and ensorcellment before us—I love it!" Adjusting his pack for about the fiftieth time, the dwarf stepped in pace beside the ranger. Quint smiled but said nothing.

Quint gazed around thoughtfully, enjoying the variety of the forest. For the last several hours, the party had been moving steadily downward. Steadily, but slowly. There were a few animal paths, but no real track. They were descending the northeast side of the mountain toward the valley below. Once there, they would strike out more or less east across the Forgotten Lands toward the Perilous Mountains. The ranger supposed, or at least, hoped Shadowbender or Drake knew of a pass; there was no such pass designated on Shadowbender's map. Well, first to the task at hand: getting down the mountains.

As they descended, the ranger noticed the difference in the plant life. They had come down far enough to re-enter a deciduous zone, with only the occasional fir tree emerging from the forest floor. Soon, he knew, they would peter out altogether. Quint was intrigued by the transition, noticing the increasing occurrence of deciduous trees coinciding with the decrease of fir. He made a game of looking for fir trees.

The going was rough. Every now and then, Drake, in the lead, would have to clear the path with his short sword or hatchet. Close behind the bard, walked Shadowbender. The elf seemed lost in thought and trudged along wordlessly. Oceana followed her brother but, unlike her disinterested sibling, looked around constantly in wide-eyed wonder. To all appearances, the elf maid was out on a spring picnic, not embroiled in something as dangerous as the task before them. Despite their apparent frailty, neither elf seemed tired and walked along with unflagging dedication. Elves, Quint remembered, were woodsmen at heart. Neither elf was making more noise than a chipmunk skittering along the forest floor. Even cloistered mages, he suspected, were relatively comfortable in the woodlands, among growing things.

Roland, on the other hand, seemed to detest growing things. The dwarf was between Oceana and Quint, who had the rearguard position. No woodsman, the puffing dwarf stomped through the wood like a pony, snorting the random curse as a recoiling limb slapped him in the face or he slipped on the leaves of the forest floor. It was good thing stealth wasn't a factor during this leg of the journey, because anything within half a mile could hear the stomping dwarf. Quint himself moved quieter than virtually any human (not that it mattered when one was anywhere near Roland), but not quite as noiselessly as the elven members of the party who moved with inhuman silence and grace. Quint, taking his position as rearguard seriously, continually scanned the surrounding wood and regularly checked behind to make sure nothing was following; he was determined nothing would sneak up on them during his watch. Ahead, Drake signalled a halt.

The party stood on a stone outcropping jutting from the mountainside like a nose on a face. Roland promptly flopped down, apparently indifferent to the reason for the halt. Oceana, leaning against a tree trunk, drank from a beaded water skin. Quint walked past both of them to where Drake and Shadowbender stood surveying the land ahead.

Drake unrolled his map and compared it to the vista in front of him. He nodded in satisfaction as, comparing their current position to the map, he affirmed they were on target, or at least they appeared to be. Shadowbender stood silently to the bards' left. From the corner of his eye, he saw the ranger move beside him and heard the sharp intake of breath as Quint gazed upon the view. He was somewhat surprised at the human's reaction as the humans he had seen (apart from druids) cared little for the intricacies of nature unless they could somehow be manipulated for their own profit.

The view was fantastic. Below them, the forested mountains and foothills of the Forgotten Lands stretched to the distant horizon where one could barely make out the jutting and ragged silhouette of the Perilous Mountains. No signs of civilization marred the picturesque beauty of the primeval forest. The wilderness, from so lofty a vantage point, appeared trackless. The ranger was awestruck with its beauty and could have happily spent the rest of the day merely gazing at the view.

"There are no paths," Drake said to the ranger, "I figure we'll stick to the valleys where the going's easier. We'll head east and a little north."

"I've never seen the Forgotten Lands, before" said Quint.

"I've been there once, briefly," Drake said, "but it's been some years ago and further south."

"The Forgotten Lands were settled once?" the ranger asked; he had heard something to that effect somewhere.

"Yes. At one time, a thriving human kingdom dwelt therein. Over time, sickness and war decimated the population. Goblin raids from the east further served to destroy the civilization and, eventually, the population dwindled to nothing. There are still a few surviving traces of their civilization, or so the tales say," the bard answered.

"How safe is it, these days?" Quint asked.

"As safe as any abandoned land overrun by humanoid armies and left neglected," said Drake.

"Great!" Quint exclaimed, "I was beginning to be afraid that the first portion of our journey would be uneventful."

"The fey are present," came the quiet voice of Shadowbender. Quint had not known the mage was listening to the conversation. The mage went on, "Very few elves, of course, but some of the others.

Humanoids are present as are more fanciful creatures, if rumours are to be believed. Humans are rare, merely passing through, though it is said more enter the Forgotten Lands than leave."

Quint shuddered and cast a nervous glance at Roland. The dwarf sat on the rock. He was engaged in a conversation with Oceana and was oblivious to the conversation here. Quint breathed a sigh of relief; if Roland knew the forest held even a hint of enchantment, it would take an entire team of Duranian war horses to drag the dwarf into the wood.

"What sort of dangers can we expect?" Quint asked the elf.

"I, for one," replied Shadowbender as he turned from the two men, "would expect and be prepared for anything." The elf walked over to crouch beside his sister.

"Cheery guy," Quint remarked to the bard.

Drake smiled, "Shadowbender's all right. He's an elf for one; a mage for two—and neither acts like you or I."

After a short rest and a discussion between Shadowbender and Drake regarding the best course through the Forgotten Lands, the party prepared for another half-day march. Hopefully, they would be at the base of the mountain and upon the outskirts of the Forgotten Lands by nightfall. Quint had insisted they reach the valley by nightfall or they'd be without a fire tonight as lighting a fire on the mountainside would clearly identify them to anyone in the valley who might be watching the mountain. This wasn't entirely true as there were always ways of hiding one's fire, but it would save a lot of effort and put them much closer to the base of the mountain.

The trip down the mountain was more difficult than they had anticipated. At times, the slope was virtually vertical. This wasn't a tremendous problem for the party except Roland, who seemed to possess little dexterity. They could hold to trees and half-walk, half-climb downward, scooting from tree to tree. Roland, not surprisingly, proved the least adept at "tree-hopping" as he derisively termed it. In addition to general lack of dexterity, the dwarf, wearing heavy armour and carrying a plethora of equipment to boot, was the most encumbered of the group. After several mishaps wherein the dwarf managed to miss the tree he was supposed to use to stop his descent and had to be caught by either Quint or Drake (each man had sufficient foresight to position himself for this purpose), Shadowbender, in exasperation, suggested they tie a rope around Roland's waist and have one of the men, bracing against a higher tree, act as a "safety anchor" for the dwarf. They complied and Quint, who volunteered for anchor duty, was kept busy "catching" Roland when he slipped or missed the target tree, which happened every third or fourth attempt. The precautions they had taken prevented the dwarf from tumbling down the mountainside, but the process was tedious, and they moved at a snails' pace. At this rate, they would never make it to the valley below prior to nightfall.

Fortunately, geography soon offered a solution. Another rock outcropping, smaller than the first, blocked their way. A deep ravine or gully formed on the southern side of the outcropping and plunged down the mountainside. It had evidently been formed by water during wet periods and, therefore, was relatively smooth and free of obstructing trees. Roland sat down and slid down the gully on the leaves coating the bottom of the cleft. The others half-slid, half-walked after him. There was no danger of gaining too much momentum as the gully was deep-sided and narrow, permitting them to brace themselves against the sides. Thus, they could easily control their descent. The gully went on for some distance, traversing the steepest portion of the mountain's slope. By the time the gully petered out, they had reached the milder slope near the bottom and everyone could walk without any danger of falling. They quickly travelled down the lower slope and entered the valley below.

They camped just before dusk. Quint had chosen a well-sheltered site in a low spot near a spring head that would emit a minimum of light to the surrounding area. Drake and Roland gathered firewood. In order to figure out the most advantageous location to post a guard, Quint scouted the perimeter of the camp, trying to ascertain from what direction anyone would most likely take should they wish to approach the camp. Shadowbender and Oceana erected a small tent for Oceana to use. The men would do without the luxury of a tent. They had brought only one, for Oceana, as tents were too bulky for their purpose, namely speed. The elf, as it was, felt they were carrying far too much gear to make adequate time. Shadowbender just hoped it would not rain.

"You know," Shadowbender said softly as he helped his sister set up the tent, "I wish you would return to the Tower."

Oceana frowned at her brother's words and focused on a frayed rope she had only just noticed, "Shadowbender," she replied,

"I know how you feel, but I can't ignore the importance of what we're doing. *You* didn't ignore it—how can I? Besides, you need another musician."

"I could learn the 'canticle' easily enough," replied Shadowbender, tying one of the supporting ropes around the exposed root of a sycamore.

"I know you're worried," Oceana said, ignoring the bait, "but you can use another mage. The stronger the party, the greater the likelihood of success." She knotted the fray as she continued, "It's really no safer at the Tower and, anyway, it's not as if this is my first adventure. My goodness, it's not even *our* first adventure. If we can survive a troll and a goblin pack, I think we can handle a trek through an abandoned forest."

"It's not the same thing…" began Shadowbender, shuddering at the episode with the troll that had proven Oceana's talent for magic as well as her courage and ability to keep her wits during times of trouble. She had been young then, too, a few years into adulthood; now she was older and much stronger in magic. Maybe he *was* worrying a bit too much.

"No, it's not," interrupted Oceana, "these cultists are human and, most likely, a lot less dangerous than a troll. Relax, Shadowbender—you make it sound as if we're going to assault the keep of the Lich King!"

"Well," said Shadowbender, "I am just worried, that is all."

"I know," Oceana smiled and placed her attention on the task at hand. Sullen and quiet, Shadowbender helped her.

Shadowbender was thinking about the encounter with the troll. Oceana had only recently completed her apprenticeship and had travelled from the Elven Kingdoms in order to find him and continue her studies. It was never safe travelling in the wild, but Oceana had travelled alone across the long miles to the Tower. When he had left his homeland, Oceana had been his baby sister, still considered an adolescent by elven standards. He had not been prepared for the fully-grown elven woman who had arrived and Oceana frequently chafed under his tutelage, claiming he treated her like a child. He knew she was right, though he had never admitted it. Finally, after months of complaining from his sibling, Shadowbender had agreed to allow Oceana to go with him on a journey.

Despite possessing a preference to remain in the Tower and study, Shadowbender occasionally travelled, though never casually. Necessity of some sort always preceded travelling and, in this case, the impetus had been Shadowbender learning the location of a patch of starflower, rare plants useful in a number of concoctions. He decided a journey to procure the flowers would be worth the hassle and he had acquiesced to Oceana's request to accompany him. Unlike her brother, Oceana preferred to be outdoors rather than confined to the Tower and she frequently took walks around the edifice (after Shadowbender had determined it was safe to do so). She had been extremely excited about the trip itself and looked forward to gathering the fragrant blooms. Oceana regularly picked the wild flowers growing in proximity to the Tower and brought the bouquets inside to liven up their home. Though he had never explicitly told her,

Shadowbender appreciated the flowers and enjoyed them nearly as much as she did.

The first portion of the journey had passed without incident. They found the starflowers and harvested some, leaving the patch healthy enough to regrow and replace the plants they had harvested. They had also dug up several whole plants with the intention of domesticating them, so they could enjoy the benefits of the plants without having to make a long and difficult journey to obtain them. They had travelled less than a mile of the return trip when they were assaulted.

They were not completely surprised. Elves, perhaps more than any of the humanoid races, were at home in the woodlands, even home-bodies like Shadowbender. The first indication of trouble was a general unidentifiable feeling of "wrongness." Shadowbender, in the lead by several paces, had turned to ask Oceana if she, too, felt something amiss. He found she had already stopped and was surveying the surrounding wood intently.

"Get ready!" Shadowbender had urged as the feeling intensified sharply, though he was unsure what was about to occur.

To their right and just ahead, movement caught his eye. A large shape arose from behind the stump of a toppled tree. Shadowbender's heart sank as he recognized the gangly form of a troll. Fortunately, trolls, despite their great strength and ferocity, were among the least intelligent of the marauding humanoids and were, therefore, not particularly difficult to defeat, provided one was a mage and prepared. Trolls were fast and, though Shadowbender felt he

99

could probably outrun the creature, he opted not to run as he was less confident as to Oceana's ability to outrun the long-limbed beast. Like many natural creatures, trolls suffered from an inordinate fear of fire; a weakness Shadowbender fully intended to exploit.

Clenching his fist, Shadowbender whispered a spidery incantation and, slowly opening his hand, smiled inwardly as he saw there a flickering ball of flame several inches in diameter. He threw the sphere and smiled outwardly as the small orb struck the troll in the chest. Almost immediately, the fire spread, encompassing most of the creature, which began to wail loudly and flail its long arms attempting to beat out the flames convulsing unnaturally around its body. The magical flames were intense but would last only a few seconds. Though the creature would be injured, it certainly would not be killed, which was fine as the elf was intending to drive the creature off, not kill it. A thrashing noise from his left drew his attention.

He turned to see the shapes of half a dozen or so goblins thrashing in the underbrush that had somehow animated and had wrapped around their arms, legs and torsos and that, while not holding the creatures completely immobile, prevented them from moving toward the mage as they had obviously been doing only moments before. Most of them had dropped their weapons, mostly the curved blades preferred by the cruel folk, and grabbed futilely at the foliage holding them fast. One goblin, apparently fast enough or far enough to the forefront to have avoided Oceana's spell (for that was what it was), slumped slowly to the forest floor with Oceana's dagger sunk in its neck.

"Well done!" Shadowbender cried before turning his attention back toward the troll that was the leader of the goblin pack. He was heartened to see the troll, having been sufficiently damaged and/or cowed by the magical fire, shambling off into the wood as fast as its spindly legs would carry it.

"Let's go!" the elf cried. He leapt to the fallen goblin, yanked Oceana's dagger from its throat, and ran off down the path, Oceana running at his side.

Oceana had not only kept her wits sufficiently to notice the goblins attacking from the flank, she commanded the proper mental strength to overthrow them. She had done well, better than many (possibly including himself) might have done in the same situation, and Shadowbender was proud of her. Thenceforth, Shadowbender let Oceana travel about the Tower grounds (as he referred to the immediate area around their domicile) as often as she wished and without complaint from him. Yes, Oceana was capable of taking care of herself and he knew he should not worry about her accompanying him on his current journey just as he knew he would worry, nonetheless.

It was a tired company that sat around the small camp fire late that night. Everyone had eaten, and each seemed lost in his own thoughts. Shadowbender and Roland were smoking and the smoke from their pipes wreathed around the low-hanging boughs of the surrounding trees. Shadowbender glanced at Drake, the glow of an idea in his eyes, "Do you know any songs or tales of the Forgotten Lands, Drake?"

"Uh...yeah," Drake answered, shaken from his reverie, "I know a couple."

"Let's hear one," urged Oceana, pulling her blanket tightly around herself.

Drake opened his pack and withdrew a mandolin wrapped in oilskin. He unwrapped the instrument, deftly tuned it, and sat lost in thought, apparently mentally reciting lyrics.

"Oceana, you're welcome to join in," he said finally.

"No, thank you, I believe I'll just listen and enjoy. Besides, I doubt I'd know the tune." Oceana closed her eyes expectantly.

"This song," said Drake, "is an old, old song. It is entitled 'The Lamentation of Drusilla'." The bard began playing a slow, eerie melody on his mandolin. Then, he began to sing, his rich baritone filling the night air and holding his listeners rapt:

"Long ago

Even when

The homes of men

Were known

To the few

Elves who then

Lived within

The wood of Lyandohlia,

Lived a maid,

A pretty maid,

Lovingly called Drusilla.

She lived a woodcutter's life
For she was a woodcutter's wife,
Deep in the wood
Their cottage stood
Surrounded by a sea
Of violets.
Life was gay
In its way
In Lyandohlia.

Then winter fell
Over the dells
And icy slopes
Of Lyandohlia.
Bitter and grim
Was the frigid wind
And wolves
Assaulted the flocks
And goblin bands
Assaulted the land,
The frozen land
Of Lyandohlia.

Her husband
Was gone
And winter

Went on

Leaving Drusilla

Alone.

Sickness and woe

Toil and cold

Took their toll

In Lyandohlia.

Drusilla 'tis said

Left her cold bed

And entered the chill

And bleak forest

Of Lyandohlia.

If the tale

Is believed,

E'en in death,

She ne'er did leave

Off wandering

The barren drifts

And cold winter mists

Of Lyandohlia.

That land,

'Tis said,

Ne'er gives up

Its dead

And Drusilla

Roams it yet."

Drake left off playing and each person was left to their wild imaginings sparked by the song. Even the normal sounds of the nocturnal wood sounded eerie and surreal.

"Is the song true?" Quint asked softly.

"All songs are true, in their way," said Drake, "Lyandohlia is an ancient and long defunct realm within the area we know now as The Forgotten Lands; we'll enter Drusilla's realm over the next few days. Perhaps we'll see her," he added, winking. Roland groaned.

"Let's hope not!" Oceana countered, echoing the dwarf's sentiment. The elf maid stood up, "I'm going to bed," she said and walked to her tent and climbed in. Everyone else, except Drake whose lot fell for first watch, wrapped themselves in their blankets to sleep. Tomorrow would be their first day in the Forgotten Lands. Who knew what they would encounter? Roland, when he wasn't on watch, dreamt of phantom housewives roaming a cold winter wood.

Chapter 7

For the next three days, the companions travelled without encountering anything more remarkable than the occasional squirrel or rabbit. Mostly unconcerned with secrecy so early in their journey, the party took no extreme methods in hiding their passage. Roland thought this a mistake but said nothing. At night, around the fire, Drake had played to them for their amusement. The bard was good and knew a variety of the songs, tales, and jokes bards were obliged to know. Drake had travelled extensively throughout most of the civilized realms of the south where human and elven civilizations flourished and could credit many of his tales to those regions. He had even learned a few tales involving dwarves and had picked up a lot of woods lore, too, the dwarf noted. Hopefully, he (along with Quint) could even guide them through the Forgotten Lands without getting everyone killed.

Though the others seemed comfortable enough, Roland had no love for the untamed wilderness. It was messy, unruly, and chaotic. Like most dwarves, he was easily confused and lost in the woodlands, preferring, rather, mines or even the orderly constructions of cities which, in the largest population centres, resembled mines from a pedestrian's standpoint as the tall buildings towered high overhead, blocking much of the sunlight and creating a tunnel-like environment. Woodlands were the haunt of elves and anything favoured by those light-headed fops was sure to be without any sane rationale. Roland snorted. Quint always went on and on about trees and such; he was almost as bad as an elf. Hang a bunch of trees, anyway! Give a dwarf a good solid rock surface beneath his feet and room to swing an axe and he was the happiest creature on the face of the earth (or, preferably, below it).

As they travelled, Quint kept pointing out factors confirming the land was, indeed, once settled, almost making a game of pointing out decaying relics of civilization. Roland argued that he was not blind and could, therefore, notice such things on his own, but the ranger merrily continued to indicate the obvious. The faint trace of a path, the occasional discovery of a long-abandoned rock wall engulfed and nearly destroyed by the spreading forest, and a couple of areas filled with younger trees that had been a pasture in the distant past, all indicated men had once lived here (as Quint delightedly informed anyone who pretended to listen). Tripping over an endless sea of fallen branches, the dwarf heartily wished men lived here still. Then there would've been roads and paths and clearings and, maybe, an inn, not to mention a lesser chance of running into monsters that were drawn to uncivilized places.

At least the humans had kept them moving along at a pretty good pace the past few days. As much as possible, Drake had kept to the valleys where the travel was easier. Still, they had been forced to overcome several steep ridges (covered in trees, of course) and a couple of difficult stream crossings (mostly overgrown with trees— was there no end to the accursed things?). Trees were stupid, anyway; they looked funny, like overgrown spears with leaves sticking out of the top and they got in the way of *everything*—no wonder men, in the

107

process of civilization, always cut them down. They might be moderately useful in camp fires, but that was about the extent of their worth. As they travelled, they were frequently obliged to hack a path through the tortuous undergrowth. The dainty elves were useless at such times and Roland and the two men cleared the way with axe and sword.

Today, however, the going was a bit easier. They were in an older part of the forest with large trees and a minimum of undergrowth. In fact, they had even stumbled upon a relatively clear, though apparently little used, path. Quint had been loath to use it for fear of encountering something upon it. Shadowbender, ever paranoid, had voiced his agreement. Everyone else promoted the path. In the end, the path was chosen as expedient and they had now been travelling along it the better part of a day. Roland didn't care if they did encounter something upon it. After all, they were well-armed, and he knew he and Quint, at least, could fight. The elves would be useless in such an encounter, but—so what? He was more than ready for anything that might happen along, as long as it wasn't one of those hideous walking tree-creatures Quint swore existed in some of the older forests.

As evening approached, they searched for a suitable camp site. They were all tired. Even Oceana's eternal bounciness was lessened (much to Roland's approval—the lass chattered like a rocky brook most of the time). Drake stopped suddenly, throwing his hand up in a cautionary gesture. Ahead, nearly invisible within the encroaching wood were the dilapidated, leaf and moss-covered remains of an old homestead.

It was a cottage. Made of roughly hewn stone, it appeared long abandoned, but more or less intact. A broken circle of stones marked the site of an old well. There was no movement within or about the old cottage and no sound issued forth. There appeared to be no danger. With a motion indicating he wanted everyone else to stay put, Quint moved stealthily toward the cottage.

As he approached, Quint could perceive no one had been within the cottage in some time. Leaves and dust remained undisturbed around the doorway. It was against his nature, however, to be careless and the ranger treated the cottage as a potential danger, despite its abandoned air. Quint listened intently. No sound from within. He knew, when he entered the cottage, his vision would be virtually nil, stepping from light to dark. Adrenaline pumping and senses on alert, he stepped through the doorway.

After a few moments, his eyes partially adjusted to the dim light. The doorway and two windows admitted enough light to faintly illumine the cottage interior. As he expected, the abode had been abandoned for a long time. A leaf-covered hearth was the dominant feature. A few pieces of broken and rotting furniture lay strewn about. Leaves and other debris had blown in through the door and windows and had accumulated in piles against some hidden obstacles. The middle of the chamber held the largest pile of leaves.

Nothing appeared to have been disturbed for a long time. It was somewhat of a shame as the dwelling would make an excellent den for some animal, but it was fortunate for Quint and his companions, who could have if for their own little den tonight.

Everyone watched expectantly as the ranger slipped through the darkness of the cottage door. A short while later, Quint's head popped back into the light and he waved vigorously, beckoning them onward. The others approached the cottage with a feeling of warmth and appreciation for a roof over their heads. The idea of being inside during the night was comforting, although the nights, so far, had held no danger.

The party entered the cottage and began to inspect their home away from home. Drake began brushing off the hearth. Shadowbender was intently studying the walls and ceiling to be sure no hidden predators were lurking in the shadowy corners. Quint began gathering pieces of old furniture for use as firewood. Roland and Oceana were poking through the leaves. Without warning, the elf maiden's scream reverberated throughout the cottage.

Everyone turned, weapons drawn. The elf-maid, however, appeared to be in no immediate danger. She stood, one hand clamped over her mouth, the other pointing toward the ground. Roland stepped over and peered intently into the leaf pile at her feet. Roland glanced up at the questioning faces of his companions and said simply, "Skeleton."

After an exhaustive search, a total of seven skeletons was found beneath the leaf litter. All were human. Four were adult, and three were children, one of them an infant. They appeared to be from different times as some of the bones were yellowed and brittle, while others were still white. Also, two of the skeletons wore armour, whereas the others did not. All but one showed signs of violence. Several weapons, rusted, old, or broken lay scattered throughout the debris.

"Odd," remarked Shadowbender.

"Yeah," said Quint, "I wonder what happened here?"

"Doesn't matter, now," shot Roland, "I guess we'll never know." About the last thing Roland wanted to do was stand around in some ensorcelled wood looking at a bunch of skeletons and trying to figure what had killed them. Whatever it was had certainly been gone a long time and the thought of wondering over pointless trivialities irritated him; they had better things to do with their time—making supper, for instance.

"They died at different times," said Drake, "that much is obvious and some, or perhaps, all of the adults appear to have been armed."

"It is odd," Shadowbender repeated.

"Who cares?" Roland responded.

"*We* should care," Shadowbender said thoughtfully as he examined the remains, "considering we are preparing to camp in a location wherein at least two groups of people have been killed on two different occasions. I would say that bears some relevance."

"Oh," said Roland. He hadn't thought about it like that and what the elf was saying did make sense, though the dwarf hated to think of the mage making a valid point.

"Whatever it was," said Drake, "it was a long time ago and I doubt we are in any danger presently." Shadowbender and Roland nodded agreement.

After a short discussion, it was decided the best course of action would be to bury the remains. This coveted task fell to Quint and Roland, while everyone else set up camp for the night. Drake began preparing a meal with Shadowbender's 'help', which consisted primarily of indifferent supervision. Tying an extra cloak around the end of Shadowbender's staff to form a makeshift broom, Oceana swept as many of the leaves as possible without the cottage. She was a little embarrassed by her screaming earlier and was trying to make up for it by being useful.

It was a tired (especially the grave diggers) and appreciative party that gathered around the hearth that night. It had begun drizzling an hour or two earlier and the crackling fire and shelter cheered them. All looked forward to a cosy, restful night.

"I think we need a song to cheer us," Quint said to Drake after the evening meal was eaten and a crackling blaze warmed the hearth and bathed the interior of the cottage in its warm glow.

"I think," interjected Shadowbender, "we should discuss a watch as we are now in dangerous territory."

"Oh, Shadowbender! You worry too much," said Oceana.

"No," Drake said in Shadowbender's defence, "he's right, but I think the discussion can wait for a song, can't it my friend?" he looked at Shadowbender with respect. The elf nodded in reply and

Drake rummaged into his backpack pulling out, this time, an ornate flute.

"How many instruments is this guy carrying around?" Roland whispered audibly to Quint. The ranger shrugged.

"How about an elven song?" Drake said raising his eyebrows in expectation while looking at Oceana and Shadowbender.

"*Da Shariada*," said Shadowbender.

"Ah," said Drake, "The Journeying Song. Good choice." Drake nodded and placed the flute to his lips. Slowly and melodically, he played as the music was enchanting and made one think of a journey full of leisure and happiness. Shadowbender, his voice timeless and musical as the singing voices of elves are, began:

"Beneath the moon
The gentle breeze
Stirs the trees
A haunting, sylvan tune.

Who can know
What sights I'll see
Or where I'll be
When, on this path, I go.

Knowledge and lore
And wisdom deep
Are mine to seek
As this land, I explore."

Shadowbender stopped singing and Oceana continued the song, her voice feminine and wild:

"Beneath the sun
Forest creatures play
And plants display
The nurturing love of the sun.

I belong here
Amongst brethren of my soul
Where woods and wild rivers roll.
I belong here.

I am one with the world
As I move through it.
As I drift through it,
I am one with the world."

Drake stopped playing and everyone sat silently for a full minute, lost in the magic of the moment. Finally, Quint broke the silence. "That was beautiful," he said gently, "I've never heard the like."

"It is an ancient elven song. Elves travel upon the world but are also a part of the world. We seek to live in harmony with nature, not subjugate it like men and dwarves."

Quint nodded in agreement. Roland, surprisingly, said nothing.

"Well," said Drake, breaking the spell, "I guess we still have the piddling matter of the watch to finalize."

After a short discussion, it was determined Roland would take first watch, Quint second, and Shadowbender the last. Everyone except Roland soon wrapped themselves in blankets and drifted off to sleep.

During his turn at watch, Shadowbender absently poked at the embers in the hearth, silently debating whether or not to add fuel and build a fire. He was over an hour into his watch and the fire would be welcome, but he was somewhat leery over the attraction a fire would almost certainly be to anything coming near the cottage. He was alert to any sounds and his eyes were sharp. A fire would also interfere with vision. Lost in thought, the mage almost did not notice something was happening before it was too late to react.

The realization crept up on him. The embers gave off a faint glow, a glow that seemed to be brightening. Chills ran up and down the elf's spine as he realized the glow was not only getting brighter for no apparent reason, but it was greenish, not the reddish glow coals would normally emit.

He slowly turned. The entire cottage was glowing with a greenish phosphorescence. Outside the window, it appeared to be day, but with the same bizarre greenish tint, like some dream scape; too blatantly surreal to be real. Something was happening, thought the elf, and, whatever it was, it was not going to be good. Shadowbender moved to awaken his companions when, without warning, the scene drastically changed. His heart leapt as a domestic scene materialized before his eyes.

A human male in homespun sat in a wooden chair facing the hearth. In his lap, he held a small child bundled in a cotton wrap. The man's wife worked on a table behind him, cutting apples. Two young girls scampered around the cottage. The man looked toward the fire as if Shadowbender were not there. In fact, no one in the family gave any indication they were aware of any of the companions despite the fact they lay scattered about the floor. The girls practically stepped on Drake without so much as glancing at the snoring bard. If he looked hard, the elf could perceive they were translucent, the deteriorated surroundings barely visible through their bodies.

Shadowbender awakened each party member by placing his hand over his mouth to stifle any possible cry and giving him a quick shake. One by one, the party members grabbed their weapons and wordlessly faced whatever danger awaited.

Now, they all stood wide-eyed with pounding hearts staring at the scene before them. Shadowbender's mind was working frantically, trying to assimilate the information and work out possible reactions. It was clear the phantoms (if such they were) were oblivious to the party. A rattling sound arrested his attention. Turning, he saw Roland. The dwarf was white as a sheet, his eyes large as saucers. He barely maintained his grasp on his axe as he literally shook hard enough to rattle his armour. In fact, it appeared the dwarf would fall over in fear at any moment. Shadowbender shook his head in impatience and resumed his frenzied contemplation.

Suddenly, the phantom woman screamed. Grabbing one of the girls who happened to be within reach, she pointed to one of the windows. The opening framed a leering goblin face. The other windows were quickly filled with the struggling forms of goblins trying to gain entry into the cottage. The cottage erupted into a frenzy of motion and noise as the husband grabbed a burning branch from the fire (nearly touching Quint who quickly stepped out of the way) and a hatchet from the mantle. His wife herded the children into the corner before running to the table and grabbing a large carving knife and a cast iron skillet. In addition to wriggling through the windows, goblins began battering at the door.

"Stop!" Shadowbender called desperately just as Roland, fear replaced by battle rage, prepared to leap into the fray. Quint and Drake were right behind him. All three stopped, however, at the mage's cry.

"What?" Roland practically screamed.

"Do not fight them," Shadowbender spoke rapidly, "they are not real. This is a vision. It is not *now*; it is a re-enactment. Nothing can change the outcome." The elf's eyes were filled with sorrow, "There is nothing we can do. Participating in the battle will only endanger yourself, it will not help."

Before them, the phantom combat was joined. The man nearly beheaded the first goblin as it wriggled through one of the windows and he thrust his torch into the face of a second as it landed within the cottage. His wife ran to the second window and caved in the skull of a goblin trying to crawl in there. At that moment, the door splintered, and ten to fifteen hooting goblins squirmed through.

With a cry that reverberated throughout the cottage, Roland launched himself from the hearth and into the fray. The warrior instinct within him could not be overcome. Shadowbender jumped in front of the remaining party members with his arms outstretched to prevent them from following the dwarf. Oceana had never moved, Drake stopped upon seeing Shadowbender's face, but Quint had to be pushed back to prevent him from charging forward after Roland.

"Stop, you fool!" hissed Shadowbender, "you will only get us killed. Were you not listening? *Nothing* will change the outcome!"

"Those people are dying!" yelled Quint.

"Those people are *dead*!" Shadowbender said, "Do you want us to die uselessly, as well?" quipped the mage, "When you bring a mage along on a journey, you had better listen to him."

Oceana laid her hand on Quint's arm partly to prevent his entering the combat and partly out of sympathy.

It was all over in less than a minute. The goblins swarmed over the humans and the children, although the man killed one more goblin before falling. Roland dispatched four goblins before taking a nasty blow to the head. Disoriented, the dwarf stumbled backward, where he was caught and held by Quint and Drake. Roland fought against their hold until, without a sound, the entire scene faded into nothingness. The blood lust drained from Roland and he, again, began shaking uncontrollably.

"I told you it was futile," said Shadowbender.

"To the abyss with you, mage" Roland screamed, wriggling in the men's grasp. Quint wrapped his arms completely around Roland, or the dwarf would have attacked the elf then and there.

Finally, everyone calmed down, though sleep was out of the question. Drake piled the fire high and the cottage glowed with a wholesome light. No signs whatsoever remained of the spectral battle.

"What *was* that, Shadowbender?" whispered Oceana. Shadowbender took a sip from his water skin, "A vision," he said quietly, "Sometimes, when an event is accompanied by intense emotion, it stains an area like wine stains a cloth and it becomes permanent. Something we did must have sparked the memory, creating a replay of the incident. They are rare. I suppose Drake has heard about such things."

"Aye," agreed the bard, "though this is the first and, I hope, the last I'll ever see."

"You and me, both," murmured Quint.

Roland was silent.

"I suppose the armoured skeletons," mused Shadowbender, "the newer ones, must be the remains of those who were lured into combat and slain."

"The ghosts can kill?" queried Oceana. "Only if one accosts them," answered Shadowbender, "you noticed they ignored us and attacked Roland only after he engaged them. Had we all stayed put, none of us would have been assaulted."

"If all of us would have helped," Roland said bitterly, "those people would have been saved."

"I wish that were true," Shadowbender said.

"You don't know it's not!" Roland spat.

Shadowbender merely shrugged and busily wrapped himself in his blanket. No one said anything else for the remainder of the night. Roland stared blankly into the fire.

Chapter 8

The subdued atmosphere persisted until well into the morning. Warm and sheltering just the evening past, the stone cottage now seemed foreboding, the open doorway staring out like a misshapen eye, the entire structure an evil cyclopean monstrosity. Or, so Drake thought. Bards were like that.

Even with the events of last night, Drake felt happy. The bright morning sun was peeping through the branches into the clearing and the birds were cheeping out in the forest. It wasn't that last night didn't happen or wasn't important, but...that was last night. Today was a new day. Perhaps even a day to compose a song about last night.

Looking around, Drake was amused by what his critical eye noticed. Shadowbender appeared lost in thought, trudging along without really looking where he was going. He would probably obsess on the ethereal scene last night for the better part of the day. His sister, on the other hand, as was her custom, was aware of everything occurring in her surroundings. She seemed sobered, less vivacious than usual, which was not unusual considering what she had witnessed last night. Everyone was affected to some degree.

Quint even seemed somewhat subdued. Roland was intractable. He silently moved along, a scowl etched onto his face. With the dwarf in such a foul mood, it was only natural for the ranger to light into him with a vengeance and Drake watched the exchange with amused interest.

121

"Gee, Roland," said Quint, "I've never seen shaking like I did last night when those ghosts popped up." The ranger put his hand to his cheek in mock surprise, "I didn't even know mail could rattle so loud".

"I can't even hear what you're saying!" said Roland, looking in every direction except toward Quint.

"I didn't know you were afraid of ghosts," said Quint, lying. Even the thought of anything supernatural usually upset the dwarf.

"I wasn't scared!" Roland said heatedly, "it was some sort of spell or something."

"Right," said Quint in mock realization, "it must have been an evil spell of armour-rattling."

"It was some sort of sorcery," the dwarf insisted.

Quint laughed into his sleeve in mock discretion. Despite this little interlude, things soon returned to normal and the quest resumed.

The party continued eastward. The events of the night before had instilled a stronger-than-normal sense of caution within them, and they moved at a much slower rate without even being aware of the change. It was obvious these woods were once settled, albeit sparsely, by human settlers. Signs of this civilization still remained, notably in the path on which the party was travelling. They had managed to travel along paths and the remains of paths since entering the Forgotten Lands, which was fortunate to a group needing to make good time. Quint, however, wasn't entirely happy with their route.

"The path is still in use," Quint said, moving alongside Drake. Shadowbender listened on quietly. The bard had reached the same

122

conclusion as the path was easy to follow and relatively clear of impediments. The one potentially difficult stream crossing they had encountered had been neutralized by a log placed conveniently over it and the branches of the log had been cut by tools to facilitate crossing.

"What by?" the bard asked.

"Animals. Some humanoids." Quint looked around thoughtfully, "Enough sign is present to indicate we'll encounter intelligent life if we remain on our present course."

"Not likely," said Shadowbender glancing at Roland.

"My concern," said Drake "is we'll draw more attention to ourselves thrashing about in the wood than we will on the path. Not to mention we would fatigue ourselves terribly in doing so."

"You may be right," Quint acknowledged, "but we still need to be wary."

"Of course," said Drake, "a point man?"

Quint nodded, "I'll go." With that, he silently moved well ahead of the bard to take the point position. He made his way far enough ahead to be generally out of sight of his companions, but within range should communication be necessary. In this manner, the party travelled due east the better part of the day without encountering any danger.

Oceana watched the ranger slip off in the distance ahead. She moved her gaze from the front of the line to the dwarf stomping along in front of her. Roland had been quiet most of the day except for defending himself with obvious lies when Quint had teased him. Roland was funny. His gruffness was mostly an act, she decided, a false bravado. Of course, she had no doubts as to the dwarf's fighting ability. His movements, in general, and his action in the cottage, specifically, had demonstrated his combat prowess. She looked ahead again. Quint was out of sight. Drake hiked along with determination. Behind him, Shadowbender glided along the path in typical thoughtfulness. Smiling, she moved up to walk next to Roland.

They walked in silence for a while, the dwarf making no acknowledgement of her presence. That was no good.

"Hey," the elf maid said quietly.

Roland made a cursory glance in her direction, his pumping legs never missing a beat. Roland had to walk faster than he normally would in order to maintain the pace of the longer–legged humans and elves.

"Oh, hello, lass," he finally muttered.

"You don't care much for magic, do you?" Oceana asked.

"Ah, well, I guess, well…" the dwarf began stammering then said confidently, "No. No, I guess I don't, at that." He never looked at the elf maid, keeping his attention on the trail ahead.

"Why?" Oceana asked conversationally.

The dwarf seemed taken aback and didn't respond for some time as if mulling over his answer.

"I guess it's…unnatural," he said finally, "all obscure knowledge, dead toads, bat wings, and weird sayings and such. Not what a normal man would be involved in. Not that it's all bad, of course," he added hastily, "I'm sure some wizards are good folk, but most of them, at least the ones I've heard about anyway, aren't what

I'd consider noble or good. Too, the Mage War nearly wiped us all out. Magic is dangerous business, I suppose." The dwarf fell silent.

"Virtually all the mages I know, "Oceana said, "use their knowledge for good. There are some (like Shadowbender, she mentally noted) who are largely indifferent and consider magic apart from everything else, sort of an entity in and of itself. And," she added, "I have heard about evil mages, of course, and I think most people pay more attention to works of evil than of good. Evil is a tale to be shared; good is a closely held secret—so goes the old saying." The woman cocked her head quizzically, "The dwarves don't have magic, do they?"

"Aye," answered Roland, "dwarven clerics are fairly rare but certainly not unheard of." Oceana knew dwarven clerics were every bit as violent as dwarven culture, in general, and were frequently referred to as the "hammers of the gods," acknowledging the almost universal habit of dwarven clerics to wield bludgeoning weapons, of which, the war hammer was the culturally-acceptable example.

"Most dwarves honour the priestly arts," Roland continued, "and even those dwarves not destined to become clerics usually receive rudimentary training—history and prayers, mostly—as sort of a basic training."

Oceana knew there were two types of healing in the world: that of ordinary means performed by ordinary people, by far the most common, and that of faith-based healing magic. Ordinary healing ranged from the rudimentary skills, such as binding a wound, that virtually everyone knew how to do (at least in concept) to formally trained healers who could diagnose and treat substantial or complex wounds and sickness. Most healers were female as women seemed to inherently possess a greater talent for healing than men. A common proverb, at least among the elves, was that men cause wounds and women heal them. Clerics, however, possessed the ability to magically heal wounds or counter sickness. Mostly militant warrior-priests, clerics were granted this power (which did not qualify as arcane power, at least to wizards, as the ability did not come from the arcane "fabric" underlying the world from which wizards drew their power) directly from the gods or the cleric's tremendous faith in some higher power or ideal. Thus, though Oceana did not truly understand it, some clerics were able to heal by drawing power from their faith in concepts such as "nature" or "good." In keeping with the role of priest, many clerics were formally trained in non-magical healing which was then bolstered with faith-based magical healing. The abilities of such clerics were amazing though, except in very rare instances, they could not heal extreme wounds.

The terms "priest" and "cleric" were not synonymous as far as the elf knew. "Priest" was a generic term for anyone making a career of following and serving a specific deity or concept. Sometimes, priests were charged with serving a congregation (usually within a certain geographic region) and operated from a church or other formal place of worship, though this was by no means universal. A great many priests travelled in service to their deity as teachers or proselytizers. The exact distinction between priests and clerics was a little hazy, but it seemed clerics were a subclass of priest. Clerics seemed to be militant priests trained to fight on behalf of their god's ideals. In elven society, a culture much more focused on peace and art than fighting, there were some priests but few clerics. Elven deities were largely focused on nature and their priests, largely (and, sometimes, completely) pacifistic, rarely carried weapons at all. More prone to ponder the intricacies of magic than the philosophical subtleties of religion, elven wizards were much more common than priests, though priests were respected by virtually all elves. Only the priests of Ralynian, the elven war god, supported a small sect of clerics and even these tended to focus on the "artsy" aspects of fighting such as archery and a beautifully complex fighting style resembling dance. Despite its martial talents, this group was largely introspective and few of its adherents fit the mould of proselytizing warrior clerics.

"But the dwarves," Oceana asked, "don't have arcane skills or so I've heard."

"No," Roland answered, "I'm not aware of any dwarven mages."

"I wonder why that is?" Oceana mused. Roland didn't answer. In fact, the dwarf seemed a little uncomfortable with the topic. Oceana decided to change the subject.

"Have you and Quint been friends long?" she asked.

This was a topic the dwarf was more comfortable with, and Oceana could actually see the dwarf relax as he answered, "Yeah. We've been together a little over ten years now," the dwarf took a swig from his water skin, "ever since I saved his tail from a lynch mob. 'Course, he's saved mine a time or two since."

"A lynch mob?" Oceana frowned.

"Yeah," Roland laughed, "a group of villagers thought he had killed their cattle. Sometime, when you're in the mood for a long, drawn out tale, ask him about it; it's a pretty funny story, you know, looking back on it."

"I'm sure," said Oceana.

"Can I ask *you* a question?" queried the dwarf.

"I don't see why not," answered the maid.

"Why do you choose to be a mage?"

It was Oceana's turn to be surprised and unsure of her response.

"One doesn't really choose to be a mage," she said thoughtfully, "it's kind of something you just *are*." She nodded more certain of her view, "*You* didn't choose to be a dwarf, for example, it's simply your identity; what you are."

Roland obviously heard but didn't respond to the elf maid's words. They walked a bit further before Oceana picked up the conversation where they had left off.

"I think elves are prone to mage-craft like dwarves are prone to combat. Just as all dwarves aren't full-fledged warriors (I guess), but still have an inherent understanding of military matters; virtually all elves have a rudimentary understanding of wizardry. It's a basic part of our education. We live longer than most races and can, potentially, become great wizards. Most don't, though, tending to follow scholarly and nature-oriented pursuits."

"You and your brother are unusual, then?" the dwarf asked. It was a legitimate question and wasn't asked in a negative way.

Oceana smiled quickly, "Not for what we are, but—yes, because of the level of skill attained. I would say I'm more advanced than most my age. Shadowbender, though, is truly one of the greatest, if not *the* greatest illusionist from the elven kingdom. He's wise, and obsessive, I think. But the obsession has led him to more knowledge and quicker thinking than most people ever acquire. And, he's still young, by elven standards."

Later that afternoon, they stopped in a small glade to eat and confer about their course. Ahead, the Perilous Mountains were growing larger by the hour. For the past few hours, the increasing elevation was quite noticeable. They could feel it in their legs.

The forest was thick with undergrowth and the tangled wood rarely opened into a glade or open area like the one they now enjoyed. Ravines and clefts zigzagged across the mountains. Many were impassable or nearly so, and they were forced to work around such obstacles several times over the course of the day. Thus, they were all tired and needed a rest.

A small stream meandered through the glade. Most of the companions sat alongside it or under the shade of the trees eating, drinking, or merely resting. Roland was lying with his feet nearly in the stream, his head cradled in his arms, which were crossed behind his head forming a makeshift pillow. The dwarf's eyes were closed against the afternoon sun and he was breathing deeply in a rhythmic pattern, and Quint thought the dwarf, though not snoring, was probably dozing or nearly-dozing, lulled to sleep by the steady droning of bees that filled the glade with a restful undertone.

Shadowbender sat beneath a scraggly dogwood facing away from the others and facing the forest. His head was reclined and lying against the trunk of the tree. His eyes were also closed, and he seemed to be resting, though his posture, fairly erect with arms straight out and resting atop bended knees, indicated he was not asleep. Quint had always understood elves needed less rest than other races and the time spent with Oceana and Shadowbender seemed to confirm this as both elves usually retired later and awoke earlier than the rest of them without any sign of adverse effects.

Oceana knelt by the stream. Her hair hung over her face as she refilled her water skin. She looked like a gentle yearling just learning the ways of the wondrous world. The bard, too, noticed Oceana and watched the elf maid from his seat against the stump of a long-fallen oak. With a last contemplative look around the glade and the elf maid, who was now bathing her face and neck with the cool water, Quint took a seat next to Drake. The bard glanced at the ranger as the man sat down.

"So far, so good," the bard said quietly, referring, Quint presumed, to their journey hitherto. "Aye," affirmed the ranger, "I suppose so." Both men sat silently for a bit, both pretending to be on guard and watching the glade while surreptitiously watching the elf maiden bathing in the watercourse. Finally, Quint broke the silence with a deep sigh.

"How did you meet," said Quint, "you and Shadowbender, I mean?"

The bard glanced toward the mage resting some distance away. Drake smiled in obvious remembrance and shook his head almost imperceptibly.

"A long time ago and a long way from here," he replied. "It was actually in the Barony of Crystalmere," continued the bard, warming to the tale, "before Oceana had come to live with him. Bards travel quite a bit, as I'm sure you have heard..."

"Not a bad life, I imagine, living wild and free," Quint nodded.

"Aye," confirmed the bard, "or, at least, an illusion of freedom. Anyway, I had been travelling through the frontier areas of the Barony playing mostly for individual families in exchange for supper and a bed by the hearth. One obtains a lot of information about a country travelling around in such a manner as frontier families, receiving visitors less frequently than townsmen, generally 'give and take the gossip' as the saying goes.

One evening, I stayed with a couple and their children in a small mountain cabin. Over the course of my stay, the man, stern and forthright as settlers tend to be, solemnly warned me to stay clear of the wood across the valley because an evil wizard dwelt therein. This wizard, the man steadfastly maintained, was sometimes seen in the form of a ravening wolf that occasionally raided outlying flocks. Just recently, he claimed, the wizard had grown bolder in his depredations and had attacked a shepherd, who barely escaped with his life.

I assured him I'd be careful and declared, truthfully, that I had no desire to meet with such a creature. Later that night, as I went for a load of wood, I encountered the woodman's youngest daughter on the porch. I jokingly told her she'd better be careful coming outside as she didn't want to be out-of-doors with a wizard about. She laughed and said all the adults had it wrong. I feigned surprise and she conspiratorially whispered that she had twice seen the wizard out in the nearby wood. I asked her if she had been frightened and she admitted she had been at first but had quickly gotten over her fear because she was, as she proudly declared, going to be nine years old the very next month.

She went on to say the man was somewhat strange-looking, wearing a big grey cloak, but that I should try to find him. I asked her why she so thought and she, in all the guileless innocence of childhood, told me I should find him because the man had the power to summon butterflies, not only the regular kinds, but great big ones that would alight on your hand and in your hair."

"That's strange," interjected Quint.

"Yes," Drake laughed with a glance toward the still-resting mage, "though I doubt not that Shadowbender could summon butterflies if he wanted to do so. As you can probably figure out," continued the bard, "I was curious as to the wizard and, after taking my leave of the family the next day, I set out for the area where the girl had told me she had seen the 'butterfly-man,' as she called him."

I wandered around the wood for several days without finding anything and I had nearly given up, deciding the presence of the wizard was naught but hollow rumour; after all, virtually all communities harbour tales of a wizard or troll or other beastie living just beyond the bounds of their authority."

"I have noticed that, myself," Quint affirmed.

"Well," continued Drake, "just as I had decided to give up, I stumbled across a faint path. Reasoning it must lead somewhere, I followed the path for a mile or so until, to my surprise, I found nothing less than a short two-story tower in a small meadow covered with wild flowers. I don't know if they were summoned or not, but a great number of butterflies flitted amongst the blooms in their silent and beautiful way.

I assumed I had found the wizard's abode. First, it was several days travel from the nearest homestead, indicating its inhabitant valued privacy. Secondly, the tower obviously had been built supernaturally as if featured new stone and a slate floor, yet there was no sign these materials had been transported to the site. And, it should be remembered, the structure was a *tower*, which are frequently found as parts of fortresses, but rarely as stand-alone edifices...except as the abodes of wizards. I have never figured out why wizards seem to prefer towers—no one else does—and they're jolly hard to construct and maintain. I imagine, were I a mage, I'd understand their preoccupation with the things. Despite being ignorant as to the nuances of wizardly architectural preference, I felt sure I had discovered the home of the sorcerer, though whether he was an evil shape-changer, or a benign summoner of butterflies remained to be seen.

I knocked boldly on the only door, figuring a mage, if present, would surely have been aware of my presence by that point. As I half-expected, no one answered my knock. I turned to leave and found a man standing at the edge of the meadow, watching me closely.

"I seek the mage rumoured to live in the tower," I called to the man, "is he home?"

"Why would you expect to find a wizard here?" the man queried.

I told him about the tales I had heard. He frowned deeply as I detailed the story of the wolf but smiled broadly at the description of the child's tale. He asked me why I wanted to meet the mage, offering that this particular personage was not within.

"To share music, food, and warmth," I called, "and wandering bards know quite a bit about the murmurings of the countryside—I had hoped to share information."

"Very well, then," responded the other as he began gingerly picking his way toward the tower. Later, I discovered this man was, himself, the mage, as I'm sure you've guessed. Isolated as he was, he was hungry for news; otherwise, I expect he would've run me off forthwith.

The next few days were rainy and, after spending the evening in fellowship, Shadowbender allowed me to stay overnight. We became fast friends and, although I soon left, I returned several times over the following couple of years. It was during one such visit

Shadowbender was assaulted by a group of elves, wizards from the Elven Kingdoms who held a vendetta against Shadowbender," the bard shook his head sadly at the memory, "we defeated them, barely. Due to this incident, I learned somewhat about Shadowbender's past."

"What?" Quint queried, eyebrows arched quizzically.

"It would make a worthy song or tale should it be recorded," the bard said.

"What happened?" Quint urged.

"Have you heard anything about the Elven Council?" the bard asked softly.

"A little," the ranger, who actually knew nothing about it, answered.

"Well, as you know, the mages of the Elven Kingdoms are governed by a council. Shadowbender was a member of this council and, despite his youth, one of its leading members. Shadowbender hoped to head the council and, when the current leader retired, Shadowbender announced his desire to take over that position. Another mage wanted the position and, possessing an ability to politick that exceeded Shadowbender's skill in that area, was ultimately selected to head the council.

Shadowbender accepted the leadership of the other with no bitterness, but the newly-appointed leader held a grudge and continued to view Shadowbender as a threat. To make matters worse, Shadowbender had been openly courting the other's sister for some time and the relationship had sufficiently progressed to the point the couple wanted to wed."

"Uh-oh," the ranger whistled.

"The head of the council, of course," continued Drake, "forbade the marriage and, as doomed lovers are wont to do, Shadowbender and his lady eloped, planning to marry as soon as they had escaped the borders of the realm. They would be exiles, of course, but they willingly accepted this sacrifice if it allowed them to be together. They expected loss, but a tragedy far greater than they could have anticipated awaited them.

The second evening of their flight, they camped alongside a rushing boulder-strewn stream. Giddy with love, they frolicked in the soft moonlight only a few miles from the border. Disaster struck. The lady, elated as soon-to-be brides are, made a game of hopping from boulder to boulder, calling all the while for Shadowbender to chase her. Laughing, he sprang after her; as nimbly as a fleet-footed deer, she evaded him—him the pursuer and her the prize—they bounded from rock to rock.

Perhaps she couldn't see in the semi-darkness or she was distracted, for she sprang onto a boulder slick with moss and the water's spray. Her feet flew out from under her as she landed, and she cracked her head against the unyielding stone.

Shadowbender couldn't save her. He tried to bind the wound to no avail; her life's blood trickled through his fingers and was carried away by the cold water to a place beyond ken. He held her through the night, but even his titanic will could not undo what had been done. She never regained consciousness and, sometime in the lonely night, her spirit flew to its new home.

Shadowbender carried his lover's body back to her brother's home and left her wrapped in a blanket near the door along with a short missive stating what had happened. He expected retribution and, unwilling to bring danger to his own sister and family, Shadowbender left the Elven Kingdoms, never to return."

"They hunted him down," Quint said quietly.

"Aye," the bard confirmed, "he had fled to Crystalmere and built the small tower where I first met him. The lady's brother and his companions eventually found Shadowbender and tried to kill their foe. Only one of them survived the battle, the brother as fate would have it, and he believed he had killed Shadowbender. Thus, the elf departed, believing his mission accomplished.

Within months, Shadowbender abandoned the tower in case his enemies ever returned. In this way, he would not be found alive and well in the tower; furthermore, the building would suffer from neglect and appear to have been left uninhabited as a result of his 'death.' He selected the site of the current tower due to its isolation; only random chance would bring anyone to it and, even if someone did approach, such a person would be unlikely to recognize the mage as he only then assumed the name of Shadowbender and the appearance he now wears."

"I thought 'Shadowbender' was an odd name," said Quint, "for a couple to name their child—what is his real name?"

"Elves do not give their real names to any but their nearest relatives. Frankly, I know neither his nor Oceana's real name."

"Isn't the new tower," asked the ranger, "awfully close to the Elven Kingdoms; I mean, I thought Shadowbender wanted to avoid being detected?"

"He does. The difficult terrain of the mountains effectively shields him; he is several days' worth of hard travel from the border of the Elven Kingdoms, but the border is likewise far removed, a week's journey, at least, from any permanent elven habitations, and even those are far removed from Shadowbender's original home. He is quite safe there due to both the location and his altered appearance—even Oceana didn't recognize him when she first saw him in his new form."

"How did Oceana find him at all, considering he had taken such pains to hide?" the ranger asked.

"After Shadowbender completed the tower, he secretly sent word to her that he was alive. She expressed a desire to leave the Elven Kingdoms and live in self-exile with him. Long did Shadowbender resist, but he eventually acquiesced; in retrospect, I think the tower's location was largely selected in order to accommodate his sister's arrival without her having to travel a long distance. Around three years ago, Oceana arrived at the tower and has been there ever since. The enmity of the council, I think (I have not been expressly told), prevented Oceana from advancing and she had learned as much as she could from her tutors. Coming to live with Shadowbender not only reunited her with her brother, it furthered her career, at least in the way wizards perceive such things."

"So," said Quint, "Oceana and Shadowbender are both exiles."

"Not officially," the bard declared, "but, for all practical purposes, you are correct. Oceana could return, perhaps, but Shadowbender cannot so long as his foes are still alive."

"Elves live practically forever, don't they?" Quint asked.

"Practically," the bard said, gazing sadly at the elf-maid who, her bathing complete, sat next to her brother, the two of them softly talking.

An obstacle before them was the topic of conversation, and the entire party was soon engaged with the dilemma. Ahead, a quarter mile from the glade, a deep ravine cleft the mountainside. The ravine was impassable due to both width and depth. The source of concern, however, was something else entirely.

An old, weather-worn swinging bridge spanned the ravine. Tied to trees on either side, the rope was spotted with mould or fungus. The boards were warped, weathered, and, in some places, gone altogether.

Roland was opposed to using the bridge at all. They had gone to the bridge prior to returning to the glade. Looking at the decrepit bridge over the dizzying drop into the rock-cluttered ravine, the dwarf had flat out refused to cross. Drake didn't blame him, feeling a bit uneasy about it, himself. Oceana whole-heartedly agreed with the dwarf. Quint didn't like the look of the bridge but didn't want to look like a coward (especially in front of the elf maid) and cast his vote for crossing. Shadowbender merely shrugged, giving no indication either way.

Unfortunately, there was no simple means of bypassing the bridge. According to the map, and as evidenced by a brief foray by Drake and Quint in both directions alongside the ravine, it would take hours of travel in either direction to avoid the obstacle and return to the path. After a brief (and emphatic on Roland's part) counsel, the majority of the group decided the bridge, despite its condition, was the only viable method of getting across the ravine.

After a brief meal, the party progressed to the bridge. The bridge swayed gently in the breeze, creaking softly.

"We're all going to die, you know that!" growled Roland.

"We're not going to die, Roland," urged Quint, "It's going to be fine." The ranger frowned at Roland and then nodded at Oceana, communicating to the dwarf he was frightening the woman. Roland frowned even more deeply—if that were possible—but said nothing further.

"How *are* we going to cross?" Drake asked Quint.

"We have enough rope," said Quint, "I suggest one of us carry the rope across and secure it so the rest of us can walk across holding to the rope should something happen."

"Good idea," said Drake, "Who'll be the one to go?"

"The one who has wings," said Roland, "but, since none of us happens to boast a pair, I suggest whoever is lightest."

"Leave it to you to come up with a description that just happens to leave you out!" Quint joked.

"That would be me—I'm the lightest!" the elf maid's voice was strong but quivered slightly and her eyes widened in fear.

"No," said Shadowbender, "I will go. I am nearly as light as Oceana and I have a magical contingency should I fall."

No one seemed eager to argue and Oceana, despite trying to mask herself in stoicism, looked relieved, so the elf took the rope and stepped gingerly onto the bridge. Roland actually jumped as the bridge groaned like a banshee under the elf's weight. Shadowbender drew a sharp breath and held it, but the bridge held. In slow motion, the mage crept across the chasm.

There were several terrifying moments when the boards sagged beneath his weight, but they held. The nervousness was contagious and those on land shifted and glanced around uncomfortably. Shadowbender breathed a sigh of relief as he stepped onto the solid ground on the other side and stood there shaking in the after-effect of fear and danger.

Oceana was next. After Shadowbender had tied the rope around a large maple on the far side of the chasm and Quint had similarly secured it on this side, she felt much more confident. Holding on to the rope with one hand, she glided daintily across the span. Drake followed once she had reached solid ground.

The human bard was a good bit heavier than Shadowbender and a lot heavier than Oceana. Tightly gripping the rope with both hands, Drake moved slowly across the bridge. Between the slats, the bard could look into the depths of the ravine. Way below him, the silver thread of a stream glistened. He watched in awe and fear as the tiny forms of distant birds soared *below* him. Gulping, Drake focused on putting one foot in front of the other, pointedly ignoring the depth beneath him. He was almost halfway across. Soon, he thought, it would be over.

With an eerie thud, an arrow embedded itself in the boards a few feet in front of Drake. The bard, as scared and focused as he was, simply stared at it stupidly, not realizing its portent. A million miles away, Oceana's scream drifted to him and the sound brought him back to reality.

Shadowbender had been watching Drake's progress. The whine of the arrow pricked his senses and, before the arrow made impact on the bridge, the mage had dropped and spun around. He heard Oceana scream.

Roland and Quint were also watching the bards' progress. They heard the thud and they saw the arrow quivering at the bard's feet. They saw Shadowbender spin around and heard Oceana scream. They also saw the cause of the alarm. About a dozen masked figures, some with bows, emerged from the wood on the elves' side of the ravine.

"Quint, we've got company," Roland said grimly.

"I know," said Quint looking across the ravine.

"No," said the dwarf, "our side."

Quint spun around as a score of men converged from the surrounding forest. With a sinking feeling, the ranger recognized the lizard-like mask each man wore.

"Your dragon men, I presume?" Roland said as he brandished his axe.

"Yeah," Quint drew his long sword, "and they've got us between the hammer and the anvil."

Drake looked up in time to see the men emerge beyond Shadowbender and Oceana. He turned to cry a warning to Quint and Roland, stopping short as he saw they were in the same situation. *Come on!* The bard was in anguish. Which way should he go? Quint and Roland were definitely better equipped to deal with attackers. In an instant, the bard began running, one hand still on the rope, toward the elves.

The cultists moved toward Quint and Roland.

"I hope these guys don't know how to fight," Roland said grimly. They awaited the assault. Sticking together, they might have a chance. They had fought as a team many times and both knew they stood a better chance together where they could protect each other's back. The cultists moved into melee range. Quint struck out with his sword and, without a word, the combat was joined.

In an instant, Shadowbender assessed the situation. He and his sister were no match for a dozen armed men, especially bowmen who had the drop on them. Shadowbender, eyes never leaving the enemy, quickly reached and touched his sister, mumbling some arcane words. Oceana disappeared.

A ripple of surprise coursed through the cultists. "Mage!" cried one. The cry was repeated by several of the cultists as they spread out warily. The disappearance of the elf maid obviously disturbed them as they looked around wildly. Perversely,

Shadowbender regretted they wore masks; their expressions would certainly be priceless.

"No more magic!" the foremost cultist said, his voice strangely hollow from within the mask. His bow was drawn back and pointing at Shadowbender's chest.

"Of course not," Shadowbender said mildly. The elf held out his arms in a submissive attitude.

On the other side of the bridge, Quint and Roland fought desperately. Three cultists lay dead at their feet. They had been forced onto the edge of the bridge but were temporarily holding their own. Roland had a light cut on his face and Quint had taken a hit from a mace in the shoulder. They were on the losing end of the battle and both were experienced enough to know it.

Drake ran along the bridge, his feet pounding the rotten boards. With a crack, the slats beneath him gave way. Fortunately, he still held the rope; otherwise, he would have fallen to his death. As it was, he dangled breathlessly over the yawning abyss, legs flailing empty air. 'Some help I am,' he thought vaguely.

Oceana grimly prepared a spell. She wasn't about to allow her brother to be taken. She had recognized the invisibility spell as he had cast it and realized no one (including Shadowbender) could see her. She hadn't moved but was ready. She would become visible if she cast a spell or otherwise attacked, so she waited. There was no telling what Shadowbender would do and she didn't want to interfere with his plan. If he had one. Trying to breathe quietly, Oceana waited.

Meanwhile, the combat on the opposite side of the bridge grew fiercer. Roland's height made him a difficult opponent for men unused to blocking attacks from below. The cultist in front of the dwarf suffered from such inexperience and Roland grunted as his axe gutted the man before him. Screaming, the man sank to his knees and fell over the side of the cliff. Roland focused on the next opponent.

Quint parried frantically. He faced two opponents, both armed with long swords. A well-placed kick sent one careening into the press of cultists behind him. Quint slashed wildly at the second cultist, who managed to deflect the blow (and keep his head). Momentum carried Quint's blow aside, and the blade sliced through the rope they had tied across the gorge. "Whoops!" he thought as he regained his balance.

Shadowbender had been in losing situations in the past and recognized a no-win position when he saw it. Oceana should be fine as long as she kept quiet and did not do anything stupid like cast a spell. He slowly glanced back to where Quint and Roland fought. They were on the bridge, but seemed to be holding their own, at least for the moment.

Drake was dangling from the rope, the boards beneath him broken. He was still alive, though, and should be fine as he obviously had a firm grip on the line. With an amused smile, the mage realized a plan. He was doing no one any good just standing here. With an eerie chuckle, Shadowbender stepped backward over the edge of the cliff and fell from view.

Drake tried to pull himself back onto the bridge. He gripped the rope with both hands, trying to leverage himself up by pulling with his arms and pushing against the next unbroken board with his feet. He had almost gotten up when the pressure proved too great for the slat. With a crack, the slat broke and Drake, again, dangled in mid-air.

With wide-eyed wonder, Oceana watched her brother step into mid-air. He fell. He spoke some arcane words and, abruptly, he ceased free-falling and began slowly drifting downward. Oceana smiled as the cultists began a confused chorus of calls and questioning. Apparently, having one elf disappear and another step off a cliff was difficult for them to accept. She watched, amused, as they spread out and tentatively began searching for her.

Drake stretched his leg, but couldn't reach the nearest unbroken slat. He began walking hand-over-hand along the rope, moving nearer the boards. He glanced at Shadowbender and Oceana. They were gone. There was no sign of either elf and the cultists were fearfully walking around. Drake began to wonder what had happened when something else happened. The rope, no longer tied on Quint's side of the gorge, went slack. Drake's stomach pushed into his throat as he began to fall.

Quint grimaced as a sword nicked his arm. He and Roland were fighting valiantly to be sure, but they were outnumbered too badly. A sudden realization dawned on Quint. The cultists were shouting more forcibly than they had been. Quint couldn't spare the attention to get a good look, but those cultists in the back ranks turned their backs toward the bridge. Something had them riled up. It was Roland who said something about it: "I think your rangers are here!" the dwarf grunted in between axe swings. Quint fought with renewed vigour. They were going to make it after all. Screaming, Drake fell. Of course, the other end of the rope was still tied, and, with a jerk, Drake was pulled in an arc toward the cliff face. Drake saw the rocky face approaching and realized what it meant. Bracing himself, the bard swung toward impact.

Oceana quietly made her way to a tree; in fact, it was the same tree Shadowbender had used in anchoring the rope. She didn't notice the rope hung limply as she was keeping a wary eye on the searching cultists, but she did notice the tree had low, wide branches. Oceana scampered into the tree beyond the reach of her enemies. The cultists were dismayed at the arrival of Quint's rangers. With foes before them and foes behind, their courage failed them. Crying in desperation, the cultists fled. Several were cut down as they ran. Quint lowered his sword joyfully. Pursuit wasn't an option. From across the bodies of ten or so cultists, six bearded rangers saluted. Smiling, Quint returned the salute.

With a resounding thud, Drake slammed into the cliff side. The impact knocked the wind out him and he slid several feet down the rope but managed to keep from falling. He was going to have some bruise. He looked down from the dizzying height and felt sick. Looking up toward the climb awaiting him, he nearly fell off the rope in surprise. A dozen yards above him and to the left, Shadowbender clung to the side of the rocky precipice. The elf seemed calm, which was unusual in itself. He looked at Drake with concern.

"You okay?" Shadowbender asked.

"Yeah," Drake grimaced, "you?"

"Fine."

"What are you doing here?" Drake demanded.

"Same as you," Shadowbender said quietly, "By the way, do not climb up. You will never make it."

"Great. Like I'm going to make it, hanging here all day!" Drake muttered.

"Do not fall," Shadowbender cautioned, "I will not be able to save you."

"Well," said Drake looking again into the depths, "my plan was to fall, but, since you recommend otherwise, I guess I won't." A few moments of silence passed.

"I don't suppose you have a plan?" Drake grunted in exertion, shifting his grip on the rope. He was beginning to get fatigued.

"Ah, no," said Shadowbender, "but I am working on it." A shower of small rocks tumbled past them. Both looked up to see the mask of a cultist peering down at them.

"Better work fast," Drake hissed.

Oceana intently watched the goings-on of the cultists. Most were focused on the action on the other side of the bridge. She saw the arrival of the rangers and the subsequent retreat of the cultists fighting Quint and Roland. Then, she saw a cultist peering over the brink on her side. She took an appraising look around. The cultists on her side were quietly and animatedly discussing the events on Quint's side of the gorge. No one was looking for her anymore. She wasn't sure what Shadowbender had done, but she saw the limp rope and felt a pang of fear for Drake. Whatever the curious cultist was doing, it wasn't good for either Drake or Shadowbender. Concerned for their safety, she opted to cast a spell in their defence despite the effect of her becoming visible. Hopefully, the tree branches would shield her from discovery. Oceana began a spell.

The cultist saw both men hanging onto the cliff. He turned to tell his commander. Before he could say a word, an invisible force slammed into him. He was off balance to begin with, and he was knocked several feet over the side. His screams echoed within the gorge as he fell.

The mage and bard watched the man plummet past them, arms and legs flailing.

"I guess Oceana's all right!" quipped Drake.

"I suppose," said Shadowbender.

At that moment, the twanging of bowstrings filled the air. Both men turned their heads to see. From the other side of the gorge, half a dozen bearded men fired bows across the span at the cultist. Quint and Roland looked on in concern. After a few rounds, the men stopped firing. Quint cupped his hands around his mouth and cried, "You can climb up now, the cultists have fled."

"That's the best news I've heard all day," Drake offered. The mage and bard began their ascent.

Roland shook his head in disbelief. The bard was climbing normally up the rope. Shadowbender, on the other hand, was crawling up the rock face like a spider. "You know," he said to Quint, "that mage truly frightens me."

Chapter 9

Quint stepped forward to clasp hands with one of the men, his erstwhile companion, Davyn ap Gwyn. The two men had met a number of years ago. Quint had been a young man then, barely in his twenties. The soon-to-be ranger had been apprised of a nearby wildfire by a woodcutter as he was wandering in the Barony of Crystalmere. In fact, Quint had smelled the faint odour of wood smoke but had mistakenly attributed it to a camp fire. Upon learning of the conflagration, he set out in the direction the woodcutter indicated.

Soon, he could see the smoke covering the woodland like a shroud. As he drew closer to the blaze, animals fleeing the fire began to run past him, paying no heed to the man whatsoever. He was nearly trampled by a frantic deer.

To his surprise, he found men fighting the fire. Around a dozen men were working hard at cutting a fire break. Most were settlers, but three were full-fledged rangers. One of the latter was Davyn ap Gwyn.

'Hello!' a cheerful looking man with large eyes and a Duranian styled pony tail called out.

'Thought you might need a hand,' Quint returned over the roar of the flames.

'What we really need is some rain,' the man said with a wink, 'but we'll take what the gods give us!' The man offered his hand, 'I'm

Davyn ap Gwyn.' 'Quint Longbow'. 'A ranger?' 'I haven't decided yet!' Quint said, coughing.

'You'll come around sooner or later,' Davyn had laughed. Quint was quickly incorporated into the effort. In the end, the blaze was thwarted by rain. The work had been difficult: blistering heat, lung searing smoke, falling timber, and panic-stricken wildlife. One of the men fighting the fire had died and two were sick from smoke inhalation.

Quint and Davyn became fast friends and Davyn probably saved the young, soon- to-be ranger's life by knocking him away from a falling tree the fire-focused man neglected to see coming. Quint had never forgotten his debt to Davyn and both had agreed to come to the other's aid if ever necessary.

Quint had remained with Davyn for the better part of two months. The older ranger had a wealth of knowledge and, more importantly, a willingness to share this information. Quint learned much; he was an eager and intelligent student. Davyn had a small cabin in a thick pine forest high in the mountains and it was there, while fishing the fast-moving streams, tending Davyn's small garden, or simply talking late into the evening on the blocks of rough-hewn logs Davyn had the audacity to call chairs, Quint had learned about the plants, animals, and the delicate, yet resilient, balance that kept them all alive. It was during this time Quint learned about the loose brotherhood of the rangers and the possibility of summoning them in times of dire need such as forest fires or. . .dragons. Quint had even met a few other rangers including a young ranger named Cullen the

Brown. Quint and Davyn stayed in touch irregularly, but Quint had known the other would come and he was pleased Davyn had brought help. They might stand a chance against the Cult of the Wyrm, after all.

"You feel confident we will not be found?" Shadowbender demanded for the third time. The elf was not convinced about the ability of Quint's ranger companions despite the obvious wood craft displayed in their ten-hour march from the bridge. Quiet and perceptive, the rangers moved with almost elven grace.

"We're as safe as can be expected," Quint replied nonplussed.

The group, accompanied by the rangers, had made good time. They were now at the foot of the Perilous Mountains. It was dusk. Unwilling to risk the dangerous crossing in the dark, they had found a sheltered camp site and settled down for the night. Fearing unfriendly eyes in the forest, they lit no fire.

It was a cheerless evening. Two of the rangers were on guard at all times. The gaiety of the trip had been snatched away by the assault at the bridge. Each was lost in the thought that what they were doing was not only dangerous, but important. One or more of them easily could have been killed if not for the timely arrival of Quint's ranger acquaintances. The rangers, over the course of the day, were told about the party's quest and its ramifications. Most of them seemed somewhat sceptical. Davyn ap Gwyn was the leader of the rangers and, as he seemed content to aid the group, the others seemed content to do so, too. A dark man of the west, Davyn had grown up learning folk tales and he believed in dragons but wasn't so sure about the quest.

"Do you really believe this scroll will prevent an awakening of the dragons?" he asked Quint as the two stood alone a short distance from camp. Quint looked up at the towering peaks of the Perilous Mountains, watching their crests disappear into the clouds.

"I believe Shadowbender believes so," he responded slowly. Davyn ap Gwyn nodded solemnly. "I believe," Quint continued, "no such quest, with such motives, executed with valour and faith, can go unrewarded. At worst, we can eliminate a few weirdo cultists; at best, we can save our world," Quint shrugged, "with those odds, I think it's a safe gamble to finish our mission."

"We rangers," Davyn responded, "have answered your summons. We are honour-bound to comply. Doubtless, you would do the same." Quint nodded affirmatively. "Regardless of what we personally think, and some of us think this is a merry will o' wisp, we will stand by you until the end."

Quint laid his hand on the others' shoulder, "Thank you, Davyn."

Both men were silent for a couple of minutes, each lost in his own thoughts. A breeze, refreshing in the still night, blew from the north.

"The north blows with chill fang.
The south with a sharp sea tang.
The east blows with faeries' breath.
The west proclaims the dragon's death."

Davyn ap Gwyn repeated the children's rhyme thoughtfully, "I guess there's some truth in old wife's tales, huh?" Without waiting for a reply, the western ranger walked off toward the camp proper. Quint peered up at the looming mountains, lost in thought.

Roland looked at his companions. Quint was off somewhere, but the rest sat within a rocky hollow at the eastern edge of the Forgotten Lands. Shadowbender sat in the shadows of a hemlock and was only visible to the dwarf because Roland knew he was there; otherwise, the dwarf would never have seen him. Oceana sat wrapped in her cloak. She made no movement, but the dwarf saw her eyes gleam in the moonlight as she gazed around curiously. Drake sat with his back against a large boulder holding a poultice Quint had prepared against his bruised side. A dulcimer rested on his outstretched legs, but he made no attempt to play. Wise, Roland thought, no telling what evil the sound would draw. Two of the rangers sat quietly aside, absently chewing jerked meat. Erik and Alan were their names. Two other rangers stood guard hidden somewhere about the camp. Another two were out sleeping, he thought. The sound of someone approaching drew Roland's attention.

Davyn ap Gwyn walked to the other rangers, accepted a piece of jerky from Erik, and sat down.

"Quint?" Roland questioned.

"He's outside the camp," Davyn replied, "he'll be back, soon."

"Where are you from?" Oceana asked Davyn.

"The coast of Duran. The shore didn't suit me. I entered the forest when I was sixteen and I haven't come out yet."

"How old are you now?"

Davyn smiled. "I don't know, for sure. I think about forty."

"That's old for a human, I believe," Oceana murmured.

"Depends on what you consider old," replied Davyn, biting into his piece of jerky.

"What about you?" Oceana asked a black-haired ranger.

"I am Erik Willowdale," the ranger replied quietly.

"Where are you from, Erik?" Oceana asked.

"Nowhere in particular." Erik wasn't chatty. Actually, with the obvious exception of Quint, rangers generally weren't a very vocal bunch.

"And you?" Oceana asked the last ranger. After Erik's response, she was going to forego asking the last ranger, but decided it might be rude. After all, he wasn't necessarily uncommunicative like Erik and it would hurt his feelings if he were left out of the conversation.

"Alan."

"Just Alan?" Oceana groaned inwardly at the familiar short answer.

"Just Alan," he confirmed.

"Not Alan of such and such?"

"No," Alan smiled, "though I'm sometimes referred to by the very creative title of Alan the Forester."

"Where are you from?" the elf maid asked.

"Ah, various places, much like Erik or any other ranger for that matter. But," he added, "I'm originally from a village in the Barony of Crystalmere."

"I've never been to Crystalmere," Oceana mused, "I've heard it's nice, in places."

"The wooded places," Alan confirmed, "though some like the sea." The ranger paused with thought, "There are a few elves in Crystalmere. Especially in Feywood."

"Rustic elves," said Oceana.

"A wilder breed than you would seem to be, no offence to you or them, tending away from the more civilized pursuits. They're good rangers and it is rumoured a few druids walk amongst them, though I believe they have no or few mages. But," Alan smiled as he continued, "you've never heard such music. They pipe like the very gods."

Oceana cocked her head quizzically, "Are the rangers a brotherhood?"

While Alan was thoughtfully chewing his lip, casting about for a suitable reply, Davyn interceded, "The rangers aren't a brotherhood, lady, not in the traditional sense. Mostly, I guess we're loners and misfits, some unfit and some unwilling to mesh with society or civilization. To survive, most learn a fair degree of wood lore. Most know or know about men like themselves, at least in their territory. Usually, you want to at least know those near you, though some are completely solitary. Sometimes," he chuckled at his private jest, "they're even friendly enough to occasionally cooperate," Davyn elbowed Alan in the ribs in a knowing way, "eh—Alan the Forester?"

"Yeah, whatever you say, Davyn," Alan replied.

"How then, did Quint summon you, if there is no organization?"

"I can answer that!" said Alan. "Not all rangers are completely nomadic. Most have at least semi-permanent dwellings and quite a few have permanent homes. It's not difficult for a ranger to get a word out if he knows any of those. Once notified, there are means of spreading the word."

"Are any more coming?" Roland interjected.

"I think not," answered Davyn, "the six of us were all that were readily accessible. By dove, I sent a summons to a few others, but they're further away and not likely to be available, anyway." Davyn stretched, "The rangers in Rockstead, for example, are currently dealing with fire and humanoid raids. Seems the goblin tribes have a bee in their bonnet over humans outside civilization."

Quint walked into the camp and sat near the other rangers. After a hasty query, it was decided they should cross the Perilous Mountains in the morning where they were. There was a known pass further north, but it was likely to be watched by someone— cultist or otherwise.

The Perilous Mountains were aptly named. Their distance from civilization and proximity to the never-ruled Wildwood, general inaccessibility, and the realm of the Lich King only a two-day journey away encouraged humanoid and other non-human settlement of the area. The elven kingdom to the north was well patrolled, but the elves rarely ventured outside their own domain. Quint had suggested bearing north and then east along the outskirts of the elven kingdoms as they would be less likely to encounter any enemies ('Other than elves', Roland added, but everyone ignored him). Shadowbender, however, cautioned against it, claiming the elves would certainly detain them and, at least, ask questions. Time was of the essence, he maintained, and any delay was to be avoided, if at all possible. Thus, it was eventually decided they would cross the Perilous Mountains here and strike out east and then north (avoiding the Elven Kingdoms) for Druidwood. Somewhere, in the largely unknown bowers of Druidwood, was the Vale of the Wyrm. Each slept that night and dreamt of primeval forests, hidden vales, and the hideous masks of the cult of the wyrm.

The next morning dawned misty. The slopes of the Perilous Mountains were observable for a few hundred yards, but, beyond that, the mist became too thick to see through. The rangers had a brief counsel. The mist would make it difficult for them to find their way as visibility was virtually nil. Waiting wasn't a desirable option, though, and it was generally agreed the mist, while certainly being a hindrance, would also serve to (hopefully) hide them from unfriendly eyes.

Most of the day, they crawled around the slopes of the mountains. The mist persisted throughout the day, clinging to the wet and weary travellers. The constant dampness and frustrating hampering of vision put everyone's nerves on edge. Fancy made every looming shape seem to be the leering visage of a cultist. The rangers, from lack of vision and with no clear map to work from, failed to find a pass. Defeated, at least for the day, they found a dreary overhang of rock as a camp.

Shadowbender slumped against the interior of the overhang, head hung in frustration. The mist permeated everything; the wall within the overhang was dark and cold. He shivered within damp clothing. It was going to be a long, cold night. He was thankful he had made the necessary precautions to his maps and papers or they certainly would have been damaged by the moisture. The worst factor of the conditions was the time it cost them. They had already lost one day blundering around. Shadowbender truly hoped for clear weather tomorrow.

Sighing, Roland flung himself to the ground beneath the overhang. He was tired. And cold. He was tired and cold and wet. And it wasn't getting any better, either.

"Hey," he snapped to no one in particular, "how about a fire?"

"I'd recommend against it," said Erik, "you never know what might be around."

"Whatever's going to be out tonight" Roland parried, "isn't going to see us in all this infernal fog and, if it can, it was going to find us anyway."

"Still." Erik shook his head, "I'd rather not." Erik was the only ranger around as the others were scouting around and so forth. Roland almost said something scathing but caught himself. He smiled inwardly as an idea came to him.

160

"Ah," Roland said, "I was, of course, concerned about the injured and the lady," he motioned toward Oceana, "I'm sure we wouldn't want the lady to freeze and take ill, would we?" Roland peered intently at Erik.

"Uh, uh," Erik stammered, glancing furtively at Oceana, who picked up well enough upon Roland's device to frown and wrap her arms around herself forlornly.

"Well, I don't suppose it would be all that much of a risk," he looked at Drake for support, but the bard simply shrugged.

"Good!" said Roland before lowering his voice, "you made the right choice, lad."

Quint shook his head. He and Davyn simply couldn't make their way through the fog. Travelling through the mist was not only irritating, it was dangerous both immediately and long term. It made it more likely for someone to slip or become ill, but it also greatly magnified the possibility of becoming lost, which was to be avoided not only for survival purposes but also because it would prevent the timely completion of the quest. Shadowbender would get his robes in a wad should they become lost.

Quint stepped into the warmth and glow of the pseudo-chamber. The overhang provided a natural roof and one wall. Someone, one of the rangers probably, had taken advantage of the natural resources and added a crude but effective lean-to 'wall' of vegetation creating a sort of tunnel. Not only was it cosier because it held in more heat and kept out the wind, it also screened the fire, so it was less visible.

The fire was cheerful, driving out the damp. Quint looked around. Shadowbender sat away from the fire lost in thought, his fingers tapping rhythmically on his knee as he pondered something (probably obscure). Oceana sat chatting amiably with Alan the ranger. Drake sat warming his hands beside the fire. Roland sat against the rock with his feet stuck out nearly into the fire. He smoked his pipe with a look of utter contentment upon his features.

"You look pretty pleased with yourself, Roland," Quint told his friend.

"Yep!" Roland laughed.

Erik Willowdale sat on watch at the far end of the enclosure. A sandy-haired ranger, named Bryon O'Dale, was on watch at the other end. Another ranger, Cullen the Brown, was waxing his bowstring against the dampness. Davyn and the last ranger, Eldon, were out on patrol guarding the camp.

After a brief discussion, it was decided, if the fog didn't lift, they would stay put tomorrow. Shadowbender was opposed, claiming they did not have the time to spare. He was outnumbered by those who felt otherwise, (the most vocal of whom was Roland) however, and he sullenly agreed before throwing his hood over his face and retreating to one of the darker corners of the shelter.

Snug and dry, the shelter seemed a paradise after the last few days. Roland, after bitterly complaining about their lack of ale, called for a song from the bard. The rangers promptly began a chorus of rebuttals. In the end, it was decided a tale would have to suffice.

162

Finally, they swapped jokes until second watch. Due, no doubt, to the snug shelter, they slept better than they had in a while.

Fortunately, the next day dawned relatively clear. Patches of mist clung to the mountains, but they were much smaller and less dense. Everything was fresh and vibrant from the moisture of the previous day and the companions were amazed the mountain that was so formidable and bleak yesterday was so beautiful today. With unobstructed vision, it didn't take long for the rangers to locate the proper path. They had wandered a bit too far to the south during their misty entombment, a problem they quickly rectified.

The going was brutal. The peaks were high and steep. The trees thinned progressively until, eventually, they surpassed the tree line altogether. Heath and grasses became the predominant vegetation. The severe slope and thin air combined caused them to rest often. After eight hours, they had gone only a couple of miles. It was enough, however, and they now stood at one of the few passes over the Perilous Mountains.

Narrowed eyes squinted menacingly. Humans. And elves. The entire group wound its way tortuously up the mountainside. A grin formed. The group would be tired and winded. Careless. More vulnerable. They were also outnumbered. The watcher liked those odds.

"Whew, am I tired!" Drake grunted, wearily stepping onto the level ground of the pass, "I never thought level ground could be so beautiful."

"It'll be even better," said Quint, slapping Drake on the back encouragingly, "when we start down the other side."

The humans and elves proceeded through the pass. Two humans, tall and bearded, held the point position. The rest followed further behind in twos and threes. The two men leading were cautious. They moved slowly and were paying close attention to any sights and sounds. The pass was a perfect place for an ambush and these men were apparently wise enough to know it. The shaman frowned. This would make things much more difficult. He signalled to his compatriots to initiate the plan for tougher groups. It was much more violent and required more work but needed to be done if any of them expected to cart any tribute back into the caverns. With a nod to the raiding party, the shaman waited for just the right moment to signal the attack.

Eldon and Cullen the Brown scanned the towering walls. The area was narrow, and the canyon walls were rough, scalable, and covered with ledges and large boulders. It was an ideal place for an ambush. A foreboding feeling increased as they pressed on. A skin-prickling danger sense crawled along their necks. Cullen stopped and motioned for the others to do the same. Something was in the rocks. Eldon drew his bow.

The shaman realized it was now or never. The humans had somehow detected them. He felt his blood boil as he unleashed his battle rage and screamed his war cry, signalling the attack.

Everyone stopped and scanned the heights when Cullen motioned. A tenseness was in the air. They jumped as a shrill cry

164

filled the air. Before the cry was over, what sounded like a hundred voices joined that of the first in a high-pitched yell that reverberated within the canyon. Before the sound had ceased echoing within their ears, a cascade of rocks poured down on the rangers on point. Screeching forms began leaping from the rocks, most lobbing a stone before beginning their descent.

"Goblins!" hissed Bryon O'Dale as he drew his bow.

The awareness of Cullen and Eldon had prevented all of them being surrounded and caught unaware. The foremost rangers were within the reach of the swarming goblins, but the rest of them were without their range. That wouldn't last long, though, as the bulk of the attackers were moving toward the main group while leaving enough to deal with Eldon and Cullen. More than enough, in fact.

As the first goblins arose from their cover behind the rocks, Eldon fired, dropping one with a hit to the throat. A moment later, as the ranger was reaching for a second arrow, the first of several stones found their mark. Eldon went down.

Cullen, miraculously, survived the barrage. He was hit solidly in the left shoulder and received a painful blow to the left arm but wasn't badly injured. He immediately turned and sprinted away from the advancing goblins and toward the remainder of the party. He never saw Eldon fall.

Those who weren't engaged saw two obvious problems. First, Cullen wasn't going to make it. The goblins were closing in too quickly and he was too far away. They would cut him off long before he reached his companions. Secondly, about fifty screaming goblins were charging toward them, fangs bared and misshapen bodies bounding along with surprising speed. Most carried clubs, though a few more sophisticated weapons (plundered, no doubt) appeared here and there.

Oceana's mind raced, grasping for an appropriate spell. Likewise, she saw from the corner of her eye, Shadowbender inwardly focusing in much the same way. Drake and Roland readied their weapons and grimly prepared for the onslaught. Quint also had his weapon drawn but was occupied in looking around wildly as if casting about for a more defensible position or, perhaps, a place to which they could escape. The four rangers with them were seasoned warriors and rarely became panicked. They were also angry at the loss of one of their kind and their grim faces belied their resolve to make the goblins pay for their affront. Four bows twanged, and four goblins fell beneath the flapping feet of their fellows.

With the rangers and her companions, they had the ability (hopefully) to protect themselves. Cullen, however, alone and surrounded, didn't stand a chance. With a quick burst of insight, Oceana began quietly chanting a spell, fingers splayed in the direction of Cullen the Brown.

Shadowbender desperately thought. Sadly, Cullen was beyond saving; the majority (including his sister) must take precedence. What were goblins afraid of? Knights on horseback, well armoured with lances. What else? Bright light. Primarily nocturnal, goblins avoided light whenever possible. The shadowy canyon and mist were ideal for them. He could not create a sun, he thought, but he could do something as good.

Another volley leapt from the bows of the rangers. Four more goblins fell. The rest, screaming wildly, pressed on. The rangers dropped their bows and brandished their swords and axes as the goblins moved nearly within melee range. The rangers looked in surprise as Shadowbender leapt to the forefront of the group and stood alone before the slavering goblins.

Cullen was sprinting as fast as he could go. He wasn't going to make it. Without stopping, he drew his sword and prepared to turn to face the encircling foes. It would be a short fight; he only hoped he could take a few goblins with him. Just as he began to turn, some invisible force jerked him from the ground. Legs still moving as if he was running, Cullen began to rise into the air.

Shadowbender felt a stab of fear as he moved to face the ensuing goblins. He ignored it. With a flourish, he spread his arms, his staff prominently held in his right hand, with his robes flapping eerily around him.

"What the..." Erik began, but Davyn grasped his shoulder to silence him.

Shadowbender shrieked some arcane words in a booming voice too loud for the quiet elf. The goblins' advance faltered slightly as the sound reverberated throughout the canyon and within their heads. Shadowbender whirled his staff in a wide arc and, as it passed by the canyon floor, flame shot from the tip. Miraculously, the flames grew. In seconds, the flames spread across the entire breadth of the canyon and roared into a wall of flame some twelve feet high. Through the pulsating flames, the companions saw the goblins stop, awe and fear etched on their faces. As a group, the goblins began hooting and screeching and suddenly wheeled and began fleeing back the way they had come. Outnumbered, weary pilgrims were one thing, but attacking a mage who could summon searing flame from the very rocks was something else altogether.

Oceana kept lifting Cullen. The goblins swiped at him with their clubs, but he was too high, having risen some ten feet. Obviously, some arcane power was at work. Several goblins bolted forthwith; those remaining either began casting about for stones to throw or simply gaped. When the wall of flame ignited, and their fellows began retreating pell-mell, the remaining goblins around Cullen, suddenly awash in decisiveness, ran with them. The shaman was in the lead. Surely, the goddess would forgive them for fleeing elven wizards who somehow commanded the power of flight and flames. Cullen, though himself surprised at his predicament, noted with some satisfaction that the fleeing goblins gave him a wide berth as they passed. Shadowbender lowered his arms and, abruptly, the flames disappeared. He turned, "Oceana, you had better put Cullen down, we have to get out of here."

Oceana lowered her arms and Cullen gently settled to the ground. Without a word, Shadowbender began jogging down the canyon. Everyone followed, Roland bringing up the rear. The dwarf shook his head. They may have saved all their tails, but those two elves were still scary.

Chapter 10

It was a tense and harried journey through the pass, but no one attacked. The goblins were either all hidden among the rocks, or, more probably, had retreated underground. Goblins, hating the sun as they did, nearly always lived underground in caves or caverns. This propensity for underground areas (such as mines) made the goblins natural enemies (and frequent combatants) of dwarves as each vied for the same territory. The overwhelming martial superiority of the dwarves was balanced by the fecundity of the goblins which resulted in a worldwide stalemate in regard to who held most of the known subterranean realm. Roland was still a little disappointed the elf had spoiled the fun of a little goblin-bashing but managed to assuage the sorrow with the mollifying fact he was still alive. There would always be goblins to bash in the future.

Eldon was dead. Roland had demanded they see to the remains, but Davyn and the other rangers insisted it was more pressing for the survivors to actually survive by leaving the canyon immediately. Roland was difficult to persuade as burial was an important ritual in dwarven tradition, but he was persuaded after a compromise was reached and they arranged Eldon's body in a show of respect. They continued on their way and, after fifteen minutes of travel, they had safely traversed the pass.

The trip down the other side of the Perilous Mountains, as Quint had earlier mentioned to Drake, was much easier than the trip up had been. In fact, had they not been sorrowed over the death of

Eldon and anxious about being pursued by goblins, the descent would have been enjoyable. The view was spectacular. Small cottony clumps of clouds clung to the crags of the Perilous Mountains like so many sheep in a rocky meadow. The air was comfortably cool and carried the scent from the forest below them. They quickly made the tree line and felt better as they re-entered the forest; crossing the tree line ended their feeling of being exposed.

The rangers were all for continuing all through the night in order to put as much distance as possible between them and the goblins, should the latter pursue. Roland did not care if the goblins caught them; he might even welcome an opportunity to crack a few goblin heads. Drake and Oceana had no firm opinion about whether or not to proceed. Shadowbender insisted the goblins, after demonstrating such fear within the pass, would hardly come charging *away* from their stronghold in order to chase the party in the less strategic terrain of the forest and suggested the party rest while they were able and avoid the dangers of nocturnal travel. Finally, a compromise was struck: they would travel until dusk so as to put some distance between them and the Perilous Mountains and then stop in order to allow everyone to get some rest. Shadowbender thought the agreement fair, though it seemed to him the rangers pressed on brutally fast in order to make up for what they perceived as lost time.

By the time dusk fell, they had travelled nearly ten miles, which was quite an accomplishment considering they were moving through virtually trackless wilderness. Roland was grumpy from the faster-than-he-could-normally-walk pace but was too tired to do anything to demonstrate his unhappiness. Oceana shambled along, too weary to even be aware of her surroundings. The remainder of the group was no better off. When Davyn finally called a halt, they gratefully complied. Roland plopped down where he stood. Drake and two of the rangers prepared a fire and the other rangers hastily constructed a camouflaging windbreak. They then settled down for what was sure to be a short meal before going to sleep.

Except they did not go immediately to sleep. Erik Willowdale, Davyn explained to his weary charges, was a skilled herbalist and could whip up a little something to refresh them. With Oceana assisting, Erik mixed the proper components, steeped them in hot water, and passed around a minty tea. Shadowbender looked at his cup suspiciously. Roland looked at his with contempt as tea was for old ladies. Everyone drank it, however, and they found it exceptionally refreshing, renewing their vigour. After a few minutes, they all felt restored as their limbs tingled with new strength. Drake laughed with Quint over some sort of tale, Oceana chatted gaily with Alan the Forester, and Davyn questioned Shadowbender about the events in the pass.

"I was absolutely stunned, I must say," said Davyn, "with the fire and the saving of Cullen. I have never seen such a thing."

"Thank you," answered Shadowbender, "though it was my sister who saved Cullen, not me. You could not see as she was behind you."

"Oh," exclaimed Davyn, "then *she* is also a mage."

"Of course. I did not realize you were unaware of that."

"Well," Davyn responded, "I don't know much about any of this for certain except Quint requested help and we're going to provide that help."

Shadowbender proceeded to detail their quest to Davyn, who listened attentively, despite having heard the tale already from Quint. Oceana, having finished her chat with Alan, arose and said she needed a few minutes to herself and left the camp after being warned by several of the others to be careful. Drake, Roland, and the rangers were soon joking and laughing. With the immediate danger of the pass behind them, they all (with the exception of Shadowbender) felt secure.

"How about a song?" Roland demanded of Drake.

"Quite right," said Drake as he retrieved his leather backpack. He quickly produced a small fiddle.

"How many bleeding instruments do you have in there?" Roland quipped.

"Enough," Drake answered off-handedly, "a bard must always be prepared." What the bard failed to mention was Shadowbender, performing a favour for his friend, had enchanted the bards' pack so that it held more equipment than it could hold naturally. The bards' repertoire of available instruments had grown immensely as a result.

"Well," said Roland, "from what I've seen, you are ready to equip an orchestra—but, who cares? We need music!"

Drake settled down, readied his fiddle, and smiled, "Any requests?"

"How about a drinking song?" asked Roland.

"A drinking song?" the bard repeated.

"Yeah. I know we don't have anything to drink (and that is a black shame), but we can pretend. Besides, there's nothing like a rousing drinking song to warm the heart and fire the courage!"

"And inebriate dwarves!" Alan whispered just loud enough to be heard. Everyone laughed.

"How about 'Women and Ale'?" Roland asked. It was a common ditty, and everyone present should know it. Just as importantly, Oceana was *not* present; it really wasn't a song he would want to sing around the inexperienced elf maid. Without further ado, Drake began to play the fast-paced tune and Roland, smiling widely, began to sing:

"Aye. This inn is among the best.

With women and ale

Doubly blest.

As my song shall tell.

Innkeep! Send us another round!

Tilt it back and drink it down!

Frothy ale goes down right,

Warms a man on a chilly night.

And a comely lass is a welcome sight;

Each is a princess come midnight.

She slapped me hard at a little pinch,

Spilt the ale;

Overturned the bench.
By the gods, I love a plucky wench!
Innkeep! Send us another round!
Tilt it back and drink it down!

I bedded the ale
And downed the maid.
Awoke to find the tab full-paid.
A perfect end to a perfect day!

Aye. This inn is among the best.
With women warm and ale so cold
A lovely tavern—doubly blest!
As my tale has told."

By the time the song was through, they were all in a merry mood. Laughing and slapping their legs in time with the music, they all (except Shadowbender) joined in by the third verse, with even Shadowbender appearing merry. In fact, they were having so much fun they sang through it another three times before being stopped short.

The first sign of trouble was Quint stopping singing. Then, a look of panic crossed Roland's face as he, too, stopped singing. Drake quit playing and everyone turned.

Oceana stood at the edge of the firelight, eyes glittering. From somewhere deep in the forest, an owl hooted ominously. A chorus of stammering and mumbled greetings erupted from the group of men.

Oceana crossed her arms, frowned deeply, and…began to laugh. Roland finally exhaled. Perhaps it is not necessary to mention the evening's singing was over, but Drake did continue to play, and they spent the evening in mirth and went to sleep feeling safe and refreshed.

Safety, however, as Shadowbender was wont to say, is often an illusion. The companions had no way of knowing it, but they were being pursued. The goblin shaman, feeling humiliated after the encounter in the canyon, had decided to chase down those responsible and make them pay, preferably slowly. He encountered everything from indifference to blatantly fabricated excuses to outright refusal from most of his tribe. Finally, he gathered up forty or so members that claimed to be willing to hunt down the humans. Accomplishing such a mission would certainly add to his influence within the tribe. He had been forced to do a little bribing and/or wheedling and a bit of threatening to gather this force, but he had it and that was all that mattered.

Now, having slipped down the mountain under cover of darkness and tracked them across the forest, the goblins were nearing the camp. Goblins, of course, are primarily nocturnal and had no problem tracking the group. Maybe the rangers and definitely the elves could have hidden their spoor enough to evade the pursuing goblins, but, with the presence of the dwarf (and, to a lesser degree, the bard), even a goblin child could have trailed them.

The goblins heard music ahead and a chorus of voices accompanying. What was that? A group of humans in a hostile forest, having just fought a contingent of goblins, should not be sitting around singing loudly. Maybe more of them had arrived and joined up with the original group and they were singing in celebration. Not only that, but there was also the wizard to be considered. The goblins (except the shaman) had not been too keen on the idea of assaulting the group to begin with. They began murmuring despite the shaman's protests. Soon, they began to make excuses as to why now was not the opportune time to attack the group. The shaman was distraught over the declining morale and attempted to bolster the goblin warriors. The groaning and hedging grew worse and worse and, then, the goblins, few at first, then en masse, simply bolted. The shaman was extremely disappointed but was not willing to attack an armed host (including a deadly wizard) alone. Cursing the group as only a goblin can, the shaman turned and slunk back toward the mountains from whence he had come. In this manner, the companions were saved without even realizing they had been in danger.

Later that same night, Oceana awoke. Some strange sound had penetrated her awareness. Softly, the strains of a lute plunking in the darkness drifted into her tent. She rolled over in an attempt to recapture sleep before it slipped away. After ten minutes of trying to force sleep, she grew tired of watching the light from the fire illuminate the side of her tent. Quietly, she arose and, throwing her travelling cloak about her, slipped into the night.

She blinked as a shift in the wind blew a blanket of smoke into her eyes. Roland sat nearby, his back to the fire, smoking his pipe. The dwarf nodded but said nothing, keeping his eyes focused on the perimeter of the camp. Suddenly, it dawned on her that they never had her stand watch. It was not that she had asked, and they had refused; they had simply never asked. She smiled, there were perks to being a female, after all. She began humming "Women and Ale", quite pleased with life in general.

Turning to the west, she attempted to locate the source of the music. A breeze played about her hair as she marked the bard's apparent location and walked toward the music. Just outside the camp, in an opening bathed in moonlight, stood a large maple surrounded by a grove of lesser trees. Here, his back against the maple, sat Drake of Allendale. Oceana was moving as quietly as only elves can when they want to avoid being heard and the bard gave no indication he knew she was there. The elf maid stopped to listen.

Absorbed, the bard plucked the strings of the lute, moving his head in time with the tinkling notes. He looked like some sort of artistic statue, Oceana thought, his clothing and skin had taken an unreal hue in the moonlight and all the colours looked brighter as he sat creating his art like some pagan god of old when the world was younger, and the forests were older. A look of rapture shone on the man's face as he lost himself in the ecstasy of his music. As she stood there, Drake began to sing, softly at first and gradually increasing in volume as the song proceeded:

"Were I the greatest musician

Who ever played,

Able to coax faerie music

From my lyre

In colour and shape
And watch the notes dance from the strings—
What mystic and vibrant hues they'd be
Should I play of you.
Were I the most graceful dancer
To ever swirl amain
Within the hidden realms of fancy,
Putting dervishes to shame,
How the blushing nymphs would swoon
Beneath the harvest moon
If I dedicated a dance worthy of you."

The bard played without words for a time and gradually increased the tempo of the music. Oceana had intended to interrupt, but the music was so haunting that she could not bring herself to do so. Instead, she stood outside Drake's vision gazing at the moonlit bard as he continued the song:

"And the gods, in adoration,
Would make you a constellation
Shining in the night sky—
A vibrant guide
To those below—
Demonstrating their wond'rous power
Perfected in you.

But I would make you a goddess,
A woman to whom all below aspire;

A new queen,

Eyes flickering like fire,

Overshadowing the paltry gods

We've already seen—

As harsh as winter

And soft as the moon;

All men's salvation

And all men's doom."

The music stopped. Both remained motionless as the chills inspired by intense beauty coursed through them. After a bit, the bard turned. Oceana had made no sound, she was sure, but the bard, perhaps by instinct, had realized her presence.

"Oceana," he said in an awe-filled voice as the elf maid stepped into the glade and fastened her gleaming eyes on the bard.

"Drake," the elf maid shook her head in wonder, "that was absolutely *gorgeous*. Is it your latest composition?"

"I've been working on it ever since arriving at your Tower," he nodded.

"It may well be your best work yet," she whispered. The moonlight was reflected in the man's eyes making them seem to shine in their own luminescence. Oceana suddenly felt other-worldly, like she was taking part in some sort of dream. The bard did not respond and merely stared at her with a look that might have been astonishment and might have been puzzlement; she could not decide which, "It will be successful, Drake, I can feel it. What sort of woman could resist such a romantic ballad?"

"What type of woman, indeed, my lady?" the bard replied softly.

"Only one with a heart of stone," Oceana shivered, "or one completely lost in ignorance." Oceana pulled her cloak closer around herself and glanced toward the camp.

"Oceana…" Drake said, rising.

"Yes?" she asked too quickly.

"I just wanted to tell you that you look beautiful tonight." Drake walked to her.

"It's the moon," she answered, "it infuses the world with beauty."

"No," he said, brushing away a lock of hair that had fallen across her face, "that's not it."

"Oh," she stammered. She was giddy. Her voice was catching, and she couldn't get her breath.

The bard cupped her chin in his warm hand and tilted her face, so she was gazing into his deep brown eyes. She could see both herself and the moon reflected therein.

"You're trembling," he said.

"Oh, Drake," she said, snuggling up against the man, who left his hand on her cheek and placed his free hand over hers. He, too, was trembling. "What are we going to do?" she asked.

"Oceana…" he began stroking her hair.

Both jumped as a tree branch snapped from within the darkness beneath the boughs of the surrounding grove. Oceana pulled away from Drake and turned.

"I'm sorry" said Quint stepping into the circle of trees. He was blinking rapidly and frowning. "I was…looking for Oceana. I was worried. I saw her leave, but she never came back. So, I came looking for her…"

"It's okay, Quint," Oceana said with a furtive glance toward the bard, "Drake and I were just…talking. We're through, now." She turned back toward Drake and smiled sadly, "I suppose I had better get back to bed. Good night, Drake."

"Good night, Oceana," the bard murmured.

Swirling her cloak around her in a fluid motion, Oceana turned and glided back toward the encampment. Drake watched her until she was gone.

Over the next few days, they moved steadily northwest. On the fourth day, partly due to Shadowbender's map and partly due to the ranger's instinct, they decided they had entered the environs of Druidwood. There were no markers delineating the forest from any other area, of course, but they had entered a forest that felt different to all of them except Roland, who scoffed at the notion and claimed all forests felt pretty much the same: bad.

Druidwood, should the legends be true, had never been civilized. Even the elven kingdom had been civilized in its own way. Elven homes were almost indistinguishable from their surroundings and, therefore, few if any trees were felled in their construction, but Druidwood wasn't permanently inhabited even by elves.

Undoubtedly, humanoids lived within the forest, but their impact on the growth of the forest was minimal. Thus, what they stood within was truly a virgin wood. The trees were large and undergrowth, at least where they were currently, was sparse. The forest exuded quietness and the nobility that is the by-product of age. Everyone except Roland was awed.

"So," Roland grunted, "how close are we?" The practical (in the sense of indifferent) dwarf cared nothing about a bunch of trees, twittering birds, and other such drivel. By the gods, he was paired with rangers, two elves, and a *poet*—it was nothing short of a miracle they had made it anywhere at all rather than light-footing it all day in some misty meadow like a bunch of faeries. The dwarf spat at the image.

"That," said Drake, "may be a bit of a problem."

"Why?"

"We're not sure exactly where it is," answered the bard.

"We don't know *exactly* where it is?" the dwarf asked incredulously, throwing his axe to the ground in disgust, "We don't know *exactly* where it is?" he repeated. "Well, at least we know *exactly* where it isn't—here! Gee, perhaps it's just me, but such a minor detail such as where you're going might be something you want to verify before you leave." The dwarf walked a few feet off the trail and began kicking leaves around in frustration. "I can't believe," he continued, "you brought me all the way out here (while being pursued by really scary guys in masks trying to kill us, I might add) and, when we get here, you don't know where we are supposed to go!"

"Why Roland," quipped Quint, "you seem upset!" Laughter echoed within the wood. Roland was even amused in spite of himself.

"He does have a point," said Drake after the laughter had subsided, "namely—how *do* we find the Vale of the Wyrm?"

"Good question," interjected Oceana.

"Yes, it is!" seconded Roland.

"There is a way," Shadowbender mused.

"The way we were talking about?" Drake whispered. Shadowbender nodded.

"What way?" Quint demanded. The ranger was somewhat upset they had been discussing something important without him. He was also curious.

"Drake and I decided," answered Shadowbender, "that meandering around looking for the vale would waste a lot of time while still not guaranteeing we would ever find it. The map I have is not very specific due, no doubt, to the fact *no one* (except our favourite cultists) ever knew its exact location. Therefore, we could look randomly for the Vale *or* ask someone we *can* (probably) locate who *should* know the location of the Vale. I propose the latter; we cannot go stumbling around the woods forever."

"Oh, I'm sure we could," Roland interjected, "but who is this person you think you *might* be able to find? I find it hard to believe you just happen to have an acquaintance of some sort just floating around out here in an unexplored forest!"

Everyone else looked thoughtful. They agreed with the dwarf, though they wouldn't have asked in the same way. Oceana had an idea who Shadowbender was talking about and chills ran up and down her spine, but she said nothing.

"The Grey Man," Shadowbender said flatly.

Roland stood there, blinking. The elf had answered so shortly and obviously expected the answer to suffice.

"Well," Roland went on, "for those of us who are less, uh, enlightened—who is the grey man?"

"I can answer that," said Drake, "or I guess I should say I *can't* answer that."

"Thanks for clearing that right up," Roland scoffed.

"The Grey Man," the bard continued nonplussed, "is assumed to be the guardian of the forest. He is apparently ageless and is said to possess powers beyond mortal ken. He appears in the annals of kings prior to the Mage War when rulers apparently sent to him for advice. If legends are to be believed, he is older, even, than the elves."

"What is he, exactly?" asked Quint.

"No one knows," Drake said with a shrug.

"I think *I* know," said Shadowbender, but the elf did not elaborate.

"What?" Roland finally demanded. The elf shrugged.

"Regardless of who or what he is," said Quint, "he'll know how to find the vale?"

"We believe so," said Drake.

"Well, I believe we'd better get started, then," said Quint to the bard, "take us to the Grey Man!"

The bard glanced at Shadowbender, who nodded slightly. With a deep breath, Drake set off in the direction where he and Shadowbender had surmised the Grey Man should be. The bard had always been a little sketchy about their ability to find the Grey Man and just how useful he would be *if* they found him. What worried him now, however, was Shadowbender's response to their decision. Was it his imagination or, when the decision was made to appeal to the Grey Man for help, was the expression clouding the features of the elf mage one of fear?

Chapter 11

None of the rangers, save Erik Willowdale, had even heard rumours of the Grey Man and Erik didn't know anything more than the idea that such a man existed, if, indeed, a man he was. If tales were to be believed, the being Erik assumed to be the same as the one for whom they were searching had lived within the wood for centuries. In the south, there were stories of an ancient Druid living in the wood named after him. Immortal or nearly so, this druid sometimes aided those travelling through the wood should their intentions be benign.

Other stories stated the druid was crazed and slew those who dared enter his domain. Erik had no idea whether either or both of these tales might be accurate, though he personally believed, if the stories had a factual basis at all, it was more likely the travellers had encountered different druids in different time periods and mistakenly assumed the various personages were the same man. Erik had encountered several druids over the years and they all possessed a similar outlook and even tended to dress in a similar manner. In other words, they were pretty much interchangeable, and it didn't take a vast stretch of imagination to reach the conclusion the "Grey Man" was actually various men in different times dedicated to overseeing the same swath of land. However, as the party seemed set on finding this person, Erik kept his opinion to himself. Not surprisingly, none of the rangers had the slightest clue where the Vale of the Wyrm was located. Its' very existence was known to few and, as far as anyone in the group knew, the Vale did not appear on any maps. To a man, they felt confident they would find it without having to ask for directions, if they just looked hard enough. After all, those experienced in woods lore shouldn't have too much difficulty in locating a valley, especially if they had a general idea of where to begin. But, if the mage and bard wanted to find some legendary old codger and ask him for directions—fine; it was their quest anyway, the rangers were just along for the ride. Thus, despite their confidence in their ability to find the Vale of the Wyrm unaided, none of the rangers said anything against heading out to find the Grey Man.

"How do we find this Grey Man?" Davyn ap Gwyn finally asked the bard. "It is said he lives on a rocky tor in the centre of Druidwood, from whence four streams flow toward the four cardinal points," Drake responded looking thoughtfully at the surrounding wood.

"None of the streams hereabouts should be running north," said Bryon O' Dale.

"You mean to tell me you want to give up on looking for an entire valley in order to go traipsing off looking for a hill?" demanded Roland of no one in particular, "you won't even know it if we see it."

"No, you'll know it," said Shadowbender grimly.

Carefully, they set out toward the northeast, as this, all the rangers agreed, should be the general direction of the centre of the wood, 'provided, of course,' noted Roland, 'we know where we are to begin with'. Cool weather, the party's resolve, and a proliferation of animal trails contributed to the party's speed. During the first day, they covered a good ten miles. Only once, when faced with an almost impenetrable tangle of briers and vines some half mile in diameter, had they been uncertain of the way to go and they never had to backtrack.

"And you were sceptical," Quint chided the dwarf as they trudged along a narrow ravine in the afternoon, "O' faithless one! We're making better time than I expected."

"We don't know where we're going," Roland growled, tugging at his pack straps.

"We're still making good time," Quint repeated happily as he moved past the dwarf in order to take his place at point. Davyn changed their marching order during the day to relieve monotony and keep everyone sharp and focused on his position.

"We don't know where we're going," Roland called loudly and slowly, carefully enunciating for clarity, "therefore, it does not matter that we are making good time!" Oceana, covering a smile with her pretty hand, slipped gracefully around the fidgeting dwarf and Roland fell in place behind her as they travelled up the path.

Fortunately for the party, Druidwood was not particularly mountainous. Lack of mountains in the immediate area was beneficial for several reasons. First, without tall mountains to impede vision, one would theoretically have an easier time seeing a high, rocky tor. This theoretical advantage was effectively nullified by the towering trees of the surrounding wood that impeded the vision of terrestrial travellers as completely as mountain ranges would have done had they been present. Quint suggested they circumvent this problem, at least partially, by using the trees like lookout towers. Whenever the party crossed a hill or other elevated area, Davyn sent someone to climb for a view if a tree conducive to this practice was present.

Shadowbender refused to climb and no one bothered to ask Roland as the dwarfs' physiological stumpiness as well as his weight made him a poor choice for such endeavours; also, Davyn felt the dwarf, as clumsy as he was, would fall out of any tree and kill himself. Erik Willowdale and Quint both volunteered in succession and both proved moderately capable at the task. Oceana, however, outdid them both. At the third "lookout tree," the elf maid stepped forward and volunteered to climb. Davyn had not considered the woman for the task but, after a thoughtful pause, acquiesced.

Oceana proved rather adept at tree climbing. In fact, though the rangers would have no way of knowing, she had lots of experience climbing trees as she (and her brother, to a lesser degree) sometimes climbed various trees, mostly to acquire spell components (such as mistletoe) found there and, at least in her case, sometimes for fun. As an elf, Oceana was instinctively more comfortable in and around trees than humans were, even the rangers. She was shorter than any of the men and occasionally had to be boosted into trees without low-lying branches but, once in the tree, her lighter weight and greater agility allowed her to climb faster and higher than anyone else in the group. This was especially true if the tree selected was a pine. With their relatively straight trunks and regularly spaced branches attached to the trunk like the spokes of a wheel, pines lent themselves to safe climbing and Oceana was light enough to ascend almost to the top, though she sometimes had difficulty seeing out past the thick foliage on the branches. Soon, the party began selecting pines exclusively and, after several attempts wherein the foliage frustrated the attempt, the elf maid began carrying Shadowbender's staff with her, tied to her back with a leather thong, which she used to push aside the inhibiting foliage in order to see out.

Despite all this effort, the use of trees as a vantage point was only moderately successful. Frequently, nothing appreciable could be seen as the surrounding wood blocked her vision. Even when she could see out, she couldn't see far, so, unless she happened to look at exactly the right place, she would not have been able to see the tor. Also, she didn't know what she was looking for, anyway. Thus, the sum of her labour was, at best, to give them a rough idea of the terrain in the immediate vicinity which, as a benefit, hardly outweighed time spent as they could more readily ascertain this information from the ground.

The second benefit of relative lack of mountains was the narrowing of possible locations of the tor as the tor, presumably, would be an offshoot of mountainous terrain and, therefore, near the few extant mountains. The benefit was dubious at best as tors are sometimes found altogether apart from mountains. Valleys, however, could only exist around mountains as valleys, by definition, would be mostly or completely surrounded by mountains or hills. Thus, the location of the tor, provided it existed as a natural geographic feature, could be narrowed to areas where mountains were present. In this way, Davyn could narrow the area in which they needed to search in order to conserve time. If he were wrong and the tor, in opposition to natural law, was not to be found near the mountains, nothing was really lost as they could switch their focus easily enough and concentrate on the less mountainous areas of the wood. If this happened, they would at least have an idea where the tor was not and proceed from thence.

Davyn was aware the elf mage seemed distraught over anything vaguely resembling a waste of time and the dwarf seemed distraught by the very existence of the wood. Due to the concerns of the mage, Davyn pushed the party at a slightly quicker pace than he would have assumed normally, but not fast enough to engender the negative consequences of fatigue or, more importantly, the increased likelihood of missing signs of the tor that might have resulted had the pace been too strenuous. Overshooting the tor in haste would be much worse than any time "wasted" in slow, deliberate searching.

The third benefit of the relative lack of mountains was the mobility it allowed the group. Without mountainous terrain to cross or have to avoid, the party could make much better time than it could have otherwise. This feature was consistently lauded by Quint, who equated movement with progress, and Roland, who viewed ease of movement as its own reward.

After half a dozen fruitless tree-climbing attempts, Davyn abandoned the idea altogether and the party, together on the ground, searched for the tor. The dwarf, surly and taciturn, stomped along without looking any further than was necessary to attend to his own welfare in the forested terrain and slouched down wordlessly during halts. The elves and rangers, however, accustomed to traversing woodlands, were quick-eyed and aware and more than compensated for the dwarf and the bard, who did fairly well in the wood, but was not as likely as the others (not counting Roland) to correctly interpret signs of the tor.

This lack of mountains paired with cautious travel, when taking into account the experience of half a dozen rangers, meant it was only a matter of time before a valley was discovered. Unfortunately, the first two such valleys, though inspected enthusiastically, showed no sign of the rocky tor wherein, legend maintained, they might find the Grey Man. Quint wasn't upset (in fact, he rather enjoyed the random exploring) and claimed not finding the Grey Man in the first two valleys was a good thing as it increased their chances of finding him within subsequent valleys. Everyone else thought the logic behind this was slightly off-base, but no one (including Roland, surprisingly) had the heart to second guess the jovial ranger's philosophy.

The third valley, composed primarily of hardwood forest filled with majestic trees, seemed more promising than the previous valleys. Firstly, the size of the trees, larger even than the surrounding folds of Druidwood, indicated this section was older than the rest, it was certainly the oldest they had in encountered. Secondly, massive veins of rock were evident, and the group regularly encountered rocky outcroppings and the occasional weathered boulder. Thirdly, it just felt right to everyone except Roland, who scoffed that 'bad' was the only thing he felt about this particular section of forest but, as he felt that way about any woodland, his feeling was not really indicative of anything.

"If there was ever a place to find a rocky tor, this is it!" Quint remarked gleefully. Still, the valley was large and Davyn expected it would take several days to thoroughly inspect it. They camped that night around a small fire beneath a large oak. After some debate, it was decided the rangers would split into two foray groups and spread out to either side of the main group consisting of the elves, the dwarf, and Davyn ap Gwyn. Neither peripheral group was to wander much further than bow shot and was not to move beyond yelling distance in any event. Spread out in this way, Davyn hoped to enhance their chances of stumbling upon the alleged tor. There was an inherent disadvantage to such an order as the party would be splintered should combat erupt, but Davyn figured their chances of being attacked in so remote a location was minimal and the ready advantage of a broader area of vision outweighed any disadvantages to the procedure.

Davyn ap Gwyn separated the party in such a way so as to minimize the disadvantages, though he did not let on this was the reason. The dwarf and the bard, the two members least likely to recognize the tor, he kept with the "anchor party." Thus, he could keep an eye on them while preventing either of them from hindering a foray group with his presence. The rangers would function better paired with rangers and this, theoretically, would enhance the overall chance of success. In fact, the only disadvantage to this order was to himself in having to remain with the "anchor group" while the other rangers on foray experienced the excitement of searching the ancient wood.

Two days later, the party approached what they assumed was the tor. The rangers had faced no real difficulty in guiding them toward the centre of the valley, which was near the centre of the overall wood. The sparseness of undergrowth, a result of the huge trees with their thick canopy, aided their progress. The forest was wild and rife with wildlife: squirrels, birds of all kinds, deer, and even a wild boar had been spotted by various members of the group as they proceeded. The rangers were keen on taking some game to bolster their supply of provisions, but Shadowbender maintained they did not have time for such pursuits and the rangers complied without noticeable complaint.

On the third day, the forest seemed unnaturally quiet, charged with electricity, pregnant with expectation. A feeling of awe and wonder assailed the group as they approached what must be the centre of the forest. By mid-afternoon, reassembled into one group, they stood looking at a rocky tor rising into the forest canopy one of the peripheral groups had spotted earlier in the day. Jagged stones rose from the ground, naturally creating a gateway marking a faint path leading to the top of the hill. Atop the hill, at the end of the path and just faintly visible over the crest was a small stone house. All the original party members shuddered in the memory of the stone cabin in the Forgotten Lands.

Surely this was the place. The location was correct, the tor was present, and a visible habitation all indicated they had, indeed, discovered the abode of the Grey Man. Davyn, however, had not survived as long as he had in the dangerous wilds by being careless. Unknown dangers often lurked in unexpected places and Davyn ap Gwyn was wise enough to know it. Back home, the ranger regularly inspected the area immediately around his home in order to ensure nothing unexpected had ventured into his territory to take him unaware. He wasn't going to forego this habit now, especially when the safety of other people relied on his judgement.

"Check the perimeter for the streams," Davyn admonished. Before them, a small watercourse trickled through the mould toward the south. Bryon O' Dale and Alan the Forester set off along the northwest perimeter of the tor while Erik Willowdale and Cullen the Brown struck out northeast. The others stood anxious guard, scanning the surrounding forest, though their gaze frequently turned toward the structure atop the hill. Both groups returned within twenty minutes and reported the presence of streams in the correct locations.

"Four streams," Bryon affirmed, "flowing toward the four cardinal points," the man shook his head in disbelief, "I still can't believe one flows north; it shouldn't be. What could cause such an aberration?"

"I don't know," Davyn answered simply. "This is your tor," he said to Shadowbender.

"So," said Roland, looking a bit pale, "do you think it's a good idea for us all to go trooping up to this guy house? After all, he's probably fairly reclusive, one would have to be, out here, and we wouldn't want to start out on the wrong foot."

"Roland--" began Quint.

"The dwarf is right," Shadowbender interrupted, "only part of us should go. "Which?" Drake asked.

Shadowbender stood thoughtfully for a minute or so before replying, "I should definitely go," he said, "I think you should go, too, Drake," the elf looked around at the other members, his gaze resting on Quint, "and you."

Roland was pleased to remain behind with the rangers and 'guard' Oceana while Shadowbender, Quint, and Drake went to talk to some crazed hermit. Roland had enough insanity to deal with in Quint and the two elf mages without having to worry with streams that didn't know where they should flow; everything should move according to its proper nature. The dwarf sat down and happily munched a piece of jerky, watching the trio ascend the hill. He shook his head as they disappeared over the crest of the hill, thinking them all a grand bunch of fools.

Drake frowned. The three of them stood before the cottage. He had knocked, but gotten no response; not surprising, as the place looked to have been abandoned for years. No footprints of any kind were about, and small, thorny weeds of some sort grew here and there in tangled patches. The thatch on the roof was in bad condition all over and in some places, missing entirely. A mildewy smell emanated from the thatch and the bard crinkled his nose at the sharp odour. Cobwebs covered the only door. A quick walk around the cottage confirmed that no one was here, and no one had been here in quite a long time.

"Maybe this isn't the place," Drake offered to the mage.

"Maybe he's dead," Quint muttered, kicking at one of numerous clumps of weeds.

"No," Shadowbender shot a disdainful glance at the ranger, "I do not think he is dead. It is more likely this is not the correct place," the elf crossed his arms thoughtfully, "though I do not know how this could not be it."

"Why do you say that?" asked Drake, "It is the dead centre of the forest, at least according to the rangers. The four streams are present. Everything is here."

"Except the Grey Man," said Drake.

"Except the Grey Man," echoed Shadowbender.

Quint was looking around half-heartedly. No one was here, a child would recognize that. The ranger was only a few yards from the other men and was taking a relatively passive part in the conversation (he was just along for the action anyway—he wasn't a man of mere words, but a thought did occur to him, so he decided to share it) "Maybe there's some sort of trick to summon him."

"What kind of trick?" demanded Shadowbender.

"I don't know," Quint shrugged, "you're the mage."

"It would have to be a good trick, indeed," said a voice behind them, "if it had the power to summon the Grey Man."

Chapter 12

A small, wizened old man sat with his back against one of the stones forming the walkway. A long beard bristled from his chin and swept down his brownish-grey robes and across his lap to rest among the leaves of the forest floor. He had certainly not been there before, and he appeared quite at ease despite having three armed men before him. His legs were crossed, and he held a long-stemmed pipe from which a rich aromatic smoke was wafting.

"Who are you?" Quint demanded. The old man looked like some sort of vagabond, perhaps a beggar even, as his clothes were old and careworn. The man himself was in worse shape than the clothes covering him. Quint had travelled a great deal and seen a great many wondrous things over the course of his travels, but he had never seen a man as wrinkled and plain ancient-looking as the man sitting before him. Quint was far from happy the man had appeared as he had, as if by magic. Magic had always made the ranger ill at ease as magic was unpredictable.

The old man chuckled, and his eyes twinkled with amusement, "That's an odd question for a trespasser to ask," he took a pull off his pipe and, after exhaling, continued, "perhaps it is *I* who should be posing that question to *you*. But no matter," he added quickly with a wave of his hand, "I know enough about you already. Names aren't important. At best, they are transient, at worst, ill-fitting or feigned. The best name is the one a man has earned for himself and is, therefore, deserved."

"Pardon our intrusion, elder," responded Drake, "if an intrusion it is. We are looking for someone and thought he lived here."

"I'd say you *have* found someone," replied the old man, "though it appears no one has lived here for some time," he added with a glance at the dilapidated hovel.

"Yes," Drake forced a small laugh, "I suppose we have, at that. Actually, we were looking for someone specific."

"Ah! You are in luck today," the man chuckled, "for you've found someone specific. I'm someone specific. You're someone specific. Your elven friend who keeps trying to hide the fact he's nervous and keeps nonchalantly gazing around fearing I'm some sort of decoy is someone specific. Seek and you shall find in abundance, the proverb indicates; it would seem to be a true saying, eh? considering you are quite surrounded by a plethora of exactly what you were looking for." The man took another puff of his pipe while Drake was thinking of a reply and Shadowbender frowned deeply.

"Of course," the man continued, "I suppose you're looking for the Grey Man." He nodded toward the cottage, "he's not home," he said matter-of-factly.

"Do…you…know where he is?" asked Quint, his voice filled with a mixture of politeness and excitement.

"Perhaps. Why are you looking for him?"

"We need directions," said Quint.

"Directions? You travelled all the way to the centre of Druidwood to find the legendary Grey Man to ask him for directions?" the old man asked incredulously.

"It is rather incredible," agreed Quint, "especially as a ranger such as myself…"

"We need directions, elder, to a hidden place, a sacred place wherein the very legends come to life," Shadowbender stepped forward, interrupting the ranger and speaking strongly and for the first time, "We seek the Vale of the Wyrm, ancestral birthplace of the mystical Dragon. We go to finish the work begun during the Mage War." Shadowbender stopped speaking and, with narrowed eyes, peered at the old man who still sat apparently unaffected, smoking his pipe. "You remember the Mage War, do you not, elder?" the elf asked softly.

The old man's demeanour changed; he appeared somehow wiser, worldlier, or more powerful. Perhaps he was all three. He smiled approvingly at the elf.

"Wise," he said, "but not a druid. You're a mage?" The Grey Man raised his eyebrows and kept smoking his pipe as before.

"An illusionist, actually, but … yes," the elf answered.

"Who better to recognize an illusion, eh?" the man asked, "What is it you want from the Grey Man that you cannot attain via spell-weaving?"

"All the poems ever written," interjected Drake, "all the songs ever sung, the entire history of the world and everything in it, but,

200

right now," the bard continued, "we'd settle for the location of the Vale of the Wyrm."

"Hmm," the Grey man smiled, "all the poems in the world wouldn't do you much good as you'd forget them all unless you wrote them down and even an elf would die of old age before they were all compiled. Likewise, the songs. Now, the history of the world wouldn't be too bad, but, then, the 'everything in it' part would take a while, of course. You know," he looked at Drake keenly, "it's too bad you're human, you know. Short life span and all that. A shame. The Vale of the Wyrm," the old man whispered thoughtfully, "I think, maybe, I can help you, there. Why is it you want to go?" The old man said the last part off-handedly, but his eyes shone with concentration. Nothing was getting past the old man despite his casual façade.

"During the Mage War..." began Shadowbender.

"Nasty business, that."

"Yes," Shadowbender responded, nonplussed and continued as if the interruption had never occurred, "during the Mage War, a spell was created to put the wyrms into a deep sleep. We feel the time is near for them to reawaken. We have a copy of the spell and we need to find the vale in order to invoke the spell."

"And you believe this dragon's lullaby will work?"

"Yes."

"And you believe you possess the knowledge, the arcane lore, the very power of a Wizard Before to be able to cast such a spell?" the Grey Man demanded.

"Yes," Shadowbender said solemnly.

"Perhaps you do," the Grey Man nodded his head absently, "perhaps you do, but you don't know the cost." The Grey Man looked at Drake sadly then shook his head, "No matter. You have the power, or you don't. Either way, I see you're going to try. If I tell you, what good will it do me?"

Quint and Drake looked at each other questioningly. Shadowbender, frowned slightly but did not respond.

"Um... we might have some items to interest you," Drake stammered before his eyes brightened with an idea, "musical instruments perhaps? Fortunately, I have several." The bard began removing his pack to retrieve his instruments.

"No," said the Grey Man, "that wouldn't interest me, I'm afraid. The world has natural music enough if you know how to listen."

"Oh," said the crestfallen bard.

"Perhaps you'd be interested in a bit of woods-lore," Quint interjected hastily.

"No," said the man, "not really."

"Well," Quint said drawing his sword and laying it across his palms for the man to inspect, "how about a nice long sword? It's real Duranian steel and was crafted by the dwarves..."

"No," said the man, "I haven't any use for such things, I'm afraid."

"How about some tobacco?" Drake offered.

"Grow my own."

"What do you want, elder?" Shadowbender asked softly. The Grey Man puffed his pipe, eyeing the elf appraisingly, taking almost a full minute to respond. When he did respond, he spoke so quietly the men had to strain to hear. The Grey Man said, as if to himself, "You weren't in the Mage War, were you? No, too young. Your father, perhaps, but not you. Actually, not your father, either, I imagine. The elves, if I remember, weren't particularly concerned with the Mage War—elves aren't generally concerned about anything not directly affecting them. The aloofness they once cultivated in order to survive in a chaotic world has become ingrained and is sometimes a terrible curse..." The old man stopped and cocked his head quizzically. Looking into Shadowbender's eyes, "Why are *you* concerned about the reawakening of the wyrms?" he asked the elf.

"Not all elves act like elves, just as not all creatures that look like men are men. Not all things are as they seem," the mage replied after a slight pause.

Few things are as they seem, if you ask me," said the Grey Man, obviously pleased or amused by the elf's reply, "do you think even one millionth of history is recorded or more than the surface emotions of a man are ever witnessed? No. No, I think not." The old man resumed smoking silently. The companions patiently waited or, in Quint's case, tried to appear to be patiently waiting.

"I'll tell you where the vale is," the Grey Man said after a bit, "but there is still the matter of what I'll get out of it to be resolved." He said nothing further, giving no indication what it was he wanted.

"I would think," said Quint at last, "our keeping the dragons from awakening would be reward enough in itself as the dragons, were they loosed upon the world, would certainly lay waste to this very wood!" The ranger looked solidly into the eyes of the Grey Man, waiting for a response.

The man returned the rangers gaze with an unwavering and, Quint noticed, unblinking look. Quint couldn't decide exactly what the man's eyes demonstrated. They were neither young nor old, happy or sad or angry or anything else. They were simply there, gazing back at him as if the man were reading his past, present, and future all at once. Quint was undeniably disturbed by the sheer *knowingness* reflected in the man's eyes. Determined not to show any sign of faltering, Quint returned the gaze determined that, when the gaze was broken, it would be because the old man broke off. Quint had no idea how long they stayed thus, he was only aware that, finally, the old man spoke. Even then, he wasn't sure who had looked away first.

"The wyrms, of course," said the Grey Man, "wouldn't pose any real threat to me—but well spoken," he nodded approvingly at the ranger, "so, I'll tell you and," he continued, "wish you luck in your endeavour, to boot." He looked at the bard before turning to address Shadowbender, "The Vale of the Wyrm, though not all creatures so name it, lies almost due east of here. It is still a beautiful place. Not all things are as they seem—eh? Anyway, once you reach the south-flowing Whitefoam River (as I believe it is called by the men of the south) and cross it, follow the river north. The headwaters originate in the Vale. The caverns you seek may be accessed a mere stone's throw from the headwaters. Therein is your object and your fate." The old man said nothing further, resumed smoking his pipe and, to all appearances, had forgotten three men stood before him.

"What dangers might we expect?" Drake said finally.

"That's a second question," said the Grey Man, "and I'd have to be a seer, indeed, to know the answer. But, I'll answer anyway." He looked piercingly at Drake, "You're a bard," he said, "and bards, though now less mystic and more worldly than they once were, are still taught wisdom as well as knowledge, thus you should know the worst dangers awaiting a man lie within himself." The old man resumed his posture as if he considered the conversation ended.

Lacking a suitable reply, the bard and the ranger both shrugged and prepared to leave. Shadowbender, however, held up his hand, indicating they wait.

"Who are you, elder?" the mage asked, peering intently at the seated figure.

The Grey Man smiled and looked at the elf, kindness flooding his features, "I think you know the answer already, faerie-kin. Search your memory, the inheritance of your forebears, and you will find you already know the answer. Before men came from the south, I was here. The first elves, when they set out to explore the new world they had discovered, found the Grey Man walking within this wood. I was here before the sires of the mightiest oaks of the forest were acorns and I will be here long after the fallen trunks of their descendants have rotted away into nothingness. I am known among the wise of your kind, though by another name. However, what you ask is a third question and one I choose not to answer. Fare ye well on your quest, illusionist." The old man said nothing further. Wordlessly, Shadowbender bowed, slowly turned, and, Drake and Quint in tow, began threading his way back down the hill.

Chapter 13

"So, let me get this straight," said Roland after hearing the full tale involving the Grey Man from Quint, "this kook living in the middle of nowhere gives us directions and we just go for it, no questions asked?"

"Pretty much," Quint nodded.

"My life has involved nothing but crazy people ever since I started following you around!" the dwarf crossed his arms and spat in disgust. Shadowbender, looking thoughtful, opened his mouth to speak.

"Here's one now!" the dwarf chimed. Shadowbender glared at the dwarf momentarily before speaking, "We would all do well to heed the voice of the Grey Man."

"I agree," murmured Bryon O'Dale. The other rangers nodded in agreement.

"Fine," said Roland, "*I* don't care. It doesn't matter what *I* think. *I* am just along as baggage and no one listens to me anyway. What do *I* know about forests? What do *I* know about psychotic hermits? What…"

"Roland!" Quint interrupted, hoping to stall what he recognized as the onslaught of one of the dwarf's tirades, "We brought you along to pummel anything that might get in our way. We need a warrior."

"Damn straight!" Roland said. The dwarf hitched up his breeches, wiggled his axe in its scabbard, and glared at the surrounding forest.

"Well," the dwarf continued, "let's go, then."

Quint had shared the Grey Man's directions with the other rangers and, after a brief counsel, they set out due east. Travel through the wood was easy for the most part.

Occasionally, the party was forced to circumvent some sort of obstacle such as a thicket or tangle of fallen trees. Only rarely were they obliged to clear their path with sword or axe, though this was a task Roland seemed to relish and the dwarf gleefully applied himself to the task when it was needed. As a result, they made good time.

Oceana was entranced. The forest was primeval, at least as old as the forests of the elven kingdoms. She loved the towering trees and the carpet formed from thousands of years' worth of falling leaves and pine needles. Birds flitted merrily from tree to tree and there were a good number of squirrels nipping about. The smell of a living forest, at once ancient and vibrant, overwhelmed the senses. It was a lively scene and her heart bubbled over. She laughed and told little jokes. The mirth was infectious and, soon, all the rangers, who had an instinctive reaction of joy toward the wood as well, were smiling and jostling good-naturedly.

"What we need," said Oceana in sudden inspiration, "is a holiday! We've been travelling and we're tired, sore, and hungry. We need to stop now, while it's still early, have a decent meal, hear some happy music, and get a little rest!" The elf maid propped her hands on her hips, indicating the request wasn't optional. She knew, of course, they'd do what she wanted; they were tired, too. More importantly, they were men and pretty girls, acting decisively, always got their way around men. Shadowbender, as her brother and, therefore, exempt from this mysterious power, might be the only exception, but he could go on alone if he didn't like it. Oceana smiled widely as, one by one (except Shadowbender, who gave no outward indication of his opinion), the men began to nod. Oceana shook her head jovially; nothing is quite as agreeable as compliance.

By mid-afternoon, they had located an ancient pine grove with a tinkling stream meandering through it. The arboreal cover and thick blanket of pine needles made the whole area virtually free from undergrowth and created comfortably open surroundings as well as a soft seat and bed as both were answered by the ground. Oceana knew this was the place.

Quint, Erik Willowdale, and Cullen the Brown went hunting. They had been wanting to hunt ever since entering Druidwood and were excited to finally be doing so. Each had claimed he would take enough game to last the rest of the journey. Alan the Forester and Bryon O'Dale fished the stream using pliant limbs of young pines as poles. Davyn ap Gwyn and Drake went off in search of herbs.

Shadowbender, not much use in hunting, fishing, or gathering, sat quietly reading through a large, leather bound tome. Roland, unfamiliar with the finer or, coming as he did from a subterranean background, indeed, *any* of the points of fishing and considered too loud by the hunters, was left behind and he smoked contentedly and stared up into the boughs of the trees towering hundreds of feet above thinking how they formed a vault not unlike some of the larger caverns of his home, albeit brighter. Oceana sat combing her hair outside the flap of the tent her brother had prepared for her. She thought it *did* seem domestic and festive.

The hunters soon returned with several squirrels and a brace of rabbits. Quint was absolutely beaming and claimed he had gotten every bit of it until Cullen piped up with the truth that Quint, in fact, was responsible for exactly none of their future meal. Of the three, Quint was the only one failing to bring down anything.

"I didn't really try!" he whispered to Roland.

"Why don't you make yourself useful and cut us some spits!" Cullen called, overhearing Quint's comment to the dwarf. With a mock salute, Quint went to collect spits and a bit of firewood. Roland, perversely eager to cut trees, went with him.

Alan and Bryon returned with a catch of a dozen fat trout. Davyn and Drake later appeared, bringing in a goodly amount of raspberries, a rabbit they had stumbled across, various spices, and even a clump of wild onions. Drake went to wash his hands in the stream. Mentioning she needed a drink, Oceana followed.

Once they were out of sight of their companions, Drake turned toward Oceana and the elf maid almost wept to see his face.

"Oceana," Drake said, moving toward her, "I've…"

"Stop!" Oceana held up her hand, "I have to say something first. I've been thinking, Drake, about the other night…"

"So have I." "...and it was a mistake."

"How can love be a mistake?"

"We're on a quest, Drake, with danger on every side. We are worried, scared, and our emotions are intensified."

"But they're there," he urged.

"Yes. No," she shook her head, "I don't know. They might be. We need to wait until our quest is over. Then, we can give ourselves time to inspect our feelings in a normal time. If we want to explore love, then we can do so unimpeded. All I am asking is that we wait a little while."

"Are you sure this is what you want?" Drake asked after an agonizing pause.

"I am."

"Well, then," said Drake, nodding "we can wait for a little while."

"For a little while," Oceana echoed.

"Let's go," Drake said, reaching out and squeezing her hand, "there's a party going on without us."

Once Quint and Roland returned with the firewood and accessories, the meal was soon cooked, and a full-fledged feast initiated.

Stomachs full, bodies warm, and hearts uplifted, everyone enjoyed the respite. The men smoked, and everyone joked and talked for several hours about things unrelated to their quest. After another round of food, Oceana called for music.

"As you wish, milady," Drake said bowing with an exaggerated flourish.

From his pack, the bard pulled out the flute and mandolin. He reached again, withdrawing a small fiddle.

"This guy absolutely astounds me!" Roland whispered conspiratorially to Quint who was quite astounded himself.

Drake kept the flute. He knew Oceana played the mandolin, so he handed the instrument to the elf-maid. Now, for the fiddle. To the bard's surprise, as he looked around, Roland slowly reached for the instrument. Davyn pulled a whistle from somewhere. Erik and Alan produced flutes of their own and, soon, the pine grove was bursting with music.

The companions, of course, had no way of knowing, but the last time music had echoed within this grove was nearly a thousand years before when a long-dead and forgotten bard played beside his camp fire during his desperate (and fool-hardy, he thought) attempt to reach the Vale of the Wyrm to stop the marauding dragons. That night, the forgotten bard played against the darkness to ward off loneliness. Tonight, the music came from people because they were not lonely. The forgotten bard would never have thought others, a thousand years later, would sit in the same grove under the descendants of the trees surrounding him performing the very mission he was struggling with. That would have been a fanciful idea, indeed. Even for a bard.

The companions, cheered by the fire and food, played well into the night, heedless of anything hearing. In fact, nothing unfriendly did hear and the moon waxed full and bright, filling the grove with a warm glow. Such nights, surreal and dreamy, were as perfect as those belonging to tales.

After a collection of traditional tunes, an elfish waltz, a couple of dwarven tunes (including a popular and innuendo-free dwarfish drinking song), and several impromptu songs, everyone was ready to settle down to sleep. Everyone felt safe and the rangers posted only one guard. This guard was Alan, who, full and relaxed, soon fell asleep on the soft ground cover. But no trouble came.

The next morning was drizzly, but, after a merry night, no one (except Roland and Shadowbender) seemed to mind. The party, once again, struck out east, making good time, much to Quint's delight. They made a brief rest at midday and, after consulting their map again, continued on until mid-afternoon before encountering the Whitefoam.

Further south in the civilized lands, the river was wide and lazy, flowing through pastures and wheat fields. Here, however, the river deserved its name. The group stood on the west bank of the river watching the water dash and churn over the rocks. Except in a few locations, mostly in river bends, the water wasn't deep, but white water was always dangerous. Davyn, Quint, and Erik Willowdale stood surveying the scene trying to pick out the best route across the river and arguing about it. Everyone else took advantage of the delay to rest, plopping down where they stood.

Bryon O'Dale shattered the silence with a shriek of pain. Dropping the water skin he was holding, he grasped frantically at an arrow that had sunk into his left arm just below the shoulder. A dozen or so arrows followed, making dull thudding sounds as they embedded in the earth or in trees. Fortunately, no one else was hit. In an instant, everyone jumped for the nearest available cover.

Roland was sitting on a large log and, when the arrows began to fall, he merely rolled to the other side, allowing himself to fall to the ground. He peered over the top of the barrier, cursing his lack of a crossbow. A few seconds later, Drake and Quint dove over the log, the bard nearly flattening the dwarf. Shadowbender appeared a moment later, calmly stepping over the log as if he were on a picnic. What an idiot. Through the trees, the dwarf could make out the shadowy forms of what had to be wyrm cultists.

"What is it with these guys?" Roland snapped at Quint, who didn't answer, thinking it basically a rhetorical question.

Roland took a quick look and appraised the situation. Oceana had run to Bryon and both were behind a smallish boulder. Foolish girl—she'd be hit, for sure, as exposed as she was. Roland grimaced in sympathy as the elf maid, one hand around the arrow where it entered the arm for support and the other just further out, snapped the end of the arrow in Bryon's arm so it would not protrude so far and be an impediment; true first aid would have to wait. Roland was impressed, and the dwarf wondered how she came to know so much about combat and its effects.

The other rangers had drawn their bows and, from behind various obstacles, were randomly firing at the cultists, though it was hard to tell whether or not they were hitting anything as the cultists were mostly hidden. Arrows flew back in response, several falling dangerously near Oceana and Bryon. None, however, appeared to have been aimed at those behind the log. Surely, they knew they were here. Who could've *possibly* missed Mr. Oblivious sauntering over the log, he thought looking at the elf.

Roland glanced at the river. In the best of circumstances (and this definitely wasn't it), the river would be dangerous to cross. The cultists were in a broad half-moon position surrounding them, figuring the river as a barrier. The dwarf watched as the figures spread above and below them, pinning them against the waterway. Crossing the river would be folly. Not only would they likely drown, they would be sitting targets in the open with no chance of effectively fighting back and no way to defend themselves. Roland ducked back behind the log.

"What cruel fate the gods have enacted!" said Quint, echoing the dwarf's thoughts.

"Ah," replied Drake, "men cannot see all things. We are actors in a play, yet we know not the plot."

"True enough," the ranger admitted.

"We are but pawns of the gods, my friend, not actors," Shadowbender murmured.

"Humph!" snorted Roland, "He who relies on the gods forfeits common sense."

"Don't believe in the gods?" asked Drake.

"Yes, by the gods!" grunted Roland, "I believe in all of them. And I've created a few of my own for good measure."

"Why aren't they shooting at us?" asked Quint, shaking his head.

"Who cares?" laughed the bard.

"They are not shooting at us," explained the elf, "because they do not see us. What do you think I was doing a few moments ago—having a picnic?"

"I thought you were having a breakdown or something—all mumbling to yourself," shot the dwarf.

"It is my illusion that is keeping you from being a target. You should be thankful."

"I think," replied Roland," you're confusing illusion with delusion."

"Well…" began Shadowbender.

"Yes, well," the bard quickly interrupted, "I suppose we better figure out what we're going to do."

"*I* think we're going to die," said Roland.

"I *know* we're going to die," said Quint, "I just don't think it'll be today. What do you say we get out of here?"

"Lead the way, O' wood-wise ranger!" said Drake.

Quint jumped over the log, followed by the others.

"To the river!" Quint cried as he sprinted for the watercourse. Davyn and Erik shot one final round and followed. Arrows fell all around them. Before them, Cullen the Brown, who had been the closest to the river and was still firing at the cultists in order to cover his fleeing companions, cried out, grasping at the shaft of an arrow protruding from his chest. Gasping, the ranger stumbled backwards,

216

his bow dropping from twitching fingers, lost his footing, and fell with a cry into the churning waters of the Whitefoam.

"Leave him!" Davyn called as Erik Willowdale slowed to run toward Cullen. They were all as good as dead, Davyn knew, with most of them, if not all, to be shot down, like Cullen, in the river crossing. At least some might make it if they moved fast enough. Cullen was gone. Erik would only get himself killed stopping for him. "He's gone, Erik," he called a little more softly as a spasm of grief crossed the younger man's face. Erik resumed running.

They were not going to make it. Shadowbender had never been as sure of anything in his life. The first ranks of the party jumped into the water with a resounding splash. Oceana and Bryon ran past him. From the corner of his eye, he saw Cullen fall. Something had to be done. The elf stopped running and turned to face the enemy.

Hands outstretched and moving in a tight circular motion, Shadowbender focused on creating a diversion. Arrows whizzed past him and he grimaced. Gritting his teeth, the elf concentrated solely upon the illusion. A thick fog began rising from the riverbank nearest the cultists. Soon, the mist was swirling around the elf and, after a few moments, he was gone from sight altogether. The cultists kept firing arrows blindly, however, as they advanced toward the river.

His spell completed, Shadowbender turned and lightly bounded into the river. Everyone else was stumbling and splashing around as they tried to fight their way across the watercourse. Roland, he noticed, was having the toughest time. Not only was he the shortest (and, therefore, deeper in the water than the others), he was also the

217

least sure-footed of the group. The dwarf slipped badly enough to thoroughly douse himself twice while Shadowbender was looking and, at the rate he was sloshing around, seemed unlikely to make it across at all.

A new volley of arrows rained through the fog bank, landing randomly within the river. A steady bombardment continued. Most of the companions, Shadowbender and Roland being the exceptions, were three quarters of the way across. It looked as if they might all make it, after all. Unfortunately, looks can be deceiving.

Three things happened almost simultaneously. First, a random arrow embedded itself in Drake's shoulder. Clutching the wound, the bard stumbled but was caught by Quint and Alan and was half carried, half dragged onward. Secondly, alarmed by Drake's cry, Roland glanced up to see what was wrong, slipped on a slime-covered stone, and tumbled head first into the rapids. Third, about a dozen cultists burst through the fog at the river's edge, bows in hand.

Davyn, along with Quint and Alan, with the stumbling bard in tow, reached the far bank and clambered onto dry land. Oceana, leading Bryon O'Dale, wasn't far behind. Shadowbender, however, was only half-way across. The cultists fired.

Oceana had reached the bank and had turned to steady the ranger as he made the final step to safety and felt the impacts vibrate through Bryon's body as several arrows sank into his back. Shuddering, eyes fluttering spasmodically, Bryon's knees buckled, and he dropped back into the swirling waters of the Whitefoam.

Oceana's shriek reverberated in the ears of her companions, sounding shrill and ragged. Quint, dropping Drake out of sight behind a small copse of brambles, turned in time to see the weakly clenching hand of the ranger slip from the elf maiden's hand and disappear into the water. Oceana knelt by the water's edge, oblivious to the goings-on around her. In an instant, Quint was appraised of the situation. He saw the cultists preparing for another barrage, saw Shadowbender in midstream (a sitting target, if he'd ever seen one), noticed Oceana's indifference and impending danger, and wondered vaguely where Roland went. Quint sprinted toward the river.

Oceana would be the next target for the same reason Bryon O'Dale was the last: she was still within range, but nearing safety. They would shoot her before focusing on the still river-bound mage. Quint began shouting as he ran.

The ranger jumped the last four feet, just as a volley of arrows thudded around him and the elf maid. Miraculously, none found their mark. Adrenaline flowing through him, the ranger practically carried Oceana up the slope.

"Where is Roland?" Quint yelled hoarsely. Oceana stared blankly. Still shocked from the loss of Bryon, Quint doubted if the elf maid even heard him. Davyn and Erik met him at the top of the riverbank. They hurriedly grasped the elf maid and ran with her to the cover of the underbrush.

"Where is Roland?" Quint demanded, looking around. Erik, engaged in carrying Oceana, failed to answer at all. Davyn, also focused on his task, shrugged absently. Panicked, Quint ran back to the riverbank, shouting for the dwarf.

Quint's concern was not lessened. Shadowbender stood in the middle of the river, his eyes closed. Quint wondered what the elf was doing, though he focused his true attention on scanning the river for traces of Roland. Downstream, the body of Bryon had gotten wedged between two large boulders, the water streaming around the gaps left by his body causing his arms to flap wildly in the current as if the dead ranger was desperately attempting to swim downstream. It was a macabre and somewhat sickening scene. Of Roland, however, there was no sign.

A robed form materialized beside him and Quint nearly ran it through before he realized the form was none other than Shadowbender. The elf, realizing he was the most viable target (and an easy one, at that) had magically transported himself to the riverbank. In this manner, he almost certainly saved himself from, and nearly scared Quint to, death.

"Where is Roland?" Quint screamed, grabbing the illusionist's arm.

"I do not know," Shadowbender replied, "but we need to get to cover!"

"Not without Roland!"

"Look," said Shadowbender, "all you are going to do by standing here is get yourself killed. Then, you will be no good to Roland or anyone else!" The cultists, recovered from their awe of witnessing Shadowbender's fantastic transportation, let loose another volley of arrows. Shadowbender saw them fire. "Come on!" he urged, grabbing Quint's arm and dragging him toward cover. Arrows landed around them as they jumped into the underbrush and the relative safety of the wood.

Chapter 14

The cultist leader smiled beneath his mask. Below him, at the water's edge, lay the nearly drowned body of the dwarven warrior. Finally, the immediate mission was accomplished; they had taken one of the infidels alive. Of course, how long the prisoner remained that way remained to be seen and the man doubted the infidel would remain alive any longer than was necessary to pump him of any and all information pertaining to the intruders' task.

The overall goal was to kill the entire group. The leader of the cultists, however, thought it would be prudent to capture an opponent, question him, and find out what the party knew. The fact the intruders were consistently moving toward the Vale indicated their intent. Still, the details of the intruders' plans were still worth having. In particular, he'd like to be able to identify the bard. The bedraggled dwarf was almost certainly not the bard (dwarves produced few musicians of the appropriate calibre) but would know who was. Personally, he expected the elf maid; the only female, she was different than the others and the men seemed very protective toward her. It was costly assaulting this group. He lost men in every encounter and achieved little success. If he could identify the bard, he could concentrate attacks on that individual, thereby increasing the chances of killing him (or *her* as the case might be).

He motioned toward two of his compatriots, who were waiting patiently to the side. In response, they hopped down the riverbank and lifted the comatose dwarf. Roland was now in the hands of the enemy.

Dimly, Roland became aware of a rocking motion. It was gentle and almost comforting. All he remembered from before was the desperate bludgeoning of the river slamming him into the rocks. He still ached; he was probably banged up pretty bad—but, he wasn't very wet, merely damp. What was going on? If he was being moved around and wasn't in the river, there were two options: he was dead, or he was being carried. He opted out on being dead. He had never been dead before and his concept of the afterlife was relatively hazy, but he was pretty sure there was supposed to be a lot of light and he was pretty sure he should be free from any pain. Since there wasn't a lot of light (although he conceded his eyes *were* closed) and he still felt battered and bruised, he assumed he wasn't in Paradise. Fortunately, there didn't seem to be any flames around, so he probably wasn't in the *other* place. Therefore, Roland decided, he was alive and being carried. The most relevant question was by whom?

Roland didn't want to open his eyes and risk being discovered by enemies without knowing more. He could feel the biting cords dig into his wrists and ankles. He was also swinging from side to side in a familiar pattern. He groaned inwardly; someone had him tied to a pole by his hands and feet. Every time that had happened before (and, surprisingly, there had been a few times) it wasn't good.

The swinging journey lasted for most of a day by the dwarf's calculation, which could be a bit off with the dunking, the time he was unconscious, and the general bludgeoning and all. Unfortunately, he couldn't figure out in which direction they were travelling, though they were obviously staying within the valleys as there was little incline. This idea was also supported by the almost constant presence of water (the Whitefoam?) he could hear in the background.

The dwarf peeked through slitted eyes a couple of times but couldn't see anything as the sudden light was overwhelmingly bright. He was afraid to open his eyes further as the men carrying him might notice. He listened intently but heard nothing that would indicate any of his companions had also been captured, though, if they were, he doubted they would make any sound.

As they progressed, Roland became aware of minute changes in the immediate environment. Deprived of sight, his hearing, sense of smell, and tactile senses gradually grew sharper. He recognized the change in the forest floor as indicated by the footfalls around him. Most of the time, leaves crunched beneath their feet and, when the crunching stopped, the dwarf assumed the men were traversing rock or bare earth. Even with closed eyes, Roland was aware of light enough to detect changes in the overall lighting. When it grew darker, the dwarf imagined them walking through shady groves and, every now and then, it grew noticeably cooler for a brief time and Roland guessed they had passed a water source, an assumption several times verified by the faint sound of running water. However, the dwarf didn't know the point of origin of the journey and he knew nothing of the terrain and, thus, all this information was pretty much useless. After a while, he ceased even attempting to ascertain his location and tried to rest. He was sure he'd need all the strength he could get once they stopped. The swinging, jostling journey continued well into the night.

Even with closed eyes, Roland could tell the change in the lighting. It also became progressively cooler and the gradual transition of sounds from daytime animals to nocturnal ones bore witness to the onslaught of night. The cultists stumbled more frequently and often bumped the hapless dwarf into a bush or other obstacle. It must have been well after midnight when they stopped, dumping the luckless dwarf unceremoniously onto the forest floor.

Unsure about the best course of action, Roland continued to feign unconsciousness. A muffled conversation took place a few yards from him, though he couldn't make out anything that was being said. Several people began moving around and, from the sounds, the dwarf realized they were building a fire. The dwarf's spirit shrank, remembering a similar occasion during which he and Quint were almost roasted by a tribe of goblins over a relatively minor misunderstanding. He was having a serious case of déjà vu, here, though this time was worse, in a way, as goblins were generally weak and inept whereas humans were much more dangerous. Within a few minutes, he heard the crackling of a camp fire, but no more talking. Roland began to worry.

"So," said a voice, finally, "this is the prisoner?" The voice was cold, echoing hollowly within the mask of the cultist speaking. Chills ran up and down Roland's back at the eerie sound.

"Yes," came a reply, "we caught him at the river during the ambush."

"The others?" said the eerie voice.

"Two definitely dead, a third possibly so, this one captured, the remainder fled into the wood."

"The mage?"

"He was one of those who escaped, sir." A thirty-second silence passed with only a low crackling of the newly-lit fire noticeable. Roland worried over who the two dead members were; he knew Cullen was one as he had seen the man fall, but he didn't know the identity of the other.

"Very well," said the leader or whatever the one with the eerie voice was, "let's question the dwarf."

"He has not yet awakened," said the other.

"He's faking," came the simple reply.

As the sound of footsteps approached, Roland wondered how Mr. Eerie Voice knew he was pretending. Not that it mattered. Roland opened his eyes.

A small clearing hosted the scene. A dozen or so wyrm cultists sat or stood around a central camp fire that threw sparks into the sky. The cultists were heavily armed and, judging from the small packs several were carrying, lightly encumbered—a war band. As he was near a light source, he couldn't see off into the forest, but that wasn't much of a problem as he doubted he'd learn anything useful even if he could see as all forests pretty much seemed identical. The cultists were clearly unconcerned with stealth as the fire was large. In fact, sparking and crackling, it was even possible the fire had been kindled expressly to be seen and was a signal fire although Roland, unable to distinguish either terrain or their location, had no way of verifying this theory.

Off to himself, sat another cultist on a wood and canvas chair, several long torches thrust into the ground on either side of him. He was apparently of higher rank than the others and was certainly Mr. Eerie Voice. Aside from the trappings surrounding him, his rank was indicated by the fact his mask was a different colour than the others; his was green, the others wore brownish masks, but he was otherwise identically attired. The source of the footsteps was two brown-masked cultists who were determinedly striding toward the captive dwarf.

Wordlessly, the two men grasped either end of the pole to which Roland was tied and lifted him off the ground. Positioning the pole on their shoulders, they carried him across the clearing toward the seated figure, dumping him onto the ground in front of the camp fire. Roland was amused that he had started this whole wretched adventure as baggage for his own companions and, now, he was baggage for the cultists.

The man seated on the chair was frightening even though his features were hidden. His manner was imposing and his eyes, the man's only visible feature, were black and shining. He sat calmly in the chair, gazing at the dwarf.

Roland cleared his throat (he hadn't had any water since early in the day—not counting what he had swallowed in the river) and croaked: "Nice place you got here."

The man in the chair said nothing. The other cultists, scattered about the camp, moved closer, apparently to hear the exchange.

"Where can I get me a chair like that?" Roland continued. Maybe, if he could keep them amused, or appear unafraid, or something, it might help.

"You won't need such things anymore, I'm afraid," replied the seated figure. He remained outwardly motionless.

"I have a rather burning question. Two actually—one, I'd like a drink of water; two—how do you eat in those masks. Also, aren't they awfully hot in the summer? Oops—that's three questions, but..."

"Bring him water," said the seated figure to one of the nearby cultists, before focusing again on the dwarf.

"I am less than amused," he said, "however, I believe we can help each other. We'll continue after your drink. "The subordinate walked to Roland and held a water skin to his lips. Roland drank deeply, took a breath, and drank a second time. With a nod to his superior, the canteen-wielding cultist returned to his place by the fire.

"Now that you're suitably refreshed," said the man, "we can continue."

"Thanks, but no," interrupted Roland, "I, unfortunately, have sort of a religious objection to being questioned. It's against my faith and..."

"Which is the bard among your party?" the man queried.

"Bard. Bard," Roland said looking thoughtful and shaking his head, "no bard. Let's see—dwarf, ranger, butcher, baker, candlestick maker…nope, no bard. Sorry."

"Let's try this again,' said the man with only a hint of menace in his voice, "and let's try to get it right. Otherwise, I shall become unhappy."

"We wouldn't want that, now would we?" Roland jested. Despite the outward appearance of bravado, the dwarf figured this was going to be his last adventure.

"No," said the man matter-of-factly, "Now, we know your companions carry musical instruments. Which of you is the bard?"

"I told you, we don't have a bard; people other than bards play instruments."

"Yes. I am quite aware of your statement. It is, however, a lie."

Again, silence filled the clearing. Even with all his gusto, Roland didn't feel like saying anything. The cultists obviously thought a bard was necessary for the spell, though Shadowbender had said something to the effect that anyone could evoke the spell so long as they knew the proper tune. Roland had no idea whether or not the cult knew this, but he was sure they weren't going to learn it from him. He also wasn't going to give away the identity of Drake. The leader of the cultists sat motionless. Whether he was thinking, trying to unnerve Roland with the silence, or both, the dwarf didn't know. Finally, the cultist leader began to laugh. A deep, resonant chuckle escaped from the confines of his mask. The laugh grew louder and his shoulders shook. The man's masked compatriots looked around, their attitude and bearing portraying the look of bewilderment that surely covered their faces.

"So," said the seated man after regaining his composure, "I've been fortunate enough to capture one of the intruders and I get this—this," he pointed at Roland in a flourishing manner, "an intractable dwarf (of all the possible races) who won't open his mouth to say anything at all concerning the 'Big Secret Mission' I'm sure *he* thinks is so important." The man focused intently on the dwarf. "You don't really think the 'canticle' will work, do you?" He clucked, shaking his head. "I am sorry for you. We've tried it, of course. It doesn't work. And your friends are walking into an ambush. We know they're heading for the caverns and a full contingent of my men are there waiting for them and there is a full contingent following them. They will be caught between the twain. What a shame that they 're going to die for naught."

"Well," said Roland, "if you think I'm going to believe the 'canticle" won't work, you're crazy. If it doesn't work, *you* wouldn't all be fired up about trying to stop us!" Roland snorted derisively, proud at his wit in outsmarting his adversary.

"No," the cultist chuckled, "you have it all wrong. We are not trying to prevent your little song; our order doesn't allow intruders. When someone enters our territory, we must eject them, with force, if necessary. So have we attempted with your group. Unfortunately, your group is skilled in the art of warfare and the cost has been staggering for both sides. I'm merely trying to save lives; if your party was aware the 'canticle' would fail, they wouldn't pursue an empty dream. If they weren't pursuing that fallacy, they would leave, and we wouldn't be forced to fight them. You," he looked at Roland, compassion bleeding into his voice, "wouldn't waste lives fighting our skilled warriors for no reason. Now, who wouldn't want to save lives?"

"Right," Roland spat, "you're a regular cleric, all right. Virtually spend all your time helping the sick, wounded, and impoverished, no doubt, rather than skulking around in the middle of nowhere plotting world destruction. Oh, yeah, while wearing funny masks, I might add."

The cultist cleared his throat before replying softly.

"Very well. You make me sad. You have a choice: you can tell me what I need to know about what you know or... you can die a slow and painful death," the man shrugged, "it doesn't really matter to me." The man waited for a response.

He didn't get one. Roland blanched visibly but made no reply. Finally, the cultist summoned two of his men over and whispered audibly, "Leave him to his thoughts until morning. If he hasn't had a change of heart by first watch, kill him."

The cultist leader nodded curtly toward Roland, arose, and walked off into the surrounding forest. Several others followed, leaving Roland with eight or nine fireside companions. The fire was blazing merrily, the stars were shining brightly. Roland was confident it was going to be a beautiful night.

Despite the hour, Roland, for some reason, couldn't sleep. He watched quietly until most of the cultists settled down for the night. Two men remained on guard while the others slept, but the leader never returned; Roland assumed he had lodged away from his command or had left on some other errand. If there was ever going to be a time to escape, it would be now.

Or maybe not. Roland discreetly tried breaking the ropes. Too thick. He tried manoeuvring into position to gnaw the ropes. Not enough contortionists' ability. He looked for a sharp rock or something to saw the ropes with. The area was devoid of any such things. Finally, Roland decided he'd have to simply wiggle out of his bonds.

It was slow work, relatively painful, and, in the end, non-productive. By midnight, his neck hurt from straining to see if the guards were aware of his attempts, his wrists were chafed to the point of bleeding, and his nerves were as frayed as he desperately wanted his ropes to be. Initially, he was encouraged, hoping the blood would lubricate the rope and promote escape. Unfortunately, it didn't work and now he lay tired, frustrated, bleeding, and suffering from a terrible crick in the neck. The situation seemed hopeless.

He thought back on the time he and Quint had been captured by the goblin tribe. He and the ranger had left a backwater inn a little too inebriated and failed to see the goblin war party before it was upon them. He had lopped one's head off and Quint skewered a second before they were taken. They were hauled to the goblins encampment to be burnt alive as a sacrifice to some grimy goblin deity.

Fortunately, a war band of one of the nearby petty lords had been tracking the group and, using the goblins focus on the prisoners to their advantage, managed to take the goblins by surprise, killing many and routing the others. Unfortunately, there were no petty warlords within a weeks' journey and Roland knew Quint and his other companions couldn't spare the time to try to save him. It would take a miracle to save him this time.

A large ember burst from the fire with a resounding crack and landed on the dwarf's neck. Roland jerked his head away and grimaced at the double pain of the burn and the resulting twinge from the crick in his neck. Roland cursed (quietly). It was a few moments before he began to smile.

An idea had occurred to him. Hopeful, he turned (more neck pain) to see if his guards were watching. Whatever gods that bothered to look out for dwarves were smiling on him tonight for both guards were apparently oblivious to his movements. One, the nearest, was asleep. Roland, of course, couldn't see his eyes for the mask, but the rhythmic breathing and soft snoring emanating from within the mask told the tale. The second guard was standing (and, therefore, awake) but was facing in the other direction. Roland felt like laughing.

He didn't, however, as it would be unwise. Instead, he gently and fairly quietly wriggled around until he was in position to lay the rope on the still glowing ember.

He missed. Roland grimaced in pain as he accidentally stuck his wrist to the coal. The second time, he did better. The dwarf anxiously watched the alert guard as the ember slowly burnt the rope, but the man gave no sign he noticed anything amiss. By the time it was burnt through sufficiently for Roland to snap his bonds, he had burnt himself several more times. But, who cared about that? His hands were free.

Chapter 15

"Let's go!" Drake shouted to Quint, "We've got to get out of here!" The ranger was looking intently at the river and was oblivious to almost everything else. The bard hesitated for a moment, then grabbed Quint, attempting to steer him into the woods and onto (hopefully) the path. As the bard had expected, Quint shrugged him off.

"We've got to find Roland!" Quint shrieked, pointing frantically toward the river.

"We need to go soon," called Davyn ap Gwyn. He, along with the two other surviving rangers, Alan the Forester and Erik Willowdale, occupied strategic vantage points around the party, but were well within hearing distance. With Quint's ranting, everything within half a mile was within hearing distance.

Shadowbender peered across the river seemingly uninterested in what was going on behind him. Once the mist had cleared, due both to the expiration of the spells' duration and the natural effect of the breeze, the mage could clearly see the opposite shore. No cultists were in sight. Shadowbender did not know if they had fled in fear or some other reason, but he did not care why they had gone, only that they had, if they had. Once his own group had reached the opposite bank, the cultists had melted away. This, acknowledged Shadowbender, was actually a wise move. The cultists, had they remained, would have been standing exposed while their opponents, including two spell-casters and several bowmen, were concealed within the foliage on the opposite bank, well within range.

The mage acknowledged their enemies may have hidden themselves or changed position and were simply out of sight rather than physically gone. The mage shrugged, whether the cultists were gone or hidden, no arrows flew across the waterway and that was the important thing.

Roland's loss was lamentable, but it was Drake (and, to a lesser degree, Oceana) who was inexpendable. The party could accomplish its objective without the rangers, the dwarf, or even... a mage. Shadowbender smiled, wryly hoping they would accomplish their objective with their mage—both of them, in fact.

Oceana stood shivering, her hood pulled over her face. Despite the cold and the soaking, she had taken in the river, the shivers were largely a result of seeing, in her memory, Bryon's grasping hand slip into the bowels of the river. She had not known the ranger well, in fact, she didn't know any of the rangers very well, but Bryon was a good man, she knew, and he didn't deserve to die unburied and unmourned so far from his home. The man was barely middle-aged and should have yet had a number of warm summers beneath the boughs of the greenwood to sing and walk and ponder the knowledge of the wise followed by the slow decline that was the fate of humans until death gently carried him out of the waking world. Then, he should have had some friend, possibly one of their present companions, to bury him beneath the mould accompanied by sweet songs to whatever god the ranger venerated, and a stone erected in remembrance to one who had once lived. She knew it was not to be; the elves knew the Whitefoam rarely gave up its dead this far north.

Drake, an idea coming to him, laid his hand on Quint's shoulder and spoke firmly but softly, "Quint, Roland pledged his life to this mission. By refusing to carry on, you're invalidating his sacrifice and dishonouring his wishes."

The ranger stood shocked and unanswering, his eyes open but displaying no evidence of sight. Drake put his left arm around Quint, took the rangers hand with his right and led the stumbling man deeper into the forest. Shadowbender, Oceana, and Alan the Forester followed. Erik and Davyn remained behind the others as rear guard.

A number of paths, presumably made by animals approaching the river, wound around the immediate area and served to obscure the true path. Keeping a wary eye out for cultists behind them and across the river, the far side of which was frequently exposed to view, the party took several of these paths in error before the rangers correctly identified the continuation of the path they had been traversing over the past day or so.

Once the path had been located, they were able to proceed at a moderate pace. The bard was wounded, and everyone was fatigued physically and affected emotionally by the death of the two rangers and loss of the dwarf during the river crossing. A brief halt was made during which Drake's shoulder was attended to by a weepy-eyed Oceana, but the rangers were desperate to put more distance between themselves and their pursuers. Thus, after a brief respite, the group resumed travelling.

Fortunately, the path more or less followed the waterway and was, therefore, relatively easy to traverse, an advantage somewhat counterbalanced by patches of heavy undergrowth the men had to cut through and, once, a blockage caused by a huge accumulation of flotsam where the river curved and flooded when the water level was high, which caused them to expend time and effort clumsily climbing over it. To further add to the misery of the party, Shadowbender managed to twist his foot on an unseen root; the mage limped on, but the party was forced to slow its pace in order to permit the mage to keep up.

That night, after it had grown too dark to safely proceed, they sat without a fire, thinking about the cost of their quest, hitherto. They hadn't even reached the Vale of the Wyrm and they had lost Roland and three of the rangers. Each hoped the price that had been paid was enough and one ranger, in particular, thought the price much too high.

The next morning, the party arose stiff and aching, cold mist from the nearby river clinging to their cloaks and damp hair. Instinctively, they knew the last leg of their journey was before them. They were tired, heartsick, and running low on food, but their determination was undented. They started out resolved to put an end to their quest and, if they were lucky, to return to their normal lives. Fortunately, Shadowbender's foot, having been tended skilfully by Oceana, was almost completely healed and the rest, though far from complete, had benefited them all, refreshing them mentally, if not physically. They set off at a rigorous pace, feeling certain the cultists knew where they were heading. The cultists would know a faster way, if one existed, and Shadowbender felt it imperative they arrive before the cult. If the cultists arrived first, they would not find it too hard to guard a cave entrance against four tired rangers, two elves, and a bard.

During the day, they allowed themselves no real stops, only periods of slower walking during which the companions regained their strength as best they could and ate cold rations and drank water from their water skins as they trudged along. The thrashing of the river interfered with their hearing and the rangers were worried the cultists would take advantage of the noise to come upon them unaware. Davyn had them walk with their weapons drawn. The men also worried about Oceana keeping up with the brutal pace, though they soon learned it was actually the frail Shadowbender they should be worried about as Oceana, though not as hardy as the humans, was certainly hardier than her brother. Breath was at a premium at such a pace and they tramped along silently. Alongside them, as the miles slipped past, the banks of the Whitefoam progressively narrowed.

"Aha!" thought Roland as the rope strands parted. Clumsily, he freed his hands. He looked around pensively, but no one had noticed. He managed to free his legs despite the tingling in his hands and fingers. The cultist nearest him was still sleeping. All the others he could see appeared to be asleep or focused elsewhere. Across the clearing, one of the cultists stirred, rolled over, and seemed to settle back into sleep. After a minute or so, he regained normal feeling in his extremities and he flexed the tired muscles to stimulate them. Roland took a deep breath. He was free.

Roland briefly entertained the idea of grabbing a weapon from one of the sleeping cultists and killing every one of them. Then, there would be no one to follow him and he could increase his personal renown. It irked him to think of leaving living enemies at his back; after all, a true dwarf left only the hordes of the dead in his wake. Prudence, however, seemed the better part of valour in this case. He *was* at a bit of a disadvantage having been nearly drowned, tied up for a day and, therefore, stiff and hungry. He was also weapon less and outnumbered. Of course, the real reason he didn't attack was lack of time. He had to find out if his friends were alive and, if so, where they were. All the inherent carnage of killing the cultists would eat up too much precious time. Assuming the party continued on without him (as inconceivable as *that* seemed), they were a full day, more or less, ahead of him. He had a lot of ground to cover.

Stealthily, at least for a hungry, weary, and stiff dwarf, Roland snuck out of the firelight and into the surrounding wood. He waited anxiously, listening to the incessant yammering of the nocturnal insects Quint always found so pleasant—the ranger was stupid like that--until his eyes grew accustomed to the inky darkness. Then he set off. Breathlessly, he crawled into the surrounding forest trying his best to avoid the inevitable rustle of leaves and snapping of twigs. He knocked his head on a low limb and was struck in the eye by a twig. Trying to maintain stealth, Roland managed to quell his desire to scream and beat the offending tree mercilessly. Once he moved far enough away that he assumed he wouldn't be heard, Roland began to run.

Dwarven stamina is legendary. None of the other races can match a dwarf in tireless, ongoing effort. Humans, with their longer legs, can run faster for shorter periods of time, but few are the humans who can run as long. Elves can match the pace if unencumbered, but dwarves had been known, in times of war (and, with dwarves, virtually all the time was a time of war), to regularly march or even run for days at a time fully armoured and with full packs. This indefatigable endurance was well demonstrated by Roland on this night. He ran until morning dawned, stopping only once to slake his thirst at a rock spring.

The site of the river ambush was well behind. He didn't even have to stop to inspect the area. Some of his party had survived and their path was easy to follow. By his reckoning, he was less than half a day behind them. They were moving steadily, but not particularly swiftly, and appeared to be making no effort to conceal their trail.

Whether they did this for his benefit or because they felt stealth no longer necessary, Roland didn't know (and, really, he didn't care). Over time and by piecing together the various footprints, Roland could tell both elves survived as did five humans. Happily, he recognized Quint's print from long association, thought he didn't know to whom the other three belonged. Hopefully, one belonged to Drake as he was fairly inexpendable in this little jaunt. Roland ran on, anxious to rejoin his friends.

"Are you sure?" the leader of the cultist hunters peered through his mask at the breathless runner before him. He could sympathize with the runner. Once, he had been a low-ranking member of the cult and had served as a runner on several occasions. The distance between the runner's home camp and his own camp was some miles and the terrain wasn't kind to runners. His thoughts, however, were more focused on the runner's missive than the runner's comfort. Various cultist groups were out on patrol due to the warning they had received regarding infidels possessing the forbidden knowledge of the song that would disrupt the balance once more and force the noble dragons into unnatural slumber.

To be effective, cultist groups needed to communicate. They used, in general, smoke signals, carrier birds, and runners. Under the current circumstances, smoke signals were a bad choice as they would alert any intruders as to the presence of the cultists. As of late, messenger birds and runners were at a premium. This particular runner had come from his subordinate who had, luckily, captured an invader and questioned him. It would be up to him to decide upon a response.

"Yes!" the other gasped, "quite sure." "So," said the first in an awed and edgy voice, "the dwarf verified they're heading for the Vale, after all. They *do* have the canticle and they intend to use it." The man grew silent, touching his fingers together as he contemplated. The runner, not at all interested in irritating his superior, quietly took the opportunity to catch his breath.

"Send a message to all the brothers within two days' forced march," decided the leader, "and have them converge upon the cave. Send a pigeon to the guards at the cavern and tell them to expect intruders. Send a second missive to His Highness detailing our plans."

"Yes, sir!" replied the other crisply before he started to run off.

"Oh, wait!" said the captain, "I almost forgot. Prepare my own company. I think it's time to deal with this foe personally."

The party continued on, taking only brief rests. The trail, as the Grey Man had indicated, continued to run essentially parallel to the river. It appeared to have been better travelled (and slightly wider) in the past though it was obviously still used by animals.

Occasionally, a startled deer or fleet elk bolted from the path at their approach. Much to the disappointment of the rangers, they didn't have the time to hunt or prepare venison. Oceana was glad, however. Deer were much too cute to be killed, though she'd eat venison as long as she didn't have to be a witness to the preparation. Shadowbender and the bard seemed uninterested and trudged along wordlessly.

On the second day since the ambush, in the late afternoon, Alan approached Davyn. Alan was rear guard, staying a few hundred yards behind the party (Erik was the point man, remaining the same distance ahead.) Concerned with the noise of the river and the increasing likelihood of encountering enemies as they approached their goal, Davyn was taking no chances and had thus arrayed the surviving rangers so there would at least theoretically be some warning should they should they encounter an enemy.

"Someone's behind us," Alan said quietly, but not secretively. Quint stopped.

"Deal with it," said Davyn, "we'll pick up the pace."

"Okay," replied the other. He stopped and drew his bow, letting the others go on. Wordlessly, Quint remained.

"Speed up!" Davyn urged as the bard passed. "Don't throw your life away," Davyn added to Alan, "if they're too many, try to lead them away from us, but you survive—understood?"

"Yes, sir," said Alan.

"Why've you stopped?" Davyn gently asked, turning toward Quint.

"I'm staying with Alan and facing whatever's coming!" said Quint, his hands clenching and eyes gleaming brightly.

Davyn glanced sadly from Quint to Alan, "Quint is going to stay, as well," he said simply. Turning, Davyn continued down the path at a quicker pace with the others.

Alan noticed Davyn didn't say anything about 'surviving' to Quint. When the other man approached, and Alan saw the look in his eyes, he understood. Alan drew his bow and camouflaged himself in a clump of laurel. Despite his having a bow, Quint drew his sword and concealed himself behind a tree just off the path. The ranger was going to kill everything he could lay his hands on and he wanted it to be personal and active; thus, the preference for the sword when a bow would serve much better. Alan had seen the blood lust before and made a mental note not to get near Quint during the pending combat as men in such a state often unknowingly killed allies in their fury. Alan just hoped there weren't many enemies approaching; that way he and Quint might eliminate them all and give Quint a chance to survive as the man would probably refuse to retreat if the battle turned against them. Hearing a branch snap nearby, Alan knocked an arrow; they were approaching.

No. *It* was approaching, Alan realized; by the sound, it was one individual. Alan waved at Quint and held up one finger. Quint, apparently oblivious, gave no indication he even noticed the motion. Whoever was approaching was running and, by the sound of it, would soon come into view. Quint heard it, for the ranger's knuckles went white around the pommel of his sword and his teeth gritted in rage. Alan felt sorry for whatever was coming.

A few moments later, a panting figure came into view. Alan relaxed his hold on his bow and smiled. By all the gods, it was the dwarf!

A few hours later, it was a happy group that gathered around a small, virtually smokeless camp fire. Shadowbender, of course, had objected to the blaze, but was cowed by both Quint and Oceana, both of whom felt Roland needed the direct comfort of warmth and indirect comfort of hot tea and hot water to treat his wounds. The latter task was attended to by Oceana. Meanwhile, Roland told of his capture and subsequent escape, giving the details twice to satisfy Shadowbender's numerous questions.

Now, fed, armed, and tended, Roland was feeling downright hospitable. Or would be, if not for Shadowbender's sulking. Quint was ecstatic to the point of near hysteria that Roland was alive and, even better, rejoined with his friends; the ranger laughed at nearly everything anyone said even if it was not funny. Roland had never seen Quint this way when sober. Oceana and Drake were glad to share in the joy and laughed at Roland's jests. Shadowbender appeared aloof if not unhappy, though he did not laugh. Davyn remarked about how glad he was to have another sword arm.

"We'll need all we can get, I think," said Davyn, "before it's all over."

"More," Shadowbender remarked.

All the men sat around smoking their pipes. Quint took the occasional puff off Roland's. Displaying his usual paranoia, the mage had solemnly warned them against smoking as the aroma, he cautioned, would certainly draw any number of evils to the camp, not the least of which was the cult of the wyrm. However, upon seeing the others ignore his advice and happily light their pipes, the mage, apparently figuring one more pipe wouldn't make any difference, resigned himself to fate and took out a long-stemmed pipe of curiously-worked ivory and smoked along with his companions.

There was no extra axe in the supplies, but Drake had an extra short sword. The dwarf preferred an axe to any sword, but it was a good deal better than nothing. Armed and reunited with his travelling partners, Roland was ready for anything. Except, of course, what was coming.

Morning saw them preparing for the final leg of their journey. The faint predawn was chilly but beautiful, the shapes of the companions barely visible in the faint light. After he and Drake consulted the map, the mage proclaimed they would certainly reach the Caverns of Sleep this day barring mischance though, as he noted, mischance was likely. Anxious to reach the Caverns, everyone packed hastily. The noise made by breaking camp covered the sound of an approaching group intent on malice.

The captain of the cultists peered through the predawn gloom. The trail the dwarf left was easy to follow, and the cultists had no difficulty tracking the group here. He had enough men to deal with the intruders once and for all. He looked to his lieutenant, who motioned, indicating all was in order. The interlopers were largely on the path with only a few to the eastern flank of his men. Silently, he gave the signal to attack.

Chapter 16

AAAIIIEEE! The screams of several dozen voices ripped through the early morning light as the cultists, weapons brandished, sprinted toward the mixed group of invaders standing shocked before them. Blood-lust and adrenaline pumped through their veins, giving them enough extra strength to move at an almost inhuman speed.

The onslaught of the cultists completely surprised the party. As the screams reverberated in their ears, each frantically tugged at his weapon in stunned confusion for a few precious moments.

The cultists, barely distinguishable from the foliage of the dark wood, swarmed toward the party. The bulk of the enemy was coming from the rear, with only half a dozen or so flanking them from the east. Davyn, more experienced in warfare than the others, had been less shocked by the screams, recovered faster, and recovered better as his immediate reaction was to take in his surroundings.

Davyn had survived many years, countless fights, and a few battles, all of which had trained him to scan the perimeter even while focusing on the visible threat. The ranger was hyper aware as adrenaline coursed through him. He realized the cultists hadn't surrounded the party as he first thought. This was certainly an error on the cultist's part unless the cultists were attempting to herd them; the error could have been unintentional but, with the arrival of dawn, it was likely the cultists chose to spring the attack prematurely rather than allowing the light to expose them.

Almost instantly, Davyn sized up the two sides and realized his party was out-classed. In reflex, he had grabbed his sword and pulled it half out of its sheath, but he pushed it back in. With his own group surprised, fatigued, and spread out at a tactical disadvantage, the ranger decided flight, not fight, was the best response.

"Run!" yelled Davyn ap Gwyn. The ranger pointed north, further along the path. "Run," he shrieked, "It's a race now!" Davyn followed his own advice and, not waiting to see if anyone followed, sprinted up the path, his cloak billowing behind him.

Everyone except Oceana and Shadowbender complied immediately, some of them dropping the packs they had been preparing and dashing off after the fleeing figure of Davyn ap Gwyn. The elves were the furthest back and, even running at the frantic speed born of fear, it was obvious to them that they wouldn't avoid being flanked. If the foremost cultists could only delay them for a moment so the remainder could catch up, all would be lost.

Thinking quickly, at a speed that even surprised herself, Oceana spread her fingers toward the foremost of the flanking cultists. Grasping a jade amulet within her robes, head bowed in concentration, she chanted a quick spell. A vine shot from the forest floor and whipped around the throat of the attacker. His sword flew from his hand as the momentum of the man caused the vine to violently jerk him to the forest floor, breaking his neck in the process with a sharp snapping sound that almost made Oceana feel sorry for him. Her spell cast, Oceana ran after the rest of the party, fully aware her brother was able to take care of himself; he could magick himself out if need be and didn't need her to remain in an attempt to defend him and possibly spoil whatever plan he might try to execute.

Ahead of her, the surviving cultists reached the fleeing party with the clash of weapons. Davyn shrieked for Drake to keep running as the ranger threw himself in the path of a cultist threatening to engage the bard. Erik Willowdale, deftly blocking a sword thrust, collided with a second antagonist and the two men crashed to the ground in a tangle of flailing limbs. Alan, Quint, and Roland viciously attacked the four remaining flanking opponents.

"Go, Oceana!" Roland cried as he cut the legs out from under his opponent. Tears filled the elf maiden's eyes as she ran. Despite the efforts of her friends, it was obvious to the woman that they would all be delayed and quickly overwhelmed by the cultists swarming from the surrounding wood. These men were sacrificing themselves in order to allow her and Drake the opportunity to escape.

Shadowbender frowned. A quick glance allowed him to see Drake and Oceana running up the path. The other party members were in a little writhing knot of combat just behind them. Shadowbender felt a stab of compassion as he realized they were engaging the cultists in order to allow Oceana and Drake to escape. Oceana and Drake might get away, but the rest of them (except him) would certainly be caught or killed. He needed to do something.

Mentally summoning the proper words and semantics, Shadowbender began a spell, smiling as he felt the magical energy course through his veins. A strong wind whipped through the wood between the mage and the approaching cultists, picking up leaves and small branches in its force. The foliage flew in the faces of the approaching cultists effectively blinding them and many fell, tripping over obstacles they could not see to avoid. All stopped moving forward and clawed at the debris covering their masks, except one, the mage noted. The leader of the cultists recognized an illusion when he saw one. Not odd, really, considering he, too, was a mage.

Whispering a short counter spell, the leaves and wind ceased before his eyes. He was mildly amused at the antics of his men tripping and swatting at leaves and debris that weren't there. He knew such a detailed illusion was a strain on even an accomplished mage. He looked at the elf and smiled; his opponent *did* seem weary and weary opponents were much easier to destroy. The elf looked him in the eye (the elf, of course, was immune to his own illusion) and the cultist nodded in mock respect. Behind the elf, he saw the last of that particular group of his men that had been engaging the intruders fall. He frowned; they just didn't make warriors like they used to.

"Shadowbender!" Quint yelled as the last of his immediate opponents was dispatched with a quick sword thrust, "let's go!" The ranger, aware of Shadowbender's magical powers and having seen the mage do strange things before, didn't seem surprised at the whipping wall of wind opposite the elf. Roland and the other rangers, having slain the cultists pressing them and having no opponents threatening to immediately impede them, sprinted off after Drake and Oceana.

"Shadowbender!" Quint called again.

"Go," said Shadowbender.

"Not without you," Quint answered.

"Yes, without me. I will have to let my spell go—they'll be after you. Go!"

With a word from the elf, the wind wall ceased. A throng of cultists gained their feet and surged forward, yelling wildly. Shadowbender jumped into the air, unnaturally attaining about twelve feet and then merely…hung there. Vastly outnumbered, Quint figured discretion was the better part of valour and he sprinted off down the path. Airborne, the mage should be fine.

"Go!" the leader of the cultists ordered to several of his subordinates who had stopped to deal with the floating mage. They hesitated for an instant before heading after their comrades who were wildly running down the path after the fleeing ranger.

"Very good," said the cultist to the floating mage.

"Thank you," said Shadowbender. The elf glanced behind him and, satisfied no one was attempting to attack him from the rear, returned his gaze to the cultist leader. This man, apparently immune to his illusion (Shadowbender, concentrating as he had been on the casting and maintenance of the spell, had not seen the cultists' counter-spell and was, therefore, unaware of the man was a wizard), would likely pose a problem.

"You know," said the cultist as he drew a thin knife from his belt, "it's almost a shame I have to kill you."

"It would be a shame to have to die," said the elf.

Suddenly, the cultist threw the knife in a spinning arc. Shadowbender, expecting this, with almost inhuman speed, plucked the knife from thin air by the handle and, in one fluid movement, flipped it back at the cultist. The man jerked aside, and the blade buried itself in the trunk of a tree and quivered there.

"I'll kill you," the cultist spat, anger burning in his eyes.

"I think not," Shadowbender replied quietly.

The cultist raised his right hand, fingers splayed toward the sky, and began an incantation. It was time to end this battle. Shadowbender frowned, realizing his opponent was a mage.

Shadowbender recognized the spell. Quickly, the elf summoned the counter spell and mumbled the words. A burst of flame erupted from the cultist's palm and rapidly engulfed his entire hand. Face creased in concentration, the man threw the fireball and the sphere hurtled toward Shadowbender.

Pushing his hands outward, a silvery globe formed just outside the elf's reach and zoomed toward the fireball. The two spheres collided in a crackle of magical energy and, in a burst of light and sparks, the two disintegrated.

Shadowbender dropped to the ground. He did not want to expend even the minute effort required to remain airborne and he needed the dexterity afforded him by being on the ground. He looked up, deflated by the knowledge his opponent also wielded magic. Arms spread wide, the cultist had already initiated another spell.

Two swords of pulsing energy appeared in the cultist's hands. With a hiss, the man threw the weapons. In an unnatural arc and spinning rapidly, the two swords flew toward Shadowbender. Quickly, the elf held up his hand in the proper gesture, bent his head in concentration, and summoned the mystic energy necessary for a spell. Shadowbender disappeared. The pair of swords passed cleanly through the space where he had been and sliced completely through several trees behind him. Such weapons, Shadowbender knew, were formed of pure energy and cut through nearly everything. They were particularly devastating in a battle as they were often cast in rapid succession in order to eliminate a wide swath of men. After a few moments, Shadowbender reappeared, having faded out of this plane to avoid the weapons he did not have the power to stop. Once launched, they moved unerringly to their target. Moving around would have been futile, so the elf had moved *out*. This deadly spell was difficult to master and the cultists' ability to cast it indicated he was a mage of some power. Shadowbender decided it was time to take the offensive.

Unfortunately, Shadowbender was an illusionist and had few offensive spells. Fortunately, he was creative, so he had no doubt he could come up with something. Unfortunately, the cultist seemed creative, as well. Blowing across his cupped hand, the cultist completed another spell, beating Shadowbender to the offensive. A vicious wind (real, this time) whipped through the clearing, throwing leaves and debris into the elf's eyes. The cultist followed the magical barrage with two spinning daggers.

Unprepared, Shadowbender was caught by the wind. He blinked rapidly as grit scratched at his eyes. Instinctively, he stepped aside as he always did when finding himself disoriented in combat. It had saved his life before and it saved his life again.

The first dagger cut his side as it passed him by, slicing through his robe and into his skin. The second dagger, due to the elf's side-stepping, missed entirely. Still blinking, Shadowbender clamped a hand over the wound. He looked at his opponent. The cultist was regarding him intently but did not seem to be casting another spell. Blood trickled between the elf's fingers. The sensation sparked a memory and an idea. Shadowbender smiled.

The cultist frowned. The elf was just standing there gripping his side and looking at him. Certainly the elf wasn't injured badly enough to interfere with his concentration to the degree it prevented spell casting. Of course, he *was* an elf and elves were supposedly the daintiest of the races. Perhaps he was too fragile to handle the pain.

Shadowbender finalized his spell with the last ingredient: his own blood. He generally did not use this particular spell because of his nominal aversion to taking life. Even now, he would not consider using such a spell without the desperation of the situation. It was vital he get back to the party; there was no way of knowing if they were caught or still running. The former was most likely; the dwarf in particular, was slow.

The cultist was completely fooled by Shadowbender's illusion. Focusing on the fake Shadowbender, he wasn't aware the real elf, invisible, had cast the complicated spell that suddenly manifested. A bright red flash as the ichor appeared a scant centimetre from his face before exploding into his eyes was the last thing the cultist saw. He jerked as the red fluid entered his eyes and hit his skin where it was instantly absorbed.

Shadowbender saw the man jerk as the blood haze erupted. Success. A twinge of regret flowed through the elf. It could not be helped, though. Shadowbender was anxious to leave; he had to get to his companions and there was nothing here he wanted to see. Concentrating, the elf again tapped into his store of arcane energy and metamorphosed into the form of a sparrow. In this new form, he launched into the air. He exited the clearing just as the cultist began to scream.

Drake wiped sweat from his eyes with his sleeve and glanced behind him. Their pursuers were still gaining on them. It seemed the cultists didn't particularly believe in the concept of giving up. Drake was in the front of the loose clump of runners that made up the remainder of the party. Shadowbender had stayed behind to cover their retreat. Drake wasn't particularly concerned about the mage as long experience had taught him Shadowbender was more than capable of taking care of himself. He was, however, concerned about the rest of them.

Oceana ran beside him, gliding along the path like a swan floating down a gentle river. She seemed full of beauty and light; her hair flowed like silk down the nape of her neck and shoulders. She seemed out of place here amidst exertion and strife and fleeing death. The talkative elf maid was silent as she conserved her air to breathe. Behind them, Quint and Roland made up the next pair. The dwarf, with his shorter legs and heavier gear, was the slowest member of the party. The dwarf puffed along like a snorting bull, a look of deadly resolve on his face. Roland was too slow and, if the race lasted long enough, the bard knew he'd be caught. Beside the dwarf, Quint loped along. The ranger was obviously capable of a faster pace but was staying beside his friend. Occasionally, he shot an encouraging word toward Roland and, frequently, he looked behind them to gauge the position of their pursuers. Coming up last were the other rangers, who were at the rear by choice. Erik Willowdale was behind Quint and Roland. A dozen or so paces behind Erik, ran Davyn ap Gwyn and Alan the Forester. Both men were originally further up in the order but had dropped back to be between the party and the pursuing stream of cultists. Should (or, perhaps, *when* was a better word) the cultists overtook them, Drake knew the rangers would turn and fight in an attempt to allow the party to escape. Drake also knew it wasn't going to work as the other cultists would simply swarm around those few the rangers might engage. It figured—this whole adventure was pretty much an exercise in futility. The bitter irony of the situation would make a great poem should he be so fortunate as to survive to write it.

Quint saw Drake look backward.

"Go on!" the ranger waved his hand forward, "Go on, we'll be fine." That was a lie if the bard ever heard one.

"We won't leave you," Drake called back between gulps of air.

"You're the only ones who have to make it!" Quint yelled back, "Go on!"

Drake glanced at Oceana. She didn't acknowledge his look and said nothing, focusing on the path before her. Quint was right, Drake knew. He raised his hand in farewell and noticeably sped up. Oceana maintained her position at the bard's side. A sparrow flew in front of him. Flitting its wings, the bird circled the bards head twice.

Chirping, the bird launched itself a bow shot ahead of Drake and dived to the ground. In a shimmer of silverish light, the form of Shadowbender appeared. Drake smiled, he *thought* the sparrow had looked familiar.

Shadowbender arose. Drake and Oceana were rapidly approaching. Behind them, the rangers and the dwarf were only paces ahead of the pursuing cultists. The elf watched as Davyn ap Gwyn and Alan drew their weapons and turned to face their pursuers. Swords drawn, the two rangers blocked the path. Half a dozen or so of the lead cultists, with insufficient time to alter their course, ran full tilt into the pair and found themselves engaged. The remainder, focused and possessing time enough to respond, swarmed into the woods and around the whirling knot of combatants and back onto the path. They were slowed only minimally.

"What're you doing?" Drake gasped.

"I am going to cause a diversion," Shadowbender answered distractedly. The elf was concentrating on his spell.

"What?" Drake said as they passed the mage.

"I am going to create a figment of their imagination," the mage stated looking down the path. Shadowbender watched as Erik Willowdale turned to face the oncoming cultists. Unfortunately, the ranger stumbled, momentarily throwing himself off balance. At exactly the wrong time, too. As Erik righted himself, the first cultist crashed into him and both went tumbling to the ground. Shadowbender smiled wryly; Erik had apparently made a career out of being tackled. None of the other cultists stopped to help the flailing cultist atop Erik Willowdale; instead, they bypassed the pair in order to chase the remainder of the party. Shadowbender frowned. The cultists knew who they were after. Looking a little further ahead, he saw Quint and the dwarf were next and would soon be engaged. Shadowbender's eyes narrowed.

The elf took a deep breath. The spell he was going to cast would be exhausting. Not only would it be complicated, it would have to affect multiple viewers. Murmuring the proper incantation, Shadowbender began his spell.

Erik Willowdale nearly dropped his sword in mid-swing. The cultist he was fighting stopped. The man stood before him staring into mid-air. He couldn't really tell about the staring part as the man's face was covered, but the posture certainly indicated such—his arms hung limp, shoulders slightly slumped, and head cocked to one side.

Puzzled, Erik frowned slightly before shrugging his shoulders. In a quick move, the ranger decapitated the cultist, creating one less pursuer. The other cultists were likewise enamoured. Briefly, Erik considered dispatching them all, but he didn't. For one, there was no telling how long the spell effect, for which he assumed Shadowbender was responsible, would last; it would be a little disappointing for them to all come back to their senses while he was in their midst. Secondly, the real point was to get away, not to eliminate the cult of the wyrm. Thirdly and most importantly, Davyn and Alan, having slain their opponents, ran by and Davyn ordered Erik to follow. The three ran on, taking advantage of the respite.

Shadowbender watched the ranger's approach. Roland and Quint had already passed. The elf noticed Alan had been wounded; the man's left arm hung limp at his side, blood running down his hand and dripping off his fingers to splash onto the leaf litter of the path below. Behind them, the enraptured cultists began to stir. Everyone ran on. Twice more, Shadowbender created an illusory diversion and, twice more, the cultists were slowed, but not stopped. Alan's wound was growing worse. On the run as they were, they had no time to attend to it properly. Davyn did what he could under the circumstances, which amounted to wrapping a wad of cloth around the wound in an attempt to apply pressure to the wound, but the man couldn't stop the bleeding. Alan began falling behind.

Drake and Oceana, running at a near-sprint, had outdistanced their companions by several hundred yards, at least.

"There!" Drake cried happily, pointing across the small valley. Clearly visible in the rocky mountainside ahead, was a large cave entrance. The bard had never been happier to see anything in his life.

"The others?" Oceana queried.

"I don't know," the bard replied looking back down the path, "I suppose we could wait for them," (he didn't mention the possibility none of them would be coming), "or, we can go on. I don't know which would be best," though the bard was fully aware going on was the logical choice.

"I think we should wait," said Oceana.

Drake didn't want to upset the elf maid, if possible, though he was more concerned with what he should do regarding their personal safety. He, too, wanted to wait for the others. However, if their companions didn't make it, they would've wasted their opportunity to enter the Caverns of Sleep without the wyrm cult crawling around. Heart won over head, eventually, bolstered as it was by the desire of the elf maid. Drake and Oceana found a hiding place just off the path and settled in to wait.

After an indeterminable time, the bard could detect the sound of approaching runners. Hopefully, his friends were making the sounds. A fleeting regret over not having a bow coursed through the bard though, if he were to regret anything, he should regret *Oceana's* lack of a bow as the elf maiden was a much better shot as she often relished demonstrating on the targets the two of them occasionally set up in the clearing surrounding Shadowbender's Tower. A movement caught his eye and the bard smiled widely as Shadowbender crested the hill at the edge of the valley.

After a few moments, the rest of the party straggled into view. Alan was leaning on Erik Willowdale and was stumbling heavily. Blood soaked the man's left sleeve and tunic. He was unnaturally pale and breathing raggedly and Drake winced, knowing the ranger's life was seeping away before him, drop by drop.

Roland pointed back down the trail from whence they came. The cultists were moving into the valley.

"Go!" Shadowbender urged, "We are almost there!" The elf saw the cave entrance across the valley and felt increasingly frustrated as he thought about being so close and (possibly) not making it. Stress and fatigue had taken their toll on the mage. The fight with the cultist wizard had sapped much of his arcane energy and the spells he had cast during their subsequent flight had virtually expended the remainder. The short and rather disappointing fact was Shadowbender did not have any magic left until he rested and studied.

"Aha!" a voice shouted from the woods to his left. Two forms emerged from a leafy hiding place as the elf drew his dagger in surprise. Shadowbender lowered the weapon and a smile crept over his face as Drake and Oceana emerged from the wood. Knowing both of them as well as he did, it was no surprise they had forfeited the advantage of distance the other party members had so dearly bought by waiting for the rest of them to catch up. Shadowbender was too happy, however, to see Drake and his sister alive to be upset over their foolishness.

"Shall we proceed to the cave?" Drake bowed in mock formality.

"Yes, I quite think we shall," Oceana replied, mimicking the tone.

"Yeah, well—you'd better hurry," said Roland as he charged by, "the cult freaks aren't far behind."

"How's Alan?" Oceana asked, concern creeping into her voice. The elf maid looked at the ranger and his wounded arm.

"No time for it now, lass" said Roland, "if we're to get there, we'd better go."

As if on cue, the first of the cultists topped the hill. Seeing the party, he let out a yell and kept on running. The yell was repeated by a chorus of voices from the other side of the hill. The party began running what would be the last mad dash for their goal: The Caverns of Sleep.

Chapter 17

"Go, go, go!" Davyn called, pushing Drake and Oceana forward and running himself. Most of the party, those who were able, complied and ran frantically along the path. Alan and Erik lagged behind.

"Go," Alan said to Erik Willowdale.

"Not without you," Erik quipped limping along with grim determination. Ahead, the other party members disappeared into the forest. He didn't know how in the world he was going to drag Alan the Forester all the way to the Caves before the cultists caught up with them, but he was sure going to try.

Once, when Erik was still in his teens, he had travelled with a group of trappers into the wilds of the sparsely settled Barony of Trevor. It had been a harsh winter and the group had been eager to accumulate their goal in pelts and get out before weather prevented travel. Fortunately, fur-bearing animals had been abundant. Thus, the group had experienced great success and had quickly accumulated as many pelts as they could transport. Winter had set in and snow blanketed the ground, requiring snowshoes for ease of travel, but not deep enough to prevent egress. They set out for the civilized lands with full sledges and high hopes of profit from the sale of the furs.

Unfortunately, Erik had slipped on a rock during a river crossing, breaking his left leg and thoroughly dousing himself in the watercourse. His companions had set the leg and tended him, but Erik had taken ill and lay in a burning fever for several days. In the end, the trappers had elected to abandon a sledge-full of furs in order to use the sledge to haul the wounded ranger. This was a costly choice in itself but, when they had pulled Erik to the nearest village, they had then sacrificed several valuable pelts to pay the village healer to nurse Erik back to health. Erik had decided he would repay these men, at least in spirit, and vowed to never leave a companion behind, regardless of the personal cost involved.

Now, Alan the Forester staggering along beside him, Erik faced a dilemma. If he stayed with Alan, they would both almost certainly be killed by the pursuing cultists, although he acknowledged there was a slight possibility the cultists would ignore the pair and pursue the others as the elves and bard were the focus of their malice. If he stayed with Alan, he would be honouring his vow but, at the same time, reneging on his promise to see the quest fulfilled. Protecting the spell casters was the point of this entire endeavour and he knew he couldn't do so if he remained with Alan; he would be abandoning the quest at a critical juncture. There were too many possibilities and he was torn in his mind as to who he should protect—Alan or the others? Briefly, he considered discarding the choice altogether and turning to fight the cultists where he stood, but he discarded the plan as recklessness. In the end, Erik decided not to decide and applied himself to dragging Alan along as if he could carry Alan to safety *and* defend the others through sheer force of will. It wasn't going to work and, though Erik had wilfully chosen to deny this fact, his companion had realized the truth and reached a different conclusion.

"Listen to me," said Alan. The wounded ranger grabbed Erik by the hair and firmly turned his head so the other had to look at him, "you're not going to make it with me. You know that. The goal is more important."

"Well…" began Erik.

"Go," said Alan, "the others need you." "I…"

"You know I'm right, Erik." Alan took a deep breath, "If you'll help me draw my sword and turn me around, I'll stay here while you go on."

Alan was right, Erik knew, but it didn't make it any easier to swallow. A sense of rage began welling within him. Alan might be right about staying behind, but he wasn't going to leave him to the cultists.

"Let's hide you in the woods and we'll get you on the way out!" Erik urged.

"They'll see us, Erik, you know that. This is the only way."

The pair stopped. With an anguish-filled sigh, Erik Willowdale drew Alan's sword and put it in the others hand, closing Alan's fingers with his own. He leaned Alan against a small tree growing alongside the path.

"Goodbye," said Erik, softly.

"Goodbye."

Erik Willowdale ran on, rage in his heart. Tears blurred the path before him and he blinked rapidly to clear his vision. Behind him, Alan summoned up the mental strength to override his physical weakness for what he knew would be his last fight.

"There's no way we're going to be able to do this," said Drake to the mage running beside him, "not with the cultists right on our tail. We won't have time to play the song!" The bard crashed through a small copse of blueberry shrubs growing across the path, grunting with the added exertion.

"I know," Shadowbender nodded.

"I'll hold the door," called Davyn ap Gwyn who was behind the pair but could hear what was being said, "me and the rangers", he continued, "the dwarf, too. We'll all hold the door while you two and Oceana enter and do whatever it is you're going to do."

"Yes," Shadowbender confirmed, "it is the best way."

"What if there are cultists inside?" gasped Drake.

"We deal with it!" Shadowbender said. Despite his sense of caution and habit of considering all possibilities, the elf had not considered cultists inside the caverns. The possibility existed, but he just could not conceive men would be living amongst sleeping dragons. Of course, stranger things existed.

The dash to the caverns was maddening. The path was barely that, a narrow ribbon of trail alongside one of the small steams that formed the headwaters of the Whitefoam. Rarely used, it was overgrown in several places. The party crashed right through the undergrowth, but this obstacle did serve to slow them down. The cultists benefited from the cleared path left in their wake and were hardly impeded by the undergrowth. Thus, the cultists continued to steadily gain on the fleeing party.

The small valley was bordered to the north by a sheer mountain range. Jagged hills enclosed the other sides, melting away into the vast wilderness in all directions. Facing the south, near the base of the mountain, was the cave. Shadowbender had a fleeting fear–what if this cave did not lead to the Caverns of Sleep? He shook off the errant thought. What difference did it make? If these were the caverns, as they should be according to the Grey Man's directions, they had arrived. If, by some unfortunate chance, these were not the caverns, then they would have a convenient place to fight the pursuing cultists. Provided, of course, there was not a bear or something inside. Soon, the cave entrance loomed above them as they approached the incline leading to the cave. Only a few hundred yards to go.

Roland glanced at the cave entrance and half-smiled. He was getting pretty sick and tired of all this running, anyway. A nice, snug cave would be a welcome change. A reverse peninsula of strong rock protecting them on three sides. It would be almost like home. Except, that is, for the dragons.

Roland desperately wished the circumstances were different. He'd keep Quint in any event and possibly the other rangers, all of whom seemed handy lads to have around in a fight. He wished to the gods, however, he could magically summon half a dozen of his stout clansmen in place of the light-boned elves and the bard, who would be valuable only to Quint if the latter could convince the bard to write some sort of epic twattle about their feats-of-arms. He and a few of his clansmen, surrounded by good, solid stone and bolstered by a nice

269

blood-rage would gleefully hack to pieces every wyrm cultist ever spawned. What a grand scene it would be—the dwarves standing immovable as the very bones of the mountain, shouting paeans to the sky, and heaping the shattered corpses of their enemies before them in homage to the gods of carnage and death and valour. On second thought, Roland decided, he'd keep the bard—it *would* be nice to have a song to commemorate such a victory.

Banishing the fanciful thought, Roland consciously brought himself back to the reality at hand. One dwarf, after all, was probably more than enough to deal with the present cultists, if only that dwarf tried hard enough. He anticipated the fight at the door. The entrance wasn't extremely wide— about twelve feet. He and the rangers shouldn't have too much difficulty holding the door and it would be enjoyable to crack a few heads. Roland had no wish to enter the mountain with the wizards to search for dragons. The cultists, though strange in their own way, were merely humans. Fighting was something the dwarf understood, not overly complicated in most cases and requiring little thought.

"Be sure to turn before you enter the darkness," called Davyn, "or you won't be able to see!" It was too bad, the ranger thought, they didn't have more of a lead on the cultists, so they could enter the cave with time to grow accustomed to the darkness and attack the cultists as the latter entered and were temporarily blinded. What a glorious occurrence that would have been. He spat. Life was so frustrating, sometimes.

The last sprint up the incline was tiring and almost everyone was fatigued. Shadowbender seemed particularly affected; the elf was leaning heavily upon his staff and panting. Drake and the elf maid were in better shape, but still appeared winded. In fact, only the dwarf seemed largely unaffected by the exertion of their flight. Davyn and Erik turned to face the approaching cultists. They were still several thousand yards behind. Roland joined them. Quint, however, hesitated for an instant, glancing nervously at the gaping mouth of the cave, "You sure you don't want me to go with you?" he asked Drake.

"No," Drake smiled, "the immediate problem is there;" he motioned toward the cultists," but, when you've cleaned up that minor detail," (the bard laughed inwardly at the unintended pun), "come in after us." Quint saluted and joined the other warriors. Davyn was arranging the surviving rangers into a semblance of order. He had drawn his sword and sunlight flashed off the naked blade as he forcefully gestured to each man's proper place in the line. Davyn was taking every possible precaution in order to enhance the outnumbered group's success; it probably wouldn't be enough, the ranger knew.

"What do you think?" Drake asked the mage.

"Proceed," said Shadowbender simply.

The bard looked past the four men and saw the approaching cultists and frowned. "You think they'll make it?" he asked softly. Shadowbender shrugged, implying he did not know, but Drake knew the mage well enough to know Shadowbender thought the rangers would be overrun. He knew it, too; the four men, as fatigued as they were, stood little chance of defeating the cultists. At best, they were

271

buying himself and the elves a little precious time to (hopefully) accomplish their objective. Drake was hopeful by nature and he still felt hopeful as to he and Shadowbender successfully casting the 'Canticle of the Wyrm'; after all, they were both skilled, they worked well together, and they had prepared as much as it was possible to prepare. But Drake, as hopeful as he was, found it hard to believe he'd ever see again the four men they were leaving behind.

The cavern mouth yawned before them. Drake could see several feet into the cave where sunlight spilled into it. Beyond that was darkness and the bard knew, once they entered, he was going to be unable to see.

Oceana pulled a glass rod from her cloak. She spoke an arcane word and the rod began glowing brightly.

"I've got light," said Oceana anxiously, "what do you say we get going?"

"Absolutely," said Drake as he stepped toward the cave entrance. The elves followed. "I hope there's not a troll in here," the bard added in afterthought as the trio plunged into the darkness.

Chapter 18

Oceana blinked in the dim lighting. The cave wasn't particularly wide, perhaps a dozen paces across, but seemed fairly deep and featured many rocky outcroppings that might conceal hidden foes. Weapons drawn, Drake and Shadowbender moved past her, Drake to the left, Shadowbender to the right, to explore the interior of the cave. The elf maid took a final, pensive glance at her friends outside the cave entrance. She hoped they would all be all right. Focusing on the task at hand, she moved deeper into the cave so Drake and her brother could benefit from the flickering light of her wand. Drake, in particular, would need the light as he did not possess the dark-vision of the elves.

Drake looked around. Oceana's wand and the light spilling through the cave entrance combined to create sufficient light for the bard to see reasonably well. The cave seemed abandoned. Keeping his eyes in constant motion, Drake explored his portion of the cave. From the corner of his eye, he could see Shadowbender doing likewise with his own portion of the cave. He and the elf had adventured together before, and they slipped into the quiet efficiency and wordless cooperation of an experienced team.

Drake, unable to see as well in the dark as the elf, took primary responsibility for keeping an eye on the perimeter areas to ensure no dangers moved upon them unaware. Shadowbender, possessing the superior dark-vision of his people, was able to make out more detail than Drake could hope to discern and, as a result, the elf tended to focus more on the immediate area, seeking details. In this way, the pair maximized their ability to accurately and safely identify a given area. They worked well together though, on this occasion, there seemed little to warrant their attention. There was no sign of any occupancy, past or present, human or animal. Odd. Surely, something would claim such a convenient den. Oh-oh. The bard's eye, scanning the floors and walls, caught sight of their first obstacle. At the back of the 'entrance' chamber, two passages forked, each leading deeper into the mountain.

"Which way?" he whispered to Shadowbender. The elf was frowning. Oceana moved beside them but said nothing. Neither passage displayed any marking or device hinting at the way in which they should go.

"I suppose we might as well flip a coin," Drake muttered.

"I have a better idea," Shadowbender said, an idea dawning upon him, "one not subject to the fickle fancy of chance; Oceana—" he turned to the elf maid, "can you cast a spell telling us which path is the most dangerous?"

"Uh, well, I guess so. But why would that help?"

"What is the most dangerous thing you know?" Shadowbender urged.

Oceana smiled in realization, her eyes sparkling in the light of the wand, "Next to love-struck bards, I suppose dragons are the most dangerous thing I know."

Oceana took a small rock from the floor and set it equidistant between the two passages. Murmuring the incantation, she set her wand upon the relatively flat surface of the rock. The wand began spinning, creating a surreal effect as the glowing aura blurred as it spans, running together, creating the illusion of a glowing spinning wheel. After a few moments the wand slowly stopped to point at the left-hand passage. Satisfied with the answer, Oceana retrieved her rod and began walking toward the indicated passage.

"Just so you know," said Drake, "I resent the "lovesick bard' comment." The bard and the mage fell in with the elf maid.

As they stepped into the passage, the shouts and sounds of combat erupted from outside and reverberated within the cavern.

"We had better hurry!" urged Shadowbender. Resolved, the trio silently entered the passageway that would, hopefully, lead them to the Cavern of Sleep.

As they walked, the sound of combat progressively softened until it was no longer audible and the sound of their footfalls and the occasional sound of their breathing the only noise within the tunnel, which seemed to go more or less straight into the bowels of the mountain. Despite their trepidation, they encountered nothing; the passage appeared uninhabited. The passage was narrow, requiring them to walk in single file and even to turn sideways at one point.

"How do dragons fit through here?" Oceana murmured, "it is so narrow."

Drake stopped abruptly and turned to face the maid, "How *do* they fit through here?" he asked.

"It does not matter," Shadowbender shrugged off the question in his haste, unwilling to delay their progress.

"No," Drake laid his hand on the mages shoulder, "I'm serious…"

"What is it?" said Shadowbender, his face looking exotic in the slightly bluish light of Oceana's wand, "We are in sort of a hurry here."

"What I mean is this: *we* are required to traverse the corridor sideways. There's no way a dragon could fit through and, if a dragon can't fit through, it can't use the tunnel, and if it can't use this tunnel, no dragon will be at the end and, if there's no dragon at the end of the tunnel, we're going the wrong way."

Shadowbender frowned, "Bards are awfully wordy."

"No," said Oceana, "he's right." The elf maid chewed her lower lip in anxiety; she knew it wouldn't have been as easy as walking right in.

"Listen, both of you," said Shadowbender, "your logic is not wrong, but I would offer the possibility that the wyrms would have more than one passage to their home as a house may have more than one door. We may be sneaking in through a window or a ventilation shaft or a crack in the wall, so to speak."

"Wow," said Drake, "I didn't know mages were so wordy". With a smile, the bard resumed their course, apparently satisfied with the proffered solution.

Shadowbender went first. Drake walked a pace or two behind the wizard, close enough to aid the elf, if need be, but not close enough to be a hindrance. Her lit wand held high above her head so as to illuminate a greater area and consciously angled in order to benefit

Drake as much as possible, walked Oceana. She was rear-guard for two reasons. One, both men felt any danger, unless the cultists broke through the rangers, would come from the front. Thus, Oceana would be the furthest from danger. Secondly, as light-bearer, it was better for her to be behind Drake, so the man's vision was not impaired. Were she in front of the bard, her wand would serve to effectively blind the bard to anything in front of the group. The trio proceeded, a small circle of light in the vast darkness.

Shadowbender had considered asking Oceana to douse the light as the wand would be a very visible sign of their presence. He and Oceana could see well enough to dispense with the light, but Drake could not do without the light without having to be led like a child through the darkness. This, of course, was not a viable option and the mage decided the advantage of everyone in the group being able to see outweighed the disadvantage of potential enemies being able to see them. With any luck, they would not encounter any enemies, though Shadowbender did not have any faith this would be the case. He had travelled into the underground fairly regularly once upon a time (several times with Drake, in fact) and he knew very few of the larger underground areas of the world were uninhabited.

The passage meandered deeper into the bowels of the mountain. There were frequent natural recesses and undulations in the passage walls and the width of the passage varied dramatically though it never again narrowed to the point of requiring them to turn sideways. There were no actual side passages. Drake was relieved; sometimes, the fewer choices, the better. After ten minutes or so, the bard noticed something gleaming just outside the circle of light centred on Oceana in what appeared to be a natural widening of the passage. The bard moved to see what it was. He heard Oceana gasp as the light fell upon the source of the gleaming.

In a widened, roughly semi-circular section carved out of the passage, was a monument of some sort: a circle of yellowed skulls, all apparently human, faced inward toward a six-foot-long dragon skull. Two large rubies filled the eye-sockets of the dragon's skull and this was what had produced the gleaming.

No one spoke immediately.

"What is it?" Oceana whispered after a bit.

"It's a group of human skulls encircling a dragon skull," the bard replied.

"I know that, Drake," the elf slapped the bard gently on the shoulder, "I mean, what is it for?"

"Who knows?" he replied, "Shadowbender?"

"I do not know."

"Take a look at those rubies, huh?" said Drake, "What do you think they're worth? They'd make a nice pair of earrings, Oceana."

"Forget them," said the mage. Shadowbender moved cautiously around the circle of skulls to where the passage continued on the other side. "Come on!" he beckoned. Oceana complied. With a final admiring glance at the sparkling stones, Drake walked on taking his place as rear guard.

The bizarre monument was both chilling and cheering. Chilling because it was eerie. A strange fascination danced within the rubies as each seemed to faintly glow in its own luminescence. To varying degrees, all three felt a compulsion to inspect the jewels, though the urgency to accomplish the mission proved stronger than this compulsion. Shadowbender recognized the compulsion as magical in origin and, because of this awareness, was able to resist the allure with more ease than the others. The monument was cheering in a macabre way as the mere presence of such a monument directly indicated the presence of the Cult of the Wyrm and, by extension, indicated they had, indeed, selected the correct passage in the entry cave. Beckoning the others forward, Shadowbender plunged deeper into the passage.

After a little while and a confusing series of turns, what appeared to be a large chamber opened before them. Silently, the trio approached the cavern. Halting at the edge of the opening, they peered around. The light radiating from Oceana's wand illumined well enough for them to see clearly for about fifteen feet. Nothing seemed to be within that area. The cavern, if this was what it was, went further past the circle of light. The floor was nearly smooth; and unusual feature in a cave. Drake stepped beside Shadowbender and prepared to enter the area but was stopped by the elf.

"Something is not right," warned Shadowbender.

"What?" asked Drake.

"I do not know," Shadowbender admitted, "but something is not right."

"What do you want to do?" Oceana asked.

"I," said a voice from the darkness, "would definitely surrender if I were you."

The cavern flooded with light, nearly blinding the startled trio. With a clanging of metal, Drake whipped out his sword. Blinking in the sudden light, they saw a dozen or so masked cultists about a bow shot away in front of them. The light came from torches in iron sconces placed strategically around the cavern. None of the cultists were near the torches, however, indicating they had been lit via some sort of magic. Oceana allowed her wand to wink out and replaced it in her belt, freeing her from the effort of keeping it lit and freeing both hands.

The cavern itself was impressive. The roof was thirty feet high. In places, stalactites hung down like giant teeth. The cavern floor extended to where the cultists stood. Behind them, a cliff or gorge yawned between the section where everyone stood and another section of floor on the other side. Spanning the gorge was a plank bridge about four feet wide and twenty feet long. The cultists, of course, stood squarely in front of the bridge.

"I'm about tired of cultists," muttered the bard, "*and* bridges."

"Is that any way to greet your hosts?" said the foremost cultist. This man, the companions noted, wore a different coloured mask than the others clustered behind him and they assumed he was a leader of some type.

"There's obviously been some sort of mistake," offered Drake, "because you seem to think we're your guests."

"You are," said the other, "we've been expecting you."

"Really?"

"Yes," the man confirmed.

"Oh," said the bard. He was going to say something witty, but glibness had quite escaped him.

"Take them," the man said almost distractedly, waving vaguely in the direction of the trio. The cultists under his command leapt forward.

There was no time for this! With a blood-curdling scream, Oceana, teeth gritted in concentration, threw her arms forward, unleashing an emotion-enhanced blast of magical energy. Two of the cultists were flipped backwards as if slapped by a giant hand and flew screaming over the edge of the gorge and out of sight.

"That's our cue!" said Drake to Shadowbender. The bard, brandishing a dagger and short sword, ran toward the approaching cultists. Shadowbender drew a dagger and, in one fluid motion, threw it at one of the cultists. He missed. He frowned briefly as his dagger disappeared into the darkness of the chasm. Not wanting to leave Drake unsupported, Shadowbender followed the bard's mad careen toward the enemy. Now, if only he could figure out what to do once he got there.

The leader of the cultists stood back while his underlings charged. His eyes widened slightly in surprise when the elf maid magically assaulted two of his men. He had found an opponent worthy of his attention; this was obviously the elven spell-caster of which his superior had warned him. It would be nice to engage a worthy opponent. Reaching into a pouch, he dipped his fingers into specially-prepared ashes. Removing his hand, he began the spell, staring at the elf maid. Just as she was beginning to run after her companions, the first of three small round balls of crackling fire appeared in the cultist's hand. In rapid succession, he threw the fireballs at the elf maid.

Oceana, focused as she was on running, saw nothing but a blur of light before she felt the pain. Something slammed into her with enough force to knock her backward several steps. A second impact left her teetering. She realized she was on fire; she could smell the acrid fumes of her clothing singeing. Then, the third fire ball hit her squarely in the chest, flipping her backward to sprawl on the cavern floor.

Drake met his first opponent. Agility is one of the many skills a good bard possesses. He used his to nimbly duck the swinging sword of the first cultist and, without stopping, ran his short sword into the man's chest, grunting in satisfaction at the impact. With his dagger, he parried the blow of the next man in line. Adrenaline flowed through him and it seemed as if he were moving twice as fast as the cultists. He was like some hero of yore cutting a swath of devastation through his foes. Swimming in battle-lust, he ha-ha'd and ho-ho'd his way through four of them before the fifth caught him in the face with the hilt of his sword. Drake dropped.

Shadowbender was only a few paces from the bard. It might as well have been a mile. The elf was fighting frantically with his staff. He was connecting rather frequently but wasn't inflicting a lot of damage. One lucky blow had downed a cultist, but the others were closing in.

The leader of the cultists strode toward the whirling knot of men. The mage was out of the way. On to the next task. He smiled as one of the two men fell, the dangerous one. The elf was whirling around and striking like mad, displaying lots of frantic movement, but little progress. The elf was no fighter; perhaps he was the bard.

Oceana beat at the flames surrounding her. She was winded from the impacts and frantically tried to draw her breath. The flames dissipated after a few moments and she was able to catch her breath. Specializing in water magicks, Oceana had special magicks in contingency against fire. These contingency spells were triggered by the flames and neutralized them without her having to take any action. She was still painfully burnt, but not mortally wounded; she knew she would have been dead if not for the contingencies. Her clothes still smouldering, Oceana crawled to her feet.

In an instant, she assessed the situation. Drake and several of the cultists were down. Shadowbender was desperately fighting off the rest. She had no idea why he was in melee at all and not staying back using his magic. She was unaware her brother had expended his magical energy during their flight to the caverns. The enemy wizard was striding toward the combatants and wasn't focusing on her at all. Good.

Oceana spat out a quick, but lethal, incantation. She pointed at the cultist mage but with a last-minute twinge of conscious, she altered the focus of her attack to the men around her brother.

A faint bluish ray of light shot from her fingers, expanding as it went. The light circumvented Shadowbender but washed over the cultists. The cultists ground to a halt, a glistening sheen of ice covering them.

Engrossed, Shadowbender noticed nothing until he struck the nearest cultist. To his amazement, the man, contrary to all reality, shattered. Still swinging, the mage realized the others, too, were not moving. As a mage, Shadowbender was accustomed to the mutable characteristics of reality and he was not as fazed as a non-mage would have been at the bizarre occurrence. It was relatively obvious Oceana was responsible for the magic and the mage noted with no little satisfaction that the spell was impeccably done; Oceana was a worthy pupil. The spell, he knew, not only covered an opponent with ice, it turned all the moisture within a body to ice temporarily. With a few quick (and enjoyable) strikes, he shattered the others and sombrely looked at the shards of cultists at his feet. That was going to be nasty after the spell wore off and the men's flesh regained its natural characteristics.

A shriek reverberated throughout the cavern. Enraged at the loss of his men, the cultist leader snatched a four bladed disk from within his robes. With adrenaline enhanced speed, he threw the disk at Shadowbender. With a cry of pain, the elf went down, bent in two where the disk had sunk into his abdomen. Snarling, the man turned to face Oceana.

The elf maid shuddered as a wave of fatigue washed over her. Powerful spells were physically (and often emotionally) draining. She saw Shadowbender fall and a cry of anguish wriggled through her clenched lips. Anger flowed through her, partially offsetting the fatigue. She hoped it would be enough.

The cultist withdrew two more of the oddly shaped disks, one in each hand, and threw both with deadly accuracy. The elf maid flicked her wrists and both disks veered several feet and embedded themselves in the cavern wall. The elf wasn't a novice, he noticed; she seemed to have a broad range of abilities and, possibly worse from his standpoint, a quick mind. He cast a protective spell before proceeding.

Momentarily stalling, Oceana threw three daggers in rapid succession. The daggers whirled toward the man. The cultist nimbly leapt aside. He kept coming. Throwing caution to the wind, Oceana unleashed the ice spell again. A ray of light shot from her finger and sped toward the cultist. Instead of freezing him, however, the beam hit an obviously magical barrier. A sphere of bluish light coalesced around the cultist before bleeding harmlessly into the atmosphere around him. Oceana cried out in frustration. The cultist kept coming.

"Oh, no!" Oceana gasped. The second wave of fatigue was more intense or, at least, weakened already, she felt it more intensely. Oceana fell to her knees. She looked up through dangling strands of sweat-drenched hair: the man was still coming. Oceana sought desperately within her mind for something that would stop her attacker. If the cultist had cast the spell she thought he had cast, a relatively simple spell was all that was needed to nullify it. Unfortunately, Oceana didn't have the proper spell components or the strength to cast it. Shaking and unable to defend herself with magic, Oceana drew her last remaining dagger and waited.

The man smirked as he approached the elf maid. Defiance shone in her eyes. He smiled. He was familiar enough with combat to detect despair swirling beneath the veil of defiance. It was almost a shame to kill such a worthy adversary. Almost. He drew his last throwing disk. The elf maid was obviously exhausted. She hadn't dispelled his magical protection, so he assumed she *couldn't* do so. Thus, he essentially faced a merely physical opponent. She was visibly exhausted and distraught. He'd make short work of her. His shadow fell across the elf maid. With a passing twinge of regret that she couldn't see his sneer behind his mask, he raised the weapon.

A shudder raced through the cultist. With only the sound of a faint exhalation, the cultist slowly, quietly fell to his knees. His wide eyes looked at Oceana, amazement swirling within them. Slowly, he toppled over onto the elf maid who, amazed and exhausted, failed to move out of the way.

With some difficulty, Oceana caught the man. With him leaning forward into her, Oceana saw the reason for the man's strange behaviour: the hilt of a sword emerged from the man's back. Confused, Oceana looked up. Standing about twenty feet away, Drake smiled wanly. She couldn't believe he had *thrown* the sword. And connected. Actually, she could see the bard was still somewhat unstable, swaying slightly, the after effects of a head bashing, and he had thrown the blade in a last-ditch effort to save her. And, by the gods, he had done it.

Oceana and Drake stood over Shadowbender. He had been hit in the abdomen and two of the blades on the oddly shaped throwing disk had sunk deeply, their angle making it impossible to remove them without inflicting more damage. It was a wicked weapon, designed to inflict injury upon impact and removal. Shadowbender was conscious but was weakened by blood loss.

Drake knew the disk would have to be removed and he grimaced in sympathy, "What's that?" he asked hastily, pointing behind Shadowbender. The mage tilted his head to see what was the matter. Swiftly, the bard grabbed the disk and, before the elf even realized what was happening, he jerked the disk from the mage's abdomen.

Shadowbender and Oceana both screamed. The mage placed a thin hand over the wound to staunch the blood. His face was pale, and his lips were nearly white, blood stained his robes to the hem and trickled into the dust of the cavern floor.

"You gonna make it, old man?" Drake asked.

The mage nodded. Oceana wiped tears from her eyes, knelt, and hastily began binding the wound.

"You think you can go on?" the bard queried.

The mage blanched, but slowly nodded.

"He's not going to make it, Drake," said Oceana, concern clouding her features.

"No..." began Shadowbender.

"No," chimed in Drake, "she's right. We'll leave you here and continue on. It can't be much further. We'll pick you up on the way back."

"Do you think you'll be safe here?" Oceana asked her brother as she finished binding the wound.

Shadowbender nodded. Oceana looked expectantly at Drake. The bard nodded and began walking toward the chasm. Oceana squeezed Shadowbender's hand in a silent farewell and followed the bard.

"Well, here we are," said Drake. The bard propped his palms on his hips and looked dolefully at the obstacle before them. A rickety plank bridge spanned the chasm.

"Here we are," Oceana echoed.

"I sure hope this crossing goes better than the last," the bard forced a laugh. Oceana said nothing, looking back toward Shadowbender, anguish etched on her face, "Do you think he'll be safe from the cultists, here, Drake?"

"Of course," Drake lied, "any cultists are still further within the caverns and their attention will be focused on us. Shadowbender will be fine."

Silently, Drake mounted the bridge. He sighed in relief. Despite its rickety appearance, the plank seemed sturdy enough. He stamped on it several times, testing its solidarity. It seemed strong. Indicating the elf maid should wait, the bard set off across the chasm. It was a harrowing experience and one the bard wished he didn't have to face a second time, though the return trip (if there was one) would prove that hope false. He took a deep breath when he stepped onto firm ground on the other side. Oceana followed him across. She took one last look back at Shadowbender, who was not moving, before she and the bard continued deeper into the mountain.

They faced another choice when two tunnels branched off the original passage. Only one tunnel seemed large enough to accommodate a creature larger than man-sized and the pair opted to travel it. Earlier, Shadowbender had offered the logical stance that the dragons could have an entrance to the mountain elsewhere and a large tunnel didn't necessarily mean they were in the correct tunnel. But, of course, thought Drake, Shadowbender wasn't here and they were going to take the largest tunnel just on general principle. He only hoped his reasoning was sound.

It was. Now, the bard and elf maid stood deep within the mountain on a small ledge overlooking an immense cavern. The torch Drake had lifted from the battle-cavern was a tiny pinpoint of light, like the tiniest visible star in an inky night sky. A musky reptilian odour pervaded the entire cavern and even though the light from the torch was absorbed into the encompassing darkness without revealing anything to his straining eyes, Drake knew they stood within the Cavern of the Wyrm. Sound rose from below them, *way* below them, he guessed—shuffling and the occasional snort. If the wyrms were yet asleep, they were restless and fitful.

"Kill the torch," Oceana whispered. Wordlessly, Drake complied. Darkness blinded the bard. Oceana was blinded as well, but not from the darkness; the elf maid had closed her eyes. After a minute or so, she opened them. Elves possessed dark-vision, a trait that allowed them to see heat and cold when not impaired by a light source. It was for this reason she had asked Drake to extinguish the torch.

Oceana looked across the cavern and gasped. Faintly, her dark-vision picked out form after reptilian form of sleeping dragons. Hundreds carpeted the floor as far as even her dark-vision could distinguish. Many were stirring, and her heart sank at the thought of them awakening.

"It's the wyrms, Drake!" she whispered in a frightened tone, sinking to the floor in a swoon of emotion.

Wordlessly, the bard relit the torch. Oceana's dark-vision was nullified; she was almost glad she couldn't see the hideous forms, although knowing they were there when she couldn't see them was no less terrifying.

Quietly, Drake removed his backpack. Kneeling, he deftly unbuckled the flap and began rummaging through it. He removed his copy of the 'Canticle of the Wyrm', spread it on the floor bracing the four corners with small rocks, and, with larger rocks, built a makeshift prop for his torch, and stabilized the torch within it. He looked at Oceana,

"You have any preference as to the instrument?"

"No" she shook her head hurriedly. Shrugging, the bard withdrew his mandolin from his pack and loosened his fingers.

290

"Well," he said in a slightly wavering voice, "here goes nothing."

"No," Oceana corrected, "here goes everything."

Chapter 19

The three men and the dwarf stared grimly at the approaching cultists. Roland's muscles tensed as the raw adrenaline of anticipation flowed through him and he rolled his shoulders and head in order to loosen up. No novice, he had been through hundreds of fights, but each was unique. Once, he and Quint had been forced to fight a huge club-wielding ogre during a thunderstorm. *That* had certainly been unique. But, that was then and *now* was what was important. Looking around, the dwarf sized up his companions.

To his right, Davyn ap Gwyn stood solidly clenching the hilt of his drawn sword. A slight twitch in his cheek was the only outward sign of battle rage (the dwarf had seen the ranger in action and assumed the twitching wasn't fear induced) the stoic ranger displayed. Davyn had a bow but, rather unfortunately, had no arrows left. The man held a long sword in his hand. Davyn could handle himself, Roland knew, and the dwarf was comfortable his right flank was in good hands.

On his left flank, Quint flexed his arms and loosened up, apparently so full of battle fury he was actually excited at the prospect of combat. The ranger held a dagger in his left hand and a long sword in his right. A lethal combination in Quint's hands, as the dwarf well knew. The ranger was right-handed and generally parried with the dagger though, in close combat, the dagger was at a profound advantage regarding agility and speed. Quint had dispatched many a foe with his dagger and the dwarf anticipated he would dispatch many more ere the sun set.

On the other side of Quint stood Erik Willowdale, holding a long sword; it seemed the long sword was the weapon of preference among ranger-kind. The normally reserved ranger shook with fury. Roland was surprised the vengeance burning in the man's eyes didn't drop a few of the cultists in their tracks. Erik, too, was an able warrior. The companions, although a little sparse in comparison to the approaching cultists, were all skilled warriors and the dwarf felt confident he stood with men of valour. Such men minimized the possibility of defeat and, if they were defeated, were the type of men it would be an honour to die among.

Roland flexed his own muscles, looking ahead. The cultists would be in range in seconds. Roland whipped out his borrowed sword, once again bitterly lamenting the loss of his axe. If only he had an axe, he could hold the cave entrance single-handedly. A long, eerie howl erupted from his left and reverberated within his ears. It took a few moments for him to realize the sound emitted from Erik Willowdale. About the time he realized this, Erik leapt forward, his hair flowing behind him like a mane and his teeth bared in rage and struck the first wave of cultists about fifteen feet ahead of the rest of his companions, his sword thrashing like a whirlwind.

Roland saw the ranger's mad attack. Erik's first blow broke the defender's sword as the cultist tried to parry and continued in its lethal arc and nearly cut the cultist in two. It was absolutely amazing what battle rage could do. Roland would have enjoyed watching more, but the cultists were upon them and the dwarf was soon engrossed in his own private war.

Like most combat, this was a seemingly endless chain of grunting, swinging, missing, hitting, parrying, getting hit, and jumping around. Senses were on full alert as were reflexes. Half the actions taken were made completely on reflex. For the most part, focus was on the immediate foe and the personal area within a weapon's reach. However, with all senses on alert, goings on all over the visible battlefield were recorded by the mind although generally not consciously noted.

Roland enjoyed a distinct advantage. Standing slightly above four feet tall, he was used to fighting foes taller than himself. His foes, on the other hand, weren't accustomed to fighting dwarf-sized opponents. To an armchair intellectual, this advantage seemed small. To a dwarf engaged in wild melee, it was the difference between life and death. His life; their death. The cultists, used to fighting humans, tended to swing too high, often neglected to adequately defend their lower body or, better yet, unaccustomed to the angle, would attack the dwarf awkwardly. Roland used all this to his advantage.

Dwarves, to be sure, were often at a disadvantage in human conflicts. Smaller than humans, they were unsuited to mounted combat and can't properly use lengthy weapons such as lances (which also required mounts) or pole arms. This frequently resulted in dwarves being on the losing end of traditional above ground combat. On foot, though, as was everyone presently engaged, dwarves generally decimated the taller humans who were felled by wounds to the legs and/or abdomen.

Such was the case today. Roland gutted his first two foes and ham stringed the third almost before he realized he had done it. The latter fell almost on top of him and Roland stepped backward quickly. The next cultist, also trying to step over his flailing companion, was forced to almost jump atop Roland. His sword was too high to bring into play, but he managed to kick out and catch Roland squarely in the chest with the flat of his foot. Roland was vaulted backward and landed flat on his back six feet away.

Fortunately for the dwarf, the cultist's forward momentum was halted by the impact, the man became tangled in the limbs of his companion, and both humans ended up in a heap on the ground. Roland had time to regain his feet without being hacked to pieces while he was prone.

Two more cultists bounded around the pair on the ground. Before they closed, Roland had an instant to appraise the situation. It wasn't good.

Erik was in the centre of a writhing knot of cultists. Several lay dead or dying around the melee but Roland couldn't really see what was going on. Outnumbered and unaided, it would be a miracle if the young ranger survived.

Quint was flanked, but seemed to be holding his own, wielding his dagger and sword effectively. One cultist, holding the stump of an arm, was writhing a few feet from the ranger and was, for all practical purposes, out of the fight. Quint seemed bursting with energy; he was "in his stride," as the man called it, and Roland knew the ranger was enjoying himself immensely.

Davyn was on the right flank. From the corner of his eye the dwarf saw Davyn fall. The ranger, seizing an opportunity, ran his sword through the cultist before him. The sword hilt apparently got tangled in the cultists' armour or clothing because, as the cultist fell backward, Davyn, clinging to the weapon, was jerked forward. There was a cultist on either side of the pair and both hit Davyn almost simultaneously. One ran a sword into the rangers left side. The second caught the ranger in the stomach, hitting so squarely and with enough force that Roland saw the red-tinted tip of his sword erupt through Davyn's back. Roland grimaced in sympathy; the ranger certainly wouldn't recover from that and their right flank would be undefended. Something had to be done and fast.

Screaming a dwarfish term to 'fall back', the dwarf charged the cultists before him to enable Quint to move back. Erik wouldn't know the command, but the young ranger, embroiled as he was and too far away, probably couldn't respond even if he did recognize the command. Hopefully, Quint could and would. Together, the two of them could hold the cave entrance if they could get there. Rushing the cultists was the only thing he could think of that would allow Quint the opportunity to move back; the cultists were between him and Quint and Roland wanted to keep their focus on him rather than his friend.

It seemed to work. The two cultists moved for the approaching dwarf. Roland sprinted until he was on top of them then dropped as both swung at him at his head level. Both blades whistled over his head. With desperate strength, Roland stabbed upward, catching the opponent to his right in the hip. The man screamed and, his leg giving way beneath him, toppled backward over the downed cultist. Roland kicked out and caught the other standing cultist. He connected with a sickening popping sound Roland recognized as a breaking knee and the man fell to the ground nearly on top of the dwarf. His sword was off angle due to stabbing the other cultist, so Roland bashed this opponent violently in the face with his fist. The man fell backward.

Quint jumped over all of them, turned almost sideways so as not to expose his back to the pursuing cultists.

"Let's go, Roland!" he called almost nonchalantly.

Looking up, Roland saw a horde of approaching cultists nearly within melee range. Muttering a curse, Roland leapt to his feet and ran full tilt for the cavern entrance. Quint was facing him (and the cultists) when he arrived, and the ranger covered for him, so he could turn around. Dwarf and ranger fighting side by side, it was almost like old times, Roland thought.

"It's just us!" Quint grunted, parrying two sword thrusts; he was at an advantage wielding two blades.

"I guess so," Roland said, lashing out at an enemy only to have his thrust parried.

"Just like old times," Quint sang merrily slicing the arm off one of his attackers, "only the odds are better."

Roland parried a blow but took a second hit in the ribs. He grunted in pain, though his armour spared him from any real damage. He didn't bother to reply.

They were in a good position. As good as it could get, anyway. Davyn was definitely dead; Erik presumably so. Roland couldn't see past the men before him, but there didn't seem to be any fighting going on outside the cavern entrance. The two of them could hold the cave entrance as it wasn't very wide. Roland slipped happily into the reflexive mode of a seasoned warrior and gleefully hacked and slashed at everything around him. This was beginning to be fun.

Quint lashed out with his long sword, one of the cultists had left his chest open after a missed blow. He connected. The cultist dropped his sword to grab at the wound cut across his chest. Almost in slow motion, as it seemed to Quint, the man sank to his knees and finally fell over, a hollow gasping cry emanating from within his mask. Normally, Quint would be enthused at the elimination of an enemy (especially one dispatched so skilfully), but he was too sharply pressed to feel any particular emotion other than immediate determination to stay alive.

The ranger wasn't feeling particularly hopeful. Roland was swinging away at his side, but, having had no opportunity to scan the battlefield as he had been almost continually engaged, he had no idea where Davyn and Erik were. He assumed they were dead or incapacitated; otherwise, they'd be here. Quint had already taken a few hits. One was a relatively minor cut to the arm; the other was a clip to his left cheek. The latter upset him as he had a strong aversion to facial wounds, finding visible scars, particularly visible scars to the face, unattractive.

Quint grimaced as another blow struck. A cultist, armed with a hammer, penetrated his defence and struck him a jarring blow to the ribs. The ranger heard and felt the rib crack. Quint stabbed the offender in the face; the creep deserved it.

The wound was bad. It wasn't life threatening in itself, in fact, Quint had twice suffered broken ribs in the past, but the collateral damage was high. With each laboured breath, the cracked rib shot a sharp pain through his body and he winced involuntarily. Such responses hampered movement and reflex and often spelled the difference between life and death in combat. He was instinctively taking shallower breaths; his body's natural method of avoiding pain. Consequently, he was having difficulty breathing and found it harder to focus. They needed to fall back or something. He had to have a moment to catch his breath. He started to call for Roland to fall back into the cave, thinking they could regroup there, but never got the words out.

Parrying a sword thrust with his dagger, he ran his long sword through the same assailant. A sharp pain jolted him through the ribs, interfering with his momentum. He recoiled involuntarily and was thrown slightly off balance. Before he could recover, another cultist ran a short sword into him, burying the blade almost to the hilt.

Quint looked stupidly at the blade embedded in his side. His right side went numb and his long sword fell from his twitching fingers. He realized what had happened, but he felt no pain. Wasn't it supposed to hurt? Realization dawned on him that shock had negated the pain, the body's self-defence to extreme trauma. Quint wanted to laugh—he'd seen opponents whom he had mortally wounded stare stupidly at him in numbed surprise—probably looking very much like he did at this moment. Then, another shock of pain coursed through him as someone else struck him in the head; he wondered vaguely who had hit him and why he, perversely, felt this blow and not the previous hit. Everything went black and Quint felt himself falling. He never felt himself land.

Roland shrieked in rage and grief. From the corner of his eye, he saw Quint fall. He took a glancing blow to his left shoulder, but never felt it. The man hitting him felt it, though, when Roland cut off his left leg just below the knee. As the man was falling, Roland kicked him hard in the chest, sending him careening backward into the men behind him.

Roland needed the moments afforded him. Teeth bared into a hideous mask of rage, the dwarf crushed the skull of the man who had stabbed Quint with the flat of his short sword, grunting in satisfaction at the resulting crunch. With amazing speed, the dwarf darted into the cave. The cultists were momentarily taken aback by the dwarf's vicious onslaught, giving the dwarf a couple of seconds of respite before they charged after him.

Oddly, Roland seemed almost detached. He was seething with rage, wounded, and hounded by a gang of pursuers, yet seemed to be thinking at the speed of light. He had to defend the entrance and he couldn't do that at the cavern's mouth. Inside was his only chance. If he were exceptionally lucky, the cave would be narrow. In any event, he would be more secure in the womb of good solid stone. Bolstered by the bones of the mountain, he'd make the bastards pay, when they did come, he thought.

Uh-oh. The dwarf had covered some distance, tripping and nearly falling over a stone his hampered vision failed to discern. The good news was the cave did, in fact, narrow. The bad news was it narrowed into *two* passages. He had no idea which passage the bard had taken. It didn't matter, he decided. Either one was small enough for him to defend. The cultists wouldn't know which passage his companions had chosen. He chose to defend the right because, when in doubt, right is right.

He stood dead centre in the opening of the right passage. The lighting was dim, but sufficient. In fact, the lack of light was a distinct advantage as the dwarf could see due to his dark-vision, or would be able to in only a few seconds, after his vision became acclimated to the new level of light, whereas the human cultists could not see nearly as well. He hoped the cultists had made amends with whatever paltry god they worshipped because he was about to send a lot of them to their final judgement. The cultists approached, spreading out and moving slowly across the cavern. Wisely, they were attempting to allow their own eyes to acclimate to the lighting. Roland had hoped the cultists, as zealous as they were, would come careening across the cavern before they had time to regain their vision. Unfortunately, these men were not impetuous brigands or poorly trained ruffians, they were skilled warriors and they would be acclimated to the light before they reached the dwarf. Then, Roland would be, again, faced with a fighting force with superior numbers. Roland counted the shadows creeping toward him. Seven. Surely he could hold out against only seven men, especially as he held the superior position (provided, of course, nothing came up from the tunnel behind him). He had to buy the bard some time to cast his song or spell or whatever. He had to hold the passage until all the cultists were dead or he was dead. Sighing, the dwarf realized the latter was most likely, but he still brandished the borrowed short sword like the paragon of death-dealing dwarven wrath he desperately wished he embodied.

Chapter 20

Sitting cross-legged in the torchlight on a rocky platform over an inky ocean sat Drake of Allendale and his companion. Oceana thought he looked small or, rather, considering she was nearby, *they* looked small: two shadowy forms within a small pinprick of light in the all-encompassing darkness. What if Drake couldn't play the song? What if it didn't work? They had come too far, lost too much, for the canticle to fail. Oceana looked and saw the bard was apparently praying with his head bowed and breathing rhythmically. It wasn't a bad idea, she thought. The sorceress took a deep breath and whispered a prayer to Sylvana, goddess of the elves, to whom she normally prayed, and, for good measure, threw one out to Valyanna, patron goddess of music, on Drake's behalf.

Drake sat with his eyes closed for a full five minutes, silently preparing himself for the most important performance of his career. He wasn't particularly religious, but he did have quite a bit of faith in himself and his musical ability. After some time, Drake reached that artistic point within himself where he and the music were inseparable. Becoming one with the music was enjoyable, he frequently referred to this state as "channelling the music" and the bard smiled as he opened his eyes. He still sat within the torchlight and Oceana was looking at him intently, but Drake noticed none of this; his fingers struck the first chords and the 'Canticle of the Wyrm' was begun for the first time in a thousand years.

The notes penetrated Oceana's soul and chills ran through her body; her skin crawled so intensely it almost hurt. The music floated into the darkness. Gradually, the sound began to reverberate throughout the immense cavern. It wasn't echoes, exactly, though it did sound as if the melody was being repeated over and over again, layer after layer, until the music filled the chamber, more palpable than the darkness.

The elf maid looked at the bard. Entranced by the music, Drake was staring at the scroll containing the song almost as if he were looking through it. He plucked the strings of the mandolin almost absently. Each note sliced through her brain, overwhelming the thought process. As Drake reached the second bar, Oceana had been thrown into a state of mind that seemed magical. She was aware of her surroundings, but, like a participant in some sort of astral projection, she could view but not respond to any outside stimulus.

The music swirled around her. Oceana swore she could see the notes spinning in eddies within the darkness, filling the cavern with compressing, coalescent, wispy musical notes. If she could've reached out, she could have cupped one in her hand. Slowly, the music began to pulse in colour. Green, yellow, and mostly red, the music or the sound or whatever it would be called pulsed throughout the chamber, thickening the air until it was noticeably hard to breathe. The scintillating colours, on the bright phase of each pulse, lit the chamber dimly. She realized the music itself was imbued with the magic the instrument evoked and, in the arcane light, Oceana could see the bodies of the dragons, row after row of reptilian hulk stretching into the distance.

In the midst of the lights and sound, the wyrms began to stir. Faster and faster they began moving until the floor was a hideous mass of writhing forms. By the gods, she thought, they're going to awaken! The chamber was filled with a maddening hum, the sound of Drake's music barely perceptible beneath it. Oceana wondered what it would feel like to die.

Well-versed in arcane lore, Oceana's training allowed her to consider what was occurring even as her normal senses were being overwhelmed. Good mages, those who tended to survive, were those possessing the ability to compartmentalize.

Compartmentalization was a quasi-mystical talent used by certain clerical sects as well as by wizards, though the latter used it mostly without the religious connotation. Essentially, this skill allowed a wizard to split his consciousness into two parts: one, the normal self, was still aware of normal sensations and could even think or act on a nominal basis; the other was an ethereal consciousness without form. This form could still think, however, and any thoughts, plans, or ideas engendered by the second consciousness remained when the two consciousnesses reunited.

Compartmentalization was dangerous. The original consciousness, still with the physical body, was greatly weakened, resulting in the physical body, though still aware, being largely unable to respond effectively to outside stimuli. It continued to breathe and could perform rudimentary tasks requiring little thought, such as standing or even walking slowly, but lacked the ability to defend itself or do anything requiring more than minimal concentration. The secondary consciousness also faced serious danger.

Essentially a mind with no physical presence at all, the secondary consciousness could not speak or otherwise communicate. The advantage, and the reason compartmentalization existed at all, was that the secondary consciousness was freed from the restraints of the physical body. Thus, a mage suffering great pain or otherwise distracted, could, with this ability, separate his consciousness, allow the secondary consciousness to work unimpeded, then meld the two back together and have whatever thoughts (usually a spell ready to be cast) the secondary consciousness had prepared in his mind and usable. Requiring an iron will, it was a dangerous practice sometimes resulting in insanity, but many mages felt it sufficiently powerful to risk learning. Shadowbender was one of these. Possessing an exceedingly rigid force of will, the mage had mastered the quasi-mystical practice. He also thought the procedure important enough to have taught it to Oceana.

Exhausted and drained from spell-casting, Oceana had been overwhelmed by the pulsing music, the pressing arcane energy released by the evocation of the 'Canticle,' and the raw fear spawned by the dragons, and had responded by compartmentalizing. Leaving her primary consciousness to drown in fear and overwhelming power, Oceana allowed her secondary consciousness to be free in order to keep an eye on the dragons and situation in general. Her plan had been to maintain vigilance, so the secondary consciousness could reunite with any necessary warning should the dragons reawaken. Either the 'Canticle' or the dragons or, at least, the combination of the two were too powerful or she was too weak to completely perform the procedure correctly. Whatever the reason, Oceana found her secondary consciousness was still affected (though not overwhelmed) by outside stimuli. This had never happened before and Oceana was less than pleased by its novelty.

Still retaining control of her will, Oceana looked down at the dragons writhing on the floor. None, as far as she could see, had opened their eyes, but the movement was more than sufficient to rouse the vile creatures from a normal slumber and possibly a magical one, especially one inspired by a disintegrating magical effect. The writhing, incredibly, grew more intense and Oceana felt for certain the dragons were awakening.

But the dragons didn't awaken. After a period of some time, it could have been minutes or hours or days—Oceana couldn't tell-- the wyrms settled back down. The humming gradually subsided and ceased altogether. Eventually, Drake's music was the only sound.

Smiling in elation, Oceana turned to the bard, words of praise tripping on her tongue, and gasped. Drake still sat cross-legged and still plucked the strings in skilled musical rapture. His expression was peaceful, but Oceana hadn't gasped because of his expression. The bard was paler than pale; he appeared almost bleached. All colour had disappeared from his lips and he appeared almost bloodless. Long ago, Oceana had experienced the misfortune of witnessing the victim of a vampire and that poor woman had retained more colour than the bard now displayed. Slowly, as she watched, a trickle of blood, shining brilliantly in contrast to the chalky skin, ran from the bard's nose, slid down the side of his face and dripped into the dust of the rocky floor. Oceana wondered mildly if she were bleeding, too.

With a sickening feeling of vertigo, Oceana's two consciousnesses slid back together. Her ears stopped ringing and she realized the music had stopped. In fact, her breathing was the only sound. She focused on the cavern floor beneath her. No sound drifted up. The wyrms must have resumed their supernatural slumber. The spell had worked! She turned toward Drake.

Drake of Allendale may have been alive and, in fact, was as she could perceive his ragged breathing, but he looked dead. He still appeared bloodless, though the trickle of blood still seeped from his nose and his eyes were staring vacantly at…nothing.

Frowning, Oceana waved her hand in front of his face. The bard's eyes didn't follow the movement. Oceana shook him gently and let forth a sob of dismay; the bard was cold.

"C'mon, Drake," Ocean urged tugging at the comatose bard, "wake up." Drake didn't respond.

"I need you," Oceana wailed, "I need you to wake up!" Still no response.

Oceana nervously ran her fingers through her hair. The bard apparently wasn't going to wake up. Why not? Shadowbender would be of little help and the man was far too heavy for her to carry by herself. Or was he? Oceana thought of a plan, almost genius in its simplicity.

308

She was tired, both physically and mentally. Fortunately, the levitation spell was not a difficult or draining spell to cast and, better yet, required no willpower to keep going once it was cast. It didn't last more than an hour, but that should be more than enough time to get the bard back outside; especially with Shadowbender's help.

Shadowbender shook his head curtly as if trying to clear his mind. He was hallucinating. Left by himself, the mage had simply lain still, trying to focus on breathing. For a while, he had tried to recite spells, but could not muster the necessary concentration to do so and, in resignation, he lay staring at the cavern roof. The torches the cultists had magically lit had remained burning and greatly added to this particular endeavour. Later, he had heard the strains of distant music (a mandolin, perhaps?) and he hoped the melody was a good sign. He did not seem to be losing any more blood and that, too, was good. But, now, he was hallucinating.

Across the chamber, he thought he saw his sister pushing a floating bard. Drake sat cross-legged as if frozen several feet off the ground. Behind him and pushing, stumbled a haggard and weary Oceana. Shadowbender frowned. Obviously, he was not doing as well as he had surmised. He had always understood people often experienced hallucinations stemming from blood loss and he had lost a lot of blood. Slowly, the phantasm approached.

"Are you able to help me?" the elf maid queried as she neared Shadowbender. Though he was looking at her, there was no response.

"Hello?" she tried again. No reply was given though Shadowbender was looking at her intently. What was his problem; all she needed was two non-responsive men to be responsible for.

"Shadowbender!" Oceana said sharply, "can you not answer me, or can you not hear me? I need help with Drake."

"Can you hear me, then?" Shadowbender asked tentatively.

"Of course, I can hear you," Oceana snipped. "You know, for a mage, you're pretty stupid sometimes."

Shadowbender smiled. It *was* the real Oceana.

As it turned out, Shadowbender ended up creating more work for Oceana, not reducing her nearly-overwhelming burden. The elf couldn't stand up on his own without his staff and, even with the staff, couldn't walk without aid. Thus, Oceana found herself pushing the bard with her right shoulder and half carrying her brother with her left arm. Progress was slow and Oceana could have torn her hair out in anxiety.

After what seemed like days of tedious travel, they reached the skulls they had passed on the way in. The rubies were still glowing richly in the darkness.

"I'm going to take the rubies," Oceana said deciding a little reimbursement was in order, "maybe I *will* make earrings out of them, after all."

"No," Shadowbender gasped.

"Why not?" Oceana demanded.

"I do not know," Shadowbender offered, "but it is not a good idea. There is something amiss."

"What?" Oceana demanded.

"I do not know for certain," Shadowbender answered, "but there is an unnatural compulsion surrounding them."

"Ah, I see," Oceana said with an intense jolt of jealousy, "you want them for yourself!"

"Oceana!" Shadowbender said quietly but urgently, "you know that is not true. Let them go." Shadowbender said nothing further but looked intently into Oceana's eyes. At first, Oceana avoided his gaze, but was then caught. She fought against his gaze for several seconds before Shadowbender saw defeat reflected therein. Oceana's will, bolstered by his own, was strong enough to resist the magical allure. Shadowbender let loose an almost inaudible sigh of relief he had not been aware he had been holding.

"Okay, okay," Oceana relented. They were pretty, though. While they were talking she had thought about taking one in spite of her brother's warning, and would have, but there was no way to do so without him seeing.

Oceana had no idea how long they had been walking. She plodded on aware only of the endless placing of one foot in front of the other. A watched pot never boils and destinations unlooked for arrive early. Dimly, the elf maid grew aware of a gradually heightening sound of combat. They must be getting close to the entrance (now the exit). And at least one of her friends was still alive or no combat would be taking place. She tried to increase their pace but found she couldn't coax any more speed from herself, much less the two men. She was exhausted, Shadowbender was no better, and

Drake seemed to be getting heavier. In fact, he was floating nearer the ground which meant the spell was wearing off. Soon, he would settle to the ground and she wouldn't be able to move him at all.

Oceana stopped. It would hardly do to go stumbling into combat dragging two invalids along. She left Drake floating. He was in no danger; even if the spell expired, he would gently come to rest on the ground. She helped Shadowbender sit down, his back against the tunnel wall.

"What are you doing?" Shadowbender asked.

"I'm going to see how we're doing. I'll be right back." With that, she extinguished her wand and slipped ahead through the darkness.

Oceana sighed. She had been watching for a minute and didn't like what she saw. Roland appeared to be the only defender; at least no one else had come into view. She could make out the situation clearly thanks to her dark-vision. There appeared to be seven cultists fighting with Roland. The dwarf moved as if he was injured, but astonishingly, was holding the cultists at bay. Beleaguered and weary, the dwarf, she noted, was mostly defending himself, rarely having the opportunity to strike back. This wouldn't do. They had to get out and there was no way Roland was going to slay all seven of his opponents. An idea came to her and she acted immediately.

She scrambled back to Drake and her brother. She noticed Drake had come to rest on the tunnel floor; the spell had worn off. She approached Shadowbender.

"Give me your talisman!"

"Which one?" Shadowbender asked.

"You have more than one?"

"Yes, I have several."

"I need the one protecting you from your own spell effects," she said.

Shadowbender reached into his robes and withdrew a small talisman shaped like a shield. It had magical runes inscribed around the border that glistened in the near-darkness of the corridor. He handed the talisman to his sister.

"Be careful," he warned.

"Always," she quipped. With that, she moved back toward the combat.

Oceana had no spells left. She also wasn't much of an asset when it came to physical combat though she was better at melee than Shadowbender. Still, an idea came to her about how she might aid the embattled dwarf. Her plan was a dangerous one and she knew it. She was going to shatter her spell crystal. It was the only way she could destroy the cultists and give herself and her companions a chance to escape. Oceana fingered the crystal hanging around her neck, trying to formulate a plan.

For centuries, the elves had kept the secret of the spell crystals hidden. So long ago that even the elves couldn't remember it, the elven mages had discovered the process of creating the crystals. Mages were powerful but faced a massive disadvantage in that casting spells drained them mentally, physically, and emotionally. Minor spells had little impact, but powerful ones were more draining, and it wasn't impossible for a mage to die when exhausting himself by spell casting. This, according to legend, was why Tolhalerion, considered the greatest mage in elven history, had died while magically protecting the elven kingdoms from Inlazard the Lich-King in the early days of the world. The elves dimly knew about this battle from legend and tradition; it was so long ago that men and the other races had no memory of the event. Though the details of Tolhalerion and his contributions weren't well remembered, one result of his death was: the spell crystals.

Tolhalerion's contemporaries and their descendants, blatantly aware of the mages' vital weakness, spent the following aeons developing a solution. These mages created a way to store spell energy in an inanimate object to be called forth at will. Thus, a mage could expend energy from the container rather than himself. Any object would work, but crystals were among the first used (combining function with the elves' innate love of beauty) and were, by far, the most popular and such items were called spell crystals regardless of their form. Solon the Wise, the great diviner, possessed a spell crystal that was a small, silver–trimmed looking-glass.

The spell crystals, each attuned to its owner over decades of careful preparation, were difficult and tedious to create requiring well over one hundred years to complete. Thus, only the elves used them regularly (though they were hardly common) as shorter-lived races didn't have the time for their construction. For this reason, the spell crystals were often fiercely coveted by other races as a spell crystal greatly magnified one's power. Oceana had inherited her own from her tutor upon completion of her initial studies in mage-craft. She had long studied the spell crystals and knew more about them than most, including Shadowbender. And she knew their flaw.

The flaw was the reason she used her spell crystal sparingly. If completely drained of energy, a spell crystal became inert, unable to be recharged. Also, and lesser known, a spell crystal, if broken, discharged all of its remaining power at once. The result, especially if the spell crystal was full, was awesome and very destructive. Several mages had destroyed themselves and their comrades by accidentally breaking their spell crystals. One mage had done so in the middle of a village and killed nearly everyone who lived there. As a result, most spell crystals were made from material unlikely to break (Solon's mirror being an exception). Another result of this accident was the widespread practice of mages living and practising their craft away from the general population. Anyway, Oceana's crystal was nearly full and she had a plan to use it. She had forgotten about it before or she would've used it against the cultists earlier, but she remembered it now and, considering her situation (unbelievably) was now more urgent, she was glad she had forgotten about the crystal. Perhaps Sylvana, in her beneficence, had blessed her now with the memory of the device.

Creeping back to the combat, she clasped her spell crystal and prepared her mind for the proper spell.

"Roland!" she called, "run this way and go past me."

Roland didn't immediately respond and Oceana, assuming the dwarf had not heard her, was about to repeat her request when the dwarf suddenly turned and lumbered down the passage.

Catching his eye, she called, "Run past me and keep going until you get to Drake! Don't turn around!" The dwarf said nothing but did run past her and disappeared into the darkness.

The cultists hesitated for a few moments when Roland retreated, but soon came running after him. Oceana waited until they all entered the tunnel. They showed no dismay upon seeing an elven woman rather than a male dwarf before them. They raised their weapons as they approached.

Drawing upon the power of desperation, Oceana cried out in the strange language of magic, uttering the necessary words to break the crystal (they were virtually impossible to break, otherwise) and, with all her force, slammed the crystal against a rock on the tunnel floor. She would be caught in the effect, she knew, but Shadowbender's talisman should protect her. She hoped.

The tunnel was filled with crackling light as an energy bolt leapt from her outstretched hand. The arc of energy shot from her hand and cut through the approaching cultists. The energy bolt jumped back and forth throughout the tunnel as it bounced off the stone walls. Oceana's hair stood on end and her skin crawled. The effect on the cultists was terrifying. The lightning-like energy ploughed into them and was channelled back and forth through them and destroyed them. The putrid smell of burnt flesh almost made Oceana retch, but it was all over in an instant.

Oceana ran back and got the others. Roland dragging Drake and Oceana supporting Shadowbender, the companions moved past the smoking remains of the cultists and exited the caverns.

Chapter 21

Outside the caverns, destruction reigned. The bodies of the cultists as well as those of their companions were scattered all over the field, faces forever frozen in hideous masks of death. Already, apparently tipped off by whatever brooding, blackened sense they possessed, several carrion crows flew in lazy circles overhead, anticipating the feast sprawled below. Bodies and pieces of bodies had bled profusely staining the ground. The smell of death was sickening and Oceana nearly vomited. Gagging, she began to search for the bodies of her friends.

The elf maiden queried the dwarf as to the general location of those who had guarded the cave entrance. Quint, the last of the companions to fall, was the furthest back. Closest to Oceana and her wards, she moved to look for him first.

Roland beat her to it. Brushing past the elf mage, the dwarf ran to where the ranger lay crumpled at the cave entrance. Slowly, Roland felt for a pulse and drew a sharp breath.

"He's alive," he choked in disbelief.

"Let me see!" Oceana urged. Feeling for and finding a pulse, Oceana set to work, doctoring the wound on the battlefield. Quint seemed to have been taken out by a head wound and a deep wound to the side—he had bled a good deal and would likely be weak for a good while but, after Oceana bound the wound, she was confident he would recover. Bathing his face with water from the ranger's own canteen and a strip of her cloak, she managed to awaken the man.

"This is just what I always envisioned Paradise to be," the ranger smiled weakly looking up at the elf maiden.

"Where does it hurt?" asked Oceana.

"Everywhere," said the ranger, dazed, "what happened?"

"What do you think happened," Roland said, placing his hand on the ranger's shoulder, "you were mincing around on the battlefield and got put down like a little girl!"

"Shut up, Roland!" Quint groaned before smiling at Oceana. Throughout the episode, Roland kept a wary eye on their surroundings lest one of the fallen cultists recover enough to attack or any new opponent arrive.

The next thing Roland and Oceana did was administer whatever aid they could to Quint, Shadowbender, and Drake. Quint, after receiving a few generous gulps of water, and Shadowbender were both cognizant and offered whatever help they could which was pretty well limited to telling them where they hurt while watching out for enemies. Drake, on the other hand, was still unconscious and caused Oceana much despair. The bard wasn't physically wounded as far as she could tell, and she pulled at her hair in frustration trying to think of something she could do to effect healing.

"I think," said Shadowbender noticing his sisters concern, "the problem will resolve itself, given a little time." Convinced there was naught else they could do for the trio, Oceana and Roland went looking for Davyn and Erik after Shadowbender and Quint promised Oceana they would call her for help if they needed anything.

Davyn they found just outside the cave entrance not far from where they had found Quint. The man was obviously dead, his hand still clenching the pommel of his sword which was impaling his last opponent. Oceana wept gently over the quiet ranger.

They buried Davyn ap Gwyn in the soft mould of a nearby pine thicket. They placed his weapons at his side, cleaned his armour, and cleaned the body as best they could. Oceana watched the dwarf carefully spread fragrant pine needles over the grave he had scraped out with Davyn's own short-handled travelling shovel. Roland apparently wasn't satisfied with the way the pine needles fell as he kept patting them down or raking small clumps of the brown needles back and forth with his fingers spread like the tines of a rake. Oceana kept thinking how futile, how hopeless, how ridiculously pointless this action was.

"The problem will resolve itself, over time," Roland said with a last despairing pat at the unruly needles. Over the grave, Roland placed a mound of creek stone he obtained from a bubbling watercourse on the far side of the thicket.

Erik was a little more difficult to find. The ranger lay beneath the bodies of several cultists. He was covered in blood and Oceana despaired of getting him cleaned up as they had Davyn. The ranger groaned as they moved him, and the startled pair nearly dropped Erik in amazement. Miraculously, he had been merely knocked unconscious with a blow to the head, had suffered no other wounds, and was unhurt beyond a splitting headache. Oceana applied a poultice and gave the man some bitter herbs to chew that would lessen the pain. Roland took the ranger to get cleaned up while Oceana returned to check on her brother and the others.

Erik washed himself in the stream while Roland related the tale beyond Erik's knowledge. The ranger smiled widely at their success though he bitterly lamented the loss of Davyn. The man requested a few minutes alone with Davyn and, when he returned from the grave, he was pale, and the dwarf could tell the man had been weeping. Roland left the ranger's grief private and the pair returned to where the other waited.

"What now?" Roland queried.

"We should leave," Shadowbender replied.

"What about the wounded, including *yourself,*" Oceana demanded, "we should stay here and let everyone rest."

"No," said Shadowbender, shaking his head, "there are other cultists. It would be foolish to remain here."

The debate went on for several minutes with Oceana requesting they remain and her brother maintaining they should leave but, in the end, Shadowbender's view was upheld. They prepared to leave. Shadowbender slowly gained his feet and stood wobbling upon his staff. Erik intently scanned the surrounding forest. As the most hale and combat worthy of the survivors, the young man had taken the welfare of the group as his personal responsibility.

Thinking of Davyn lying beneath the mould, he almost wished for an encounter with the cultists. Roland and Quint talked softly as the dwarf helped his friend regain his feet. Wincing, Quint pressed his hand against his wound even as he tried to smile. Oceana knelt over Drake. The elf maiden's scream cut through the air. Erik drew his sword and turned. Shadowbender drew his hood over his face.

"Shadowbender!" Oceana sobbed. Overwhelmed, she couldn't continue. She dropped to her knees, wracked in sorrow. Roland and Quint gently stepped aside as Shadowbender hobbled over to his sister. He placed his left hand on Oceana's right shoulder but didn't speak. Cold and unmoving, Drake was no longer breathing, his eyes staring vacantly at the sky he could no longer see. Tenderly, Shadowbender placed his fingers on the bard's eyelids and closed them. No one spoke for a long time.

After a few minutes, eyes swollen with crying, Oceana finally broke the silence, "I don't understand," she sobbed.

"You are never going to understand," replied Shadowbender bitterly, looking intently into the encroaching forest's tangled mass of undergrowth as if he expected to find something there.

"I don't understand!" Oceana practically shrieked in brokenness.

"Neither do I," Shadowbender wrapped his arms around his sister and held her through another bout of crying. The elf's eyes misted heavily, but he did not cry. Shadowbender rarely cried and, when he did, it was always in private.

"Did he know, Shadowbender?" Oceana asked almost inaudibly.

"Know?" The mage looked at the sky. Great billowing clouds floated across the heavens as hollow and nebulous as his own dreams. Below the firmament, was the deep green of a mountain forest and the soft rustling of leaves as a gentle breeze flowed around him. Perverse, it seemed, certainly out of place in a world with Drake lying cold and dead within it. "We knew there was a risk," he finally replied.

"And he did it anyway," Roland said in awe.

"He did it anyway," Shadowbender echoed hollowly.

"I guess we'd better bury him," Erik said suggestively, arriving behind the pair.

"Yes," the elf answered.

Roland and Erik, the hardiest of the party, attended to the burial. Drake of Allendale was buried beside Davyn ap Gwyn in the small pine thicket just outside the Cavern of the Wyrm. Oceana and Shadowbender, weary and sorrow-laden, stood oblivious to their surroundings. Regal, Roland thought them, timeless and somehow apart from the world in that way elves have. Before the interment, they had removed two instruments from Drake's pack. Oceana held the bard's small travelling harp; Shadowbender the mandolin. As if on cue, both elves began to play, the sounds of each familiar instrument interweaving with the other into a fresh new sound never yet heard.

The music filled the pine thicket and wove itself into the trees, the stream, and the wind until the dwarf could no longer differentiate between the music and the sounds of nature. Such was the enchantment of elven music tinged with emotion. Roland generally preferred chants such as the dwarves loved, usually martial in theme

323

and unaccompanied by instruments. Dwarves accompanied their songs with drums and sometimes wind instruments (especially bagpipes), but rarely used stringed instruments as their fingers weren't particularly suited for them. Roland had often found the music of the stringed instruments giddy and somewhat grating. He changed his mind today. Elves could embody music, legend maintained, and Roland could hear why. After some time, Roland had no idea how long it had been, the elves began to sing, their voices blending perfectly with the tinkling music. A dirge they sang, the embodiment of sorrow. The dwarf unabashedly began to weep as they played unaware the two men beside him were also weeping. The elves began to sing:

"Valyanna, we pray you guide this man home
And may his steps never falter.
Please guide his weary soul
To Paradise, to dwell with his forefathers.

Though we can no longer hear his voice,
In our hearts, we know only peace
For, with him, we shall soon rejoice
After our own souls have been released.

When pain is but a memory
And tears forgotten in the oblivion of the past,
We know he will finally see
The sun in its true splendour at last.

His harp's unstrung—
He has been chosen;
His tune broken
Here in our dying world.

But the music he has played
Mirrors the soul unstained
By the ravages of sorrow
There in the world undying
Where song never ends.

And now he must travel beyond the sky.
Please walk with him; he must travel so far.
And may the last glimmer of his eyes
Shine forever amongst the stars."

Placing the strap of the travelling harp over her shoulder, Oceana stumbled away from the grave. The dwarf and rangers slowly followed. Shadowbender remained, Drake's mandolin in his hands. They were anxious to go; should more cultists arrive, they'd be in poor shape to withstand them. No one had the heart, however, to deny Shadowbender some time alone with his friend.

Quint was heartbroken for Oceana and her brother. In all the tales, the hero survived whatever evil had beset him and returned home a hero. Half the members of the party had died during their journey. Drake, in particular, as the victorious bard, should be returning home to live and love, content in the knowledge he had saved the world from an unspeakable evil. It seemed unfair to leave him here in an unmarked grave in the wild. Maybe he was just ignorant as to how it really was for heroes in the tales, but Quint felt they had all been horribly cheated.

Shadowbender stood unmoving at the grave until the others began to worry. Finally, Oceana came to him and reminded him about the possibility of approaching cultists. Shadowbender pulled his hood over his face and, his sister beside him, turned and walked into the surrounding gloom of a strangely grey and silent world.

Chapter 22

The tattered party progressed slowly. Quint and Shadowbender were both greatly impacted by their wounds and moved with acute discomfort, and both men were usually helped along by Erik or Oceana. Erik, who was trying to fulfil the role of point man, was clearly irritated over being forced to walk with the group rather than before it, though he never complained. Roland was to help but was too short to enable the wounded men to lean on him. He more than made up for this discrepancy as he, on several occasions, hauled one or the other on a homemade stretcher he and Erik had constructed out of saplings and lengths of vine. Erik, during this time, could and did move forward to be in the point position. Still, dragging men on a stretcher is tedious at best and they only moved at half their normal travelling rate when the path was relatively clear (which was seldom) and, overall, bogged down by weight and obstructions, they did well to traverse a mile in an hour's time. At this rate, everyone knew, they would hardly return to Shadowbender's Tower by the winter solstice, providing they did not first starve to death in the wilderness.

"What is that?" Erik, who was on point, asked, holding up his hand, indicating the others should stop. It was the third day of travel and they had not, so far, encountered any intelligent creature.

"Oh-oh," Roland said peering ahead down the path. Oceana said nothing, but looked ahead, a look of surprise on her face.

"What is it?" Shadowbender asked Quint. The mage was on the stretcher being pulled by Roland. Shadowbender faced away from everyone else. 'Acting rearguard' the dwarf had termed lying on the stretcher. Quint stumbled alongside Shadowbender. He was usually looking down; weak and wounded, he was merely going through the mechanics of walking, his mind somewhere far away so as not to focus on his pain. This mental separation, vital to survival, was dangerous as it left a man vulnerable. Only because he was with protective companions did Quint allow himself the solace. Now, however, Quint was staring down the path his eyes glittering with awareness.

"The Grey Man," he finally responded to the elf's query. Oceana, Roland, and Erik, who had not seen the man before, visibly relaxed at the ranger's statement. Each had feared the strange old man before them was a cultist or allied with the cultists. Now, the sight of the withered man filled them with a sense of peace. The man said nothing but was smiling broadly. They walked forward hopefully.

"Stand before me, ranger," the Grey Man stated, standing tall in the centre of the path, a strange smile on his features. Without hesitation, Quint stepped forward. The Grey Man closed his eyes and raised his hands toward the ranger, brow furrowed in concentration. After a few moments, he relaxed.

"Amazing," whispered Quint, smiling widely, "the pain is gone completely." The ranger stretched this way and that in amazement, enjoying the re-assumption of his natural abilities. "I didn't know you were a cleric."

The Grey Man did not reply. He motioned that Shadowbender should be brought before him. Quint, now hale, and Erik moved the stretcher in front of the Grey Man and reverently backed away several paces, so the man could approach the patient.

Surprisingly, the man sat down on a log lying across the path and made no move to approach the elf. He smiled oddly at Oceana. Shadowbender saw the man seated on a log crossing the path. On the ground, Shadowbender was looking up at the man and he could see the man's silhouette against the bright backdrop of the distant sun. Shadowbender struggled to his elbows and gazed curiously at him.

"You're not a cleric, are you, Elder?"

"Not exactly," the other replied. Going through the same motions he had used with Quint, the Grey Man healed Shadowbender.

"Is the way back safe?" Roland asked, interrupting Shadowbender's train of thought in order to move the conversation back into the realm of the practical—namely, how they were going to get back to Shadowbender's Tower and finally put this entire wretched ordeal behind them.

The man did not respond immediately. Roland, thinking maybe the man hadn't heard him, had decided to ask again when the man finally replied. "No path ever is truly safe," he said thoughtfully.

Roland was unhappy with this answer and mumbled something under his breath.

"True enough," Quint quickly covered. The ranger was somewhat unclear as to the Grey Man's identity but was certain he was a man of no small power. It wasn't wise to anger someone who possessed more power than you did.

"Perhaps," Shadowbender soothed, "what the dwarf meant was this: is there any specific danger we will encounter on our homeward journey?"

"Hmm," said the Grey Man. In fact, he repeated it several times. It appeared nothing more was forthcoming.

"Yes, well," Quint said in what he hoped was a pleasant manner, "we all have to make the best of it, regardless."

"Quiet," chimed in the Grey Man, "I am no seer and that's true, but I think, I *think*, your path relatively free from danger. The dragon men aren't destroyed by any means, but they haven't the strategic placement to hinder you. Go in peace."

"Who are the wyrm cultists exactly," asked Oceana, "I mean, what is their purpose? Won't they disband now that there is no hope the dragons will reawaken?"

"It is the fate of the natural order," the man replied quietly, "that there is always a certain minority of beings who wish to dominate or destroy the rest of the world. Sometimes this minority is defeated, sometimes it is set loose on the world but checked by the actions of others, and, occasionally, this group is successful and unchecked, and it is left to the invisible hand of the natural order to eventually rectify the situation. Perhaps, one day, the forces of evil will conquer the world and institute an eternal reign, though I do not believe this will occur as evil, thankfully, is destructive even toward itself and, therefore, does not possess the capacity to do more than temporarily throw the natural order out of kilter." The man stroked his beard and smiled a wry smile, "As to hope...well, evil clings to hope every bit as firmly as do the forces that work for good. Even the very wicked cannot survive without hope." With that, the Grey Man turned and wordlessly began striding down the path away from the party. They watched him go until he finally disappeared into the foliage of Druidwood.

"I think we should camp here," Shadowbender finally said.

The remainder of the journey back was difficult but not dangerous. They ran out of food after a couple of days and the rangers were obliged to hunt for food which slowed them down but caused no more damage than delay. Everyone except Shadowbender seemed to actually enjoy this time of camaraderie, hunting, swapping tales around the camp fire, and feasting on the rewards of the rangers' hunting skills. In this manner, they arrived unharmed at Shadowbender's Tower after two more weeks.

"Don't forget to go first," Roland said to Shadowbender as they stood in the clearing surrounding the tower, "and remove the traps you placed before we left." Roland was always practical on such matters (i.e. those involving himself being killed by magic in any form) as he thought how ironic it would be should they survive the cult of the wyrm only to be killed by Shadowbender's defences once they returned home.

"Of course," Shadowbender said dryly. Roland's concern was unfounded as Shadowbender was quite aware he needed to remove the magical contingencies he had placed. The mage entered the Tower alone and, after several minutes, reappeared. "It is safe to enter," he proclaimed solemnly. Roland seemed to have his doubts as to the veracity of this statement but, when the others moved forward to enter the Tower, the dwarf accompanied them without complaint.

Shadowbender stood in the Tower's music room watching the red glow of the morning bathe the floor in warm light. He glanced at the scattered pillows arranged as they had left them when they had departed the Tower; it seemed a hundred years ago. He still had difficulty accepting Drake's death. He should not be so affected, he knew. After all, he had long been aware this day would come sooner or later. Drake was human and, even if the bard had been fated to die of old age, Shadowbender would have outlived him by centuries. This knowledge did little to ease the pain, however. Taking the mandolin he had scavenged from Drake's body, Shadowbender absently plucked the strings, letting the sound tinkle throughout the chamber. Hearing a soft cough behind him, the mage ran his hand over his eyes, placed the mandolin on a red velvet pillow, and turned around.

Oceana, Roland, and Quint stood in the doorway. He beckoned them in.

"Hello," Oceana said quietly, tears swimming in her eyes. Quint and Roland, much subdued from their normal boisterousness, entered after her.

"Erik has gone?" Shadowbender asked. The man had intended to leave at dawn to return to his own home.

"Yes," answered Quint.

"And you two are prepared, as well?"

"As well as we can be," Quint responded. The ranger hesitated before adding, "Perhaps Drake weeps for us for being stuck here while he has found peace."

A sad smile graced the mages face, "Perhaps so." After a moment of awkward silence, Roland piped up, "So, it's all over, then?"

"I know not," Shadowbender said, "the dragons are no longer an immediate threat. The cultists have no reason to attack us except vengeance."

"Which would be reason enough, I'd wager," said Roland.

"I think not," said the elf thoughtfully, "I have spent much time contemplating this very thing and I do not believe the cult would risk the men or time in a futile effort. I have taken steps to ensure they have received word the 'Canticle' has been shared with a number of people throughout the world."

"Ah," Quint laughed, "making it pointless to try to silence us. Good show, mage!"

"How do we know it will work?" Roland questioned.

"*Know*" replied Shadowbender, "we do not *know*; we speculate. Still, I believe us to be safe for the time being. At least from the Cult of the Wyrm," he added.

"So, what are you going to do?" Quint asked.

"The same thing we have always done," answered Shadowbender simply.

"And you?" Oceana cut in.

333

"Well, Roland and I are still trying to figure that out," Quint smiled, "Roland wants to travel south into Rockstead. I am a little more inclined to travel to the west to the Barony of Trevor and explore some forests I've never seen before. We may also make a trip into some town or another. I need to buy a hat; I lost mine somewhere in Druidwood. Maybe I'll get a hero's discount."

"I doubt it," scoffed Roland, "considering no one knows what we've accomplished. Besides, they'll charge you double in order to accommodate a head swollen to the size of yours."

"We'll see," the ranger shrugged.

"You're always welcome here," Oceana said.

"Thank you, dear lady," Quint said. The ranger, with a flourish, bowed and kissed her hand, "and may I say your beauty would be welcome anywhere in the world." Roland and Shadowbender both snorted.

"Promise me, Quint," Oceana said, "that you'll come back, if you are able."

"I promise," he said, reluctantly releasing her hand.

Soon, Quint and Roland left the elves' Tower. From the roof, Oceana and Shadowbender watched them go. Occasionally, though she was smiling, Oceana wiped a tear from her eye. "Is it always this hard to say goodbye?" she asked mostly to herself. Shadowbender stood in front of her, his robes flowing gently in the breeze. "No," he said quietly, "sometimes it is worse."

Both were silent for a while as they watched the two specks that were their friends grow smaller and smaller and finally disappear.

334

"Come," said Shadowbender as he turned toward the Tower, "we have work to do. And," he added, "you have a present."

"What?" "A seeing globe." "A crystal ball?" Oceana asked excitedly.

"Some call it that. You have earned it."

"Thank you," Oceana hugged her brother. She thought warmly about the time she could spend with the globe after mastering its use. Via the globe, she could travel the world, learn new things, and, she thought with a lump in her throat, maybe even check in on new friends from time to time. Oceana felt sure everything was going to be fine.

They stopped outside the laboratory door.

"You first," Oceana said with a playful bow.

"Thank you," Shadowbender said regally as he passed through the portal walking tall and straight like a victorious general riding through the gates of his home town. With a deep breath and a smile, Oceana followed her brother through the door.

About the Author

Bret James Stewart has been in love with fantasy since he was old enough to read.

He is an eclectic writer living in the beautiful mountains of Western North Carolina, where he often indulges his passion for hiking. A Christian Druid, he is active in ministry and would like to praise God for imbuing man with creative imagination.

He is an avid Dungeons and Dragons player and life-long learner. He wears many hats—poet, playwright, author of both fiction and non-fiction, and game designer. He hopes you enjoy the companions' quest as much as he did.

Learn more about him at his websites:

https://www.bretjamesstewart.com—general author's website.

https://www.blueridgehiker.com —a hiking review website for the most popular trails in Western North Carolina.

https://www.dungeoneergames.com —a classic fantasy role-playing game site.

https://www.facebook.com/bretjamesstewartauthor--Facebook Author Page

https://www.goodreads.com/author/show/13432598.Bret_James_Stewart--Goodreads Author Page

http://www.amazon.com/Bret-James-Stewart/--Amazon Author Page

https://www.smashwords.com/profile/view/BretJamesStewart--Smashwords Profile Page

https://itunes.apple.com/us/artist/bret-james-stewart/--Apple I-Books Author Page

http://www.drivethrufiction.com/browse/pub/8285/Bret-James-Stewart--Drive Thru Fiction Author Page

http://lulu.com/spotlight/bretjamesstewart--Lulu Author Page

www.ingramcontent.com/pod-product-compliance
Lightning Source LLC
Chambersburg PA
CBHW051232260626
47162CB00002B/394